MOSCODELPHIA

CHARLES RAFFERTY

MOSCODELPHIA

CHARLES RAFFERTY

Woodhall Press
Norwalk, CT

woodhall press

Woodhall Press, 81 Old Saugatuck Road, Norwalk, CT 06855
WoodhallPress.com

Cover design: Jessica Dionne Wright

Layout artist: Amie McCracken

Library of Congress Cataloging-in-Publication Data available

ISBN 978-1-949116-85-4 (trade paper)

ISBN 978-1-949116-86-1 (electronic)

First Edition

Distributed by Independent Publishers Group
(800) 888-4741

Printed in the United States of America

This is a work of creative fiction. Names, characters, places, and incidents either are the product of the author's imagination or are used fictitiously. Any resemblance to actual persons, living or dead, events, or locales is entirely coincidental. The author in no way represents any company, corporation, or brand, mentioned herein. The views expressed in this novel are solely those of the author.

For B. W.

CONTENTS

Part 1 .... **13**

Chapter 1: Her Father's Steady Chewing Confirmed Her Mother's Logic 15

Chapter 2: A Faint Browning of the Air 18

Chapter 3: The Silver Smile of the Hatchet 21

Chapter 4: The Unmistakable Smirk of Someone Who Had Been Gathering Toads .. 23

Chapter 5: Play Dead until the Last Possible Moment 25

Chapter 6: Something a Lady Might Travel With 27

Chapter 7: The Locket Full of Fingernail Clippings 30

Chapter 8: She Smelled the Brandy in His Words 32

Chapter 9: Why Do You Think God Made the Locusts? 35

Chapter 10: Jerked into a State of Semi-Levitation 38

Chapter 11: The Grass on the Way to the Outhouse Was Cold 41

Chapter 12: Knocking Was for the Weak 44

Chapter 13: A Sound of Plenty 46

Chapter 14: A Gibberish of Clicks and Meows 49

Chapter 15: The Whole Industry of Collecting Girls 53

Chapter 16: There Was Enough for Two Pies 56

Chapter 17: Fire and Honey 59

Chapter 18: The Spreading of the Rust 62

Chapter 19: Her Neck Snapped in the Thrashing of Its Rack 65

Chapter 20: The Deer Walked Backwards 68

Chapter 21: She Might Do Something Rash with the Brandy 71

Chapter 22: He Smelled the Manure inside a Passing Livestock Car 73

Chapter 23: They Had No Brother Wading through the Corn toward Them 76

Chapter 24: He Was Stung of Course, but Only Here and There 79

Chapter 25: The Ox Could Lean against the Fence of Its Corral and Be Free 82

Part 2 .... **85**

Chapter 26: You Must Keep Your Voice Like Music 87

Chapter 27: When There Is Enough of Something to Make One Person Happy 91

Chapter 28: The Creature That Emerged Had Been More Beautiful 94

Chapter 29: There Were Not Only Coins in the Box beneath Her Bed 96

Chapter 30: A Warning for the Simmering Hive 98

Chapter 31: It Was Practice for What Came Next 100

Chapter 32: Then She Threw It Sidearmed into the Sumac 102

Chapter 33: The World Felt Like a Jewelry Box 105

Part 3 .... **109**

Chapter 34: She Saw Her Father Pick Up a Shovel and Head to the Barn 111

Chapter 35: Little Pieces of Glass 114

Chapter 36: Incapable of Maintaining a Proper Fence 116

Chapter 37: Even Her Husband Called Her "Mother" 118

Chapter 38: A Trail of Dead Girls along the Train Tracks 121

Chapter 39: Then We Can Commence to Properly Starving 124

Chapter 40: A Disturbance in the Topmost Tassels 126

Chapter 41: An Hourglass of Pink Taffeta 128

Chapter 42: She Wondered What Color Flowers the Bushes Would Eventually Bear ... 132

Chapter 43: The Luxuries the City Offered Served Only to Produce Anxiety 135

Chapter 44: Make Sure It Hits the Rocks 137

Chapter 45: Why Have You Killed My Turtle? 140

Chapter 46: Her Skin Had Driven Him to Poetry 143

Chapter 47: It Would Smell the Bacon More 145

Chapter 48: Everything Else in the World Felt Muted 148

Chapter 49: She Dipped Her Fingers in Again 151

Chapter 50: The Smell of a Large Meal Left Over in the Kitchen 154

Chapter 51: Tell Me about the Last Time You Had Risen above the Smog 156

Chapter 52: The Thumb-Worn Image of a Saint 159

Chapter 53: It Was Called the Naugatonic 161

Chapter 54: The Rectangles of Purple Flowers 164

Chapter 55: The Purring Increased 166

Part 4 .... **169**

Chapter 56: He Envied How the Chocolates Kept Knocking against Her Hip 171

Chapter 57: She Placed the Nail upon Her Tongue 174

Chapter 58: Pasha Had to Remind the Ox It Must Turn Around 177

Chapter 59: It Bounced off Anton's Shoulder 179

Chapter 60: She Could Smell the Wine on Him 182

Chapter 61: But They Have Steak Here 185

Chapter 62: A Man with Business above the Clouds 188

Chapter 63: The Berry That Hangs Too Long upon a Branch Is Passed Over Even by Crows 190

Chapter 64: A Message from the Countryside 193

Chapter 65: The Barrel of His Gun Had Somehow Warped 195

Chapter 66: A World Where Toads Were Not Falling from a Poisonous Sky 197

Chapter 67: It Was a Book That Had Long Since Ceased to Be Relevant 199

Chapter 68: Why Would She Love a Thing Her Husband Cared Nothing About? 202

Chapter 69: She Would Offer Him Tea or a Lozenge of Maple Candy 206

Chapter 70: A Black Flower Blossoming 209

Chapter 71: The People Don't Want Stars.. 211

Chapter 72: He Had No Problem with Tasting His Own Spit.................... 214

Chapter 73: The Soft and Slippery Crescents... 216

Chapter 74: A Light Went on in the Far End of the House 219

Part 5 .... **223**

Chapter 75: A Single Cobalt Tile Floating in the Mortar of Josef's Life 225

Chapter 76: Even the Rivers Terminated Abruptly 228

Chapter 77: There Will Be Mountains First.. 230

Chapter 78: A Little More Sugar 232

Chapter 79: Old Ladies in the Countryside Used to Read Tea Leaves..................... 234

Chapter 80: Roast Chicken and Prawns and Freshly Shucked Raw Corn.............. 237

Chapter 81: So Many Undiluted Stars... 241

Chapter 82: Like a Bright Planet That Blinked 244

Chapter 83: He Began to Taste Anton in His Mouth................................247

Chapter 84: Then She Took Out a Beige Scarf.. 250

Chapter 85: The Light the Angel Gave Off before It Struck...................... 253

Chapter 86: No One Begrudged Her the Egg.. 256

Chapter 87: Its High, Unignorable Note 259

Chapter 88: The Color of Men and Lions 261

Chapter 89: The Few Must Be Sacrificed for the Welfare of the Many.................... 264

Chapter 90: She Could Not Discount the Fact of Angels 267

Chapter 91: His Last Evening on Earth... 270

Chapter 92: It Would Not Take Them Long to Clean the Entire Yard 273

Chapter 93: Like the Breaking of a Flu... 276

Chapter 94: The Scent of Pine Trees Filled the Van 278

Chapter 95: The Crickets Crowding the Field around Them 281

Acknowledgments 285

PART 1

CHAPTER 1:
HER FATHER'S STEADY CHEWING
CONFIRMED HER MOTHER'S LOGIC

Magda Puzanov was fifteen when she found the angel huddled in a corner of bloody straw. It looked like a pile of trash someone had been too lazy to sweep away, but when Magda reached for it with a dung rake, she noticed the stump where its left wing had been. She looked up then, and saw the hole in the barn roof.

Magda ran to tell her father what she had discovered, and he followed her back with his shotgun.

He told Magda to wait outside, and then he walked up to where the angel lay and poked it with the tip of his gun. Its white robe was torn open in the front, and he could see the fine gray hair covering its torso and legs. The angel was old and had a deep, splinter-filled gash across its belly. Mr. Puzanov saw that the light had left its eyes, so he opened the angel's mouth with the barrel and confirmed that its tongue was black. Angels' tongues, he knew, turned black as soon as they died, and he needed to be sure. An angel feigning death had been able to kill one of his boyhood neighbors—because the man had been too excited to open the angel's mouth.

"It's dead," he called back, and Magda came out from behind the barn door. "But now I'll just make sure."

Mr. Puzanov put the barrel against the angel's skinny neck and fired, and the head rolled over the straw and into the pigpen. There was a din of bleating and stamping hooves, and the chickens rose high above their nests. But the pigs were practical; they began to eat the face of the angel even before the rest of the barn had settled down.

That evening, Magda and her older brother, Pasha, sat down with their parents to feast on the angel. Ordinarily, nobody would eat such meat. It was dark and oily and smelled like turtles, but if the meat was boiled thoroughly, the water emptied out, and then the meat boiled again in fresh water, it became palatable, especially if you added red onions to deaden the musk. The thigh was the choicest part, and that went to Magda's father, but he cut out a forkful for his daughter, which she savored like a piece of candy.

"Where did the angel come from?" asked Magda.

Her mother laughed. She was a bony woman with brown hair tied up in a fraying bun. "It came from the sky, Magda. Did you not see the hole in our roof?"

As her mother spoke, she heaped her plate full of shredded angel meat. It was nothing like the dense gopher stews she preferred, but a bounty could not be turned away, and as everyone knew, angel meat would not keep. It had to be eaten the day the angel died or it would spoil. It made no difference whether you smoked it or salted it—the meat would grow rank and slippery, and the putrefaction would spread to whatever was near.

"But why did it fall through our roof?" Magda asked.

Her mother chuckled again. "The angel did not fall, Magda." She pulled a piece of dark gristle from her mouth and placed it on the edge of her plate. "The angel was thrown. Either God knew we were hungry and wanted to help, or we have angered him and he has tried to correct us with a broken roof." Her father's steady chewing confirmed her mother's logic.

"But what does it matter?" her mother continued, tucking a few loose strands of hair back behind her ears. "If you hadn't found the angel, we wouldn't have this feast. It is a blessing either way."

Just then there was a knock. It was the Petrovich family. That morning, the grandfather had seen the angel streaking down from the sky, and when he asked if he might search the property, Magda's mother told him they had already found it. Then she invited his family to dinner.

"Please," said Magda's father. "Pull up some chairs. We'll never finish all of this before midnight by ourselves."

The Petrovich family sat down and waited to be served. Magda had hoped to see Anton with them, but he was an albino, and it was common knowledge that such a boy could not dine on angel meat.

After dinner, Magda helped her father carry the scraps out to the dung pile, and she didn't complain when he told her to take the skull out of the pigpen. The hogs had picked it clean, but she understood their greed—how the next morning they would crack into the bone to eat the brains, and how they could only sicken.

Later, as she lay in bed, Magda tried to remember a time when she had been offered third helpings of anything. Her belly was distended, and she felt a torpor overtaking her that she did not wish to stop. She looked out her window at the cold stars and was thankful that God had favored them this way, though she worried about what the angel must have done in order to be flung through a barn roof. She consoled herself by reasoning that God's attention would have fallen elsewhere by now, landing on one of the other worlds that spun above her bed.

Magda rolled over and burped, tasting again the oily musk of the muscle that connected wing to back.

CHAPTER 2:
A FAINT BROWNING OF THE AIR

The next day Magda's hunger resumed. The burlap curtains blew in above her face, and the sky consisted of high puffs of white cloud stretching across the air like the streaks left over where a wet mop had touched the floor. From where she lay, they seemed not to be moving, though it was clear a wind high up must be pushing them.

She thought of her belly. There was a small gurgling that would bother her for the rest of the morning. That was always the way with angel meat.

Downstairs, the kitchen was empty, but Magda's mother had left a biscuit and a list of chores on the table. Magda picked up the biscuit and placed the pepper mill on the scrap of paper so it wouldn't blow away. Then she walked out the back door and onto the crumbling steps. She could see her father astride the red barn, hammering a board into the spot where the angel had struck. In the distance, she could hear someone at the Petrovich farm whipping an ox.

Magda looked for her mother and was thankful she did not see her. With a sky like today's, Magda wanted to make the most of it. She could clean the chicken yard later. For now, she intended to climb the hill behind their farm. At the top, she would have a good view of the surrounding plains, dotted with small farms and tiny herds of goats. Her mother often told her how it would have been cows in her own day—giant Holsteins face-down in the clover—but they had been sold off to the people of Moscodelphia long ago, and if the sky was clear everywhere, Magda would be able to see a hint of this city her mother so often talked about. It would present itself as a smudge on the horizon, a faint browning of the air. When it was dusk on days like this, jet lights would sometimes reach her because they pointed briefly in her direction as the planes circled the airport, waiting to land. They looked like lazy stars trying to escape the heavens, and this is what Magda believed them to be. Living so deep in the country, she had no conception yet of jets and men and the larger world. Of course the buildings themselves were always invisible. They were simply too far away, though Magda had heard that they reached higher than trees, that they were full of many brick rooms that, despite their great weight, refused to collapse on top of the sleeping tenants.

Magda bit into the biscuit and took off for the hill. Better to get going now before her mother spotted her. Magda didn't know why the idea of the city—its sulfuric smog, its warren of apartments—intrigued her. She knew almost nothing about it. The one enduring fact repeated to her was about the last milk cow their family had owned. The cow had kicked her grandfather in the head, so they sold it off as a bit of bad luck. Selling it to the men of Moscodelphia was the best way to make sure it never caused trouble for them again. And so the cow was taken to the city, and the city ate it and turned it into boots. The sale made Magda's family rich for many months, but her grandfather limped for the rest of his life. He remained stricken by the kick when he became bedridden for the last time just as Magda was born. She was still wet from being inside her mother when the midwife settled her into her grandfather's arms. The family allowed him to hold onto Magda for a full minute as he lay dying in the bright sunshine of the death room. This was the story they handed down.

Magda continued upward. The path was steep, and she picked up the walking stick she kept at the path's first turn to steady herself. The hill beside their farm was unique to the immediate landscape. It was only a few hundred feet above the rest of the plains, but since she was not accustomed to rising, she found it difficult. As always, by the time she made it to the top, she had lost her wind.

Magda finished her biscuit and peered into the northern sky. Sure enough, she saw the telltale smog staining the horizon. She told herself she would go to this city one day, that she would dine on cows while wearing a store-bought dress.

On the other side of the hill came the sound of more whipping from the Petrovich farm. Far below, she saw Anton standing beside an ox and smacking its flanks when it wanted to rest. He was trying to convince the ox to keep pulling the plow through the morning dirt, but the ox was getting old, and in its wisdom understood that it could not truly be forced. Although the day was already warm, Anton wore long sleeves and a floppy hat, because for Anton the sunshine was a curse. He would burn and burn, unable to tan. He was two years older than Magda, and she wondered what he would look like if his shirt suddenly fell open and she was able to gaze upon him freely. She wondered too what it would be like if she could get close enough to see the hairs on his chest, to smell the sweat coming out of him, stippling his brow like dew.

Magda had yet to speak to Anton. Her brother, Pasha, had told her he was full of albino magic, and that's why his family kept him hidden on their farm. She took a last look at Anton and licked a crumb from the corner of her mouth. Then, reluctantly, she headed back down to a world of waiting chores.

CHAPTER 3:
THE SILVER SMILE OF THE HATCHET

Mrs. Puzanov always needed help with the weed-like tenacity of her daily chores, so from a young age, Magda had been put in charge of the chickens. Every day, she had to feed them and scrub out their water trough. She had to rake out their dung. She gathered the freshly laid eggs in her apron, and she enjoyed their warmth against her belly as she walked up to the house on cool mornings.

Magda also had to kill one chicken each week. The worst one could do, her mother believed, was run headless around its pen.

Magda surprised her mother by performing this duty exceedingly well. With a succession of little kisses, she would persuade the chicken to her side. She let it peck the seed from her palm as it had done on a daily basis since the first time it left the henhouse. Then she scooped it up and took it behind the barn.

The bird never complained as she laid its head on the stump. It might have smelled the dried blood or the feathery scent of a missing companion, but Magda reasoned the recognition was comforting, as if some grand reunion were in the offing. Then the silver smile of the hatchet thunked into the wood, and the body of the bird began to flap and sprint.

Magda was always careful of the head lying in the dirt, staring up at her with the last twinklings of consciousness. Sometimes it even winked at her, and Magda spoke to the head as if she would make it better with a little extra feed, a little rub behind the ears. She was always curious to see which part would die first—the head with its roving eye or the body in search of its missing brain?

One day, Magda's mother interrupted this cycle of murder and comfort. "Magda!" she called. "Stop talking to that chicken." Magda laid the head upon the ground and stood to face her mother. "Your uncle is coming for dinner. Go get another bird."

Magda had blood on her hands, an arterial spatter across her coveralls. She wanted to clean up before returning to the chicken yard, but her mother would never stand for that. "They're just animals," she would say, as if that put them into the same category as coffee cups or grass. "They don't understand the meaning of blood."

So Magda came out from behind the barn and picked another Black Star that had stopped laying eggs. It didn't look much different from the others, but its insides had grown old. She could tell by the slight loss of glossiness in its plumage. The chicken came over when Magda made kisses in the air. It climbed willingly into her arms as if it were accepting a hug.

But then the bird became agitated. Perhaps it could smell the fresh blood, or the hunger of Magda's uncle approaching. Twice it tried to crawl up the front of her shirt, its claws cutting into her. There was much flapping and squawking, and when Magda finally got back behind the barn, she kicked at the gate but it did not catch.

As always, the hatchet came down, and the body of the bird began to run. But this time the chicken found its way between Magda's legs and out through the unshut gate. Magda hurried after it, but the remaining chickens saw its headless arrival and her bloody pursuit. The Black Star fell over in the dirt like a toy that needed rewinding.

Magda bent down to retrieve the lump of feathers and felt the blood trickling over her breast where the bird had clawed her. "Trying to walk to heaven" is what her mother would have said. Magda stood up and saw the other birds regarding her. She felt conclusions being drawn. The silence of the chicken yard blossomed around her like a strange new orchard, whose only fruit was fear.

In the kitchen window, Magda's mother scraped burned potatoes from the bottom of an iron pan.

CHAPTER 4:
THE UNMISTAKABLE SMIRK OF SOMEONE
WHO HAD BEEN GATHERING TOADS

Magda collected the toads even though her mother had forbidden it. All morning, Magda parted the overgrown grasses that ran along the back of the house where the mower could not reach. She lifted the boards of the barn that had collapsed the year she was born; she raked her fingers through the wet leaves beside the log pile. To Magda, the toads were living dirt, and it was almost like magic as she watched them transform into toad, always in the place where she was not quite looking. Just as quickly, they became dirt again. She made a game of getting them, and she didn't care that they peed all over her hand as she lifted them to her face to inhale their essential earthiness. One by one, she plucked them up and placed them in her bucket.

When the morning got warmer, Magda lay in the shade of the house and counted out her toads, peering down at them with the sweaty moon of her face. Some were the size of pennies; others were as big as Magda's fist. She tried counting them several times, but she kept ending with a different answer. Her last count was twenty-six, and she decided that was good enough. Magda felt the breeze moving over the grass and up her legs. She was getting sleepy as she stared at the toads' stillness on the bottom of the bucket, trying to see them breathe. Finally, she rapped her knuckles against the metal and brought them to attention, the bronze of their many eyes upon her.

"Magda," her mother called from the back porch. "Come finish pinning up this laundry for me."

Magda came slowly around the corner of the house, and her mother saw the dirty hands, the unmistakable smirk of someone who had been gathering toads. When Magda had climbed the three steps to the porch, her mother blocked her progress and lifted Magda's palms to her nose. Then she slapped her and told her to get cleaned up.

Magda's mother believed that toads were a danger, that they were omens, messages from dead enemies. To collect them was to bring evil into your midst, into the lives of the people who loved you. Magda didn't believe this of course, but she felt a deep guilt for having gone against her mother's wishes again. She went into the kitchen and washed her hands. She tried to gauge the redness of the slap mark brightening her cheek. It would be gone soon enough, she decided, turning away from the small mirror that hung by the metal sink.

Magda saw her mother step off the porch and go around the corner of the house, and Magda ran over to the side window to see what she would do. Her mother stopped beside the bucket of toads pretending to be dirt. Through the window, she heard her mother mutter a little prayer and then kick the bucket across the yard. The toads scattered like a bunch of ricocheting marbles but quickly settled down in the grass, invisible once again. Her mother's face wore a look of disgust. She picked up the bucket by the wire handle and brought it back around to the porch.

"Get over here and clean this up," she said to Magda.

Magda took the bucket over to the pump and scrubbed it out with a rag. When she was finished, she threw the rag onto the dung pile, which is what her mother had insisted on in the past, claiming that the toads' poison made the rag unusable.

From the porch her mother called out, "We're going to let the collectors take you if you can't learn what's right."

It was an old threat. Since Magda could remember, she had been told she would be given to the collectors when next they came to the farm— if she could not keep her room clean, if she did not turn a faucet tight, if she was foolish and left a gate open, allowing a goat to escape or a fox to sneak in.

CHAPTER 5:
PLAY DEAD UNTIL THE
LAST POSSIBLE MOMENT

Magda was forever disappointing her mother. She consoled herself by thinking back to a time when she had been helpful, when her mother had been laid up with a fever and Magda was full of small, successful gestures.

She brought her mother an egg still warm from the hen. She scraped the morning plates into the pigs' pail and rinsed them off at the pump. It hadn't frozen yet, and her mother noticed when Magda brought in fresh water, knowing that Magda had no gloves, that she felt the metal loop of the bucket cutting into her fingers as she two-handed it back to the house. Magda even did the household laundry. She understood how to boil a large pot. She knew to pour in the lye and stir her brother's drawers with a stick to get them clean.

"Keep an eye out that we don't have any angels prowling up out of the woods," her mother counseled. She was laughing, but Magda couldn't tell if she was joking or if it was delirium—or if an angel might actually be on the loose.

Magda was the only one home to help her mother. Pasha and her father had gone out hunting. They did so at this time every year. There was nothing to be done with the fields. The ground was frozen, and the animals in the surrounding woods were in their finest fur, whether coyote or fox or beaver. It was only the beginning of January, so the animals had had time to grow out of their summer coats, but the season was early enough that they weren't yet afflicted with mange or any of the other diseases that can strike a starving animal.

Mrs. Puzanov lay in her bed sweating so profusely that Magda asked if she had wet herself.

"Wouldn't that be a summer's day," she responded. "Do you think I was dreaming I was out in the pond?"

Magda looked reflexively out the window. The irrigation pond was a disk of yellowish ice surrounded by frozen mud. She hated that pond. She knew there were snapping turtles buried underneath, surviving somehow, dreaming of her toes and the ducklings that would paddle out to the pond's center, believing they were safe.

"Did father leave us with a gun?" Magda asked.

Her mother laughed again, but quickly broke down into wheezing and hacking, her face turning red enough that Magda thought something inside of her might burst.

"Would you be willing to put me out of my misery?" she asked her daughter. "You're such a good girl to me, but I don't think he left us one."

Magda tried to explain that she didn't want the gun so that she could shoot her mother but because she was worried about angels. Her mother laughed hard again until she began coughing up bloody spittle into an old rag she'd been clutching in her hand all day.

"You've never used a gun," her mother said. "The angel would get you before you ever got off a shot." She dabbed at her lips and looked into the crumpled rag. "You'd do better with a knife," she said. "Play dead until the last possible moment. That advice will do you in almost any situation."

Then her mother slipped off into fever. Magda patted her head with a wet cloth and let her lie for a time with the covers drawn off her steaming body. When she started to shiver, Magda pulled the covers back over her again. She continued her vigil for two more days as her mother slowly mended, until finally she saw her brother and her father traipsing out of the trampled corn, their shoulders heaping with the skins of the newly dead.

CHAPTER 6:
SOMETHING A LADY MIGHT TRAVEL WITH

At first Magda was afraid of Anton Petrovich. Her brother, Pasha, often spoke of the strange power of albinos. He said that if you touched one, you would get a wish. He said that the corn grew taller just for Anton's walking through it. Sometimes, when Magda was wandering through the woods between their farms looking for toads or gathering mugwort, she would arrive at the nexus of woods and field. And there was Anton, strolling through the corn beneath a large orange umbrella so that it looked like a giant marigold was traversing the field. He whistled as he walked, and the first time she had seen him doing this, she wondered if she had heard this noise before and thought it was a bird.

One day, Magda's father sent her to the Petrovich farm to pick up a tool he needed. Something in his old tractor had to be replaced, but it required a special wrench to get to the part. Magda arrived at lunchtime. The farm was quiet; everyone had secreted themselves to eat their meals or otherwise pass the hour undisturbed in the dusty heat. The largest barn's sliding door was partially open, providing a rectangle of blackness to walk inside of. She thought the barn would be empty and that she would have to try the house. Perhaps Mrs. Petrovich would invite her in. She sometimes gave Magda little candies made from pine sap, which she gathered from the trees that separated their farms.

But once her eyes adjusted, she saw that the barn was not empty. The albino sat back beside a workbench, shirtless, glowing the way one does after heavy exertion, but even more so. Magda had never seen a shirtless man who was not her father or brother. He was leaning backward on a wooden chair, eating his lunch, his shoes crossed on top of the workbench. It disturbed her.

"What can I do for Pasha's sister?" he said.

"My father would like your socket wrench," said Magda. She spoke precisely, hoping this would get the favor done more quickly, hoping she could go back to her own farm on the other side of the woods. And yet she planted herself firmly, just inside the door.

Anton took his feet off the workbench and let the chair legs grind against the barn floor. He stood up and used the shirt he held to swat at an insect that was troubling his back.

The workbench was covered with tools and with the parts of tools—a combination of oil-smeared dullness and dazzling chrome. Tools seemed to drip from the walls of the barn, hanging down from crowded bars and little hooks. It was a room in which something could be built.

"Help yourself," said the albino, who sat back down and picked up the apple he'd been eating, taking a loud bite of it.

Magda walked over to the workbench in front of him and began lifting tools and opening drawers. She kept thinking about what Pasha had told her, that she would get a wish if she touched him. Magda did not really believe that such a thing was possible. She was fifteen after all. And yet she was drawn to the pinkness of his forearms, which, despite the giant marigold he traveled beneath, had gotten a little burned. She wondered what would happen to her fingers if they suddenly came into contact with the blazing pinkness of his shoulders.

"I don't know what it looks like," she said finally.

The albino stopped chewing and looked up into the giant rectangle of light coming into the barn behind Magda, as if he was thinking about what it would feel like to be out in that light again. "The socket wrench," she said. "I don't know what it looks like."

The albino stood up and flung the apple core out into the brightness of the barnyard. He pivoted and walked to the end of the bench, picked up a box, laid it aside, and then, from under that, pulled out a clean red box that looked like a little suitcase, something a lady might travel with on her way to Moscodelphia. He took it over to Magda. She could smell the funk of him then, the sweat and dust of the farm that was caking his skin and making it rise with little welts. She could see now that what little chest hair he had was white or clear—she couldn't tell which—and his nipples were pink, like scars.

"I am Anton," he said, and placed the wrench kit in her hands.

It was heavier than it looked, and Magda almost fumbled it to the barn floor. She caught it tight with both hands and hurried away, her face burning, and as she entered the full light of day, she worried the albino would see her blushing.

"I said my name is Anton," he called after her, laughing, but Magda would not turn back around.

CHAPTER 7:
THE LOCKET FULL OF FINGERNAIL CLIPPINGS

Anton Petrovich was missing the smallest toe on his left foot because his neighbor, Mr. Laconovich, had cut it off when Anton was just a baby, sleeping in his crib. Mr. Laconovich had seen Anton's father outside trying to persuade the family ox to pull a tree stump out of the dirt where another acre of soybeans would soon be planted. At the same time, Anton's mother was pinning sheets up on the line to dry, but the day was windy. It made it easy for Mr. Laconovich to step out of the woods, find Anton, and remove the toe before anyone could stop him. Now he wore the toe around his neck, and seventeen years later, the toe looked like a small piece of driftwood, dangling from a chain so tarnished no one could tell what kind of metal it was.

Anton would have lost more toes and fingers had his parents not thought quickly. Word of the albino's birth spread across the countryside like locusts. His parents shaved off all his fine, nearly translucent hair and had locks of it waiting inside folded slips of paper for when strangers came knocking, looking for a charm. Even when Anton was older, he never went anywhere without the locket full of fingernail clippings hung around his neck. Such efforts were the only thing standing between him and his own dismemberment.

Albinism ran in the Petrovich family, and there were many stories of relatives murdered for a charm. Anton's great-uncle had been cut apart and sold in the market when he was only nine. Everyone said it was a miracle he had lasted as long as that.

Sometimes, Anton and Mr. Laconovich would meet—out in the woods between their farms or on one of the dusty roads. At such times, Anton always tried to correct the small limp he had; for his part, Mr. Laconovich would let his hand float up to tuck the little toe inside his shirt collar. It was a matter of decorum. They would help each other with packages or confer about the dryness of the soil and whether the rains might come. But both of them knew that if Mr. Laconovich's luck ever took a definitive turn for the worse, he would be coming for another toe.

"Here," Anton would say as they came to the junction where their paths would part, "take this fingernail for luck." Anton would click open the locket, select the largest nail, and hand it to Mr. Laconovich.

"Thank you kindly," Mr. Laconovich would say, placing the nail into his mouth. He would grind away at it with his molars as he walked toward his home, extracting and dissolving whatever luck there was inside it. The nail was a gesture he had come to expect.

Anton had never felt any rancor toward Mr. Laconovich. He couldn't remember the violation, and even his parents said nothing untoward about the old man. If anything, they blamed themselves for their lack of vigilance. After all, Mr. Laconovich was only acting out of self-interest. He saw an opportunity and he took it. It would have been unnatural to do otherwise. In fact, their families remained cordial, and Mr. Laconovich was often heard praising young Anton's industry in the fields and his ingenuity when it came to balancing his large umbrella behind the seat of a rumbling tractor.

Anton continued on his way. Every now and then he would turn around to see if anyone was following him. This was his habit. His body could make someone rich if they knew what they were doing—if they understood how to cut and preserve. His head alone, it was rumored, could buy an entire farm.

Anton took note of the ragged trees. A breeze pushed over them, bringing with it the scent of something industrial—a whiff of oil or asphalt. A crow flapped out of an oak as Anton approached, calling to its brothers, who must have still been hiding. Then the black bird aimed the arrow of itself into the gray horizon.

CHAPTER 8:
SHE SMELLED THE BRANDY IN HIS WORDS

After Magda got over her shyness before Anton, she began to invent reasons for them to be together. If her family found themselves with a surplus of strawberries, she would offer to take them to the Petrovich farm to see what she could barter. If her father was in need of another special tool, Magda volunteered to fetch it.

It went on like this for weeks, until Magda followed Anton Petrovich into the evening corn. She wasn't a fool. She was careful to wait on the edge of the woods until the green fog of the field had fully absorbed him. Her father wouldn't stand for having an albino courting his daughter. At first she wasn't sure if she was even in the same row as Anton, and she worried that he must think her stupid to become lost in a maze that led only in one direction.

As she walked toward the center of the field, the stars announced themselves at unpredictable moments in the sky above her. It was dusk, but still too early for mosquitoes, and because there hadn't been rain in several days, they might not come at all. Some of the leaves had yellowed at the edges, and they scraped at her upper arms as she traveled between the rows of head-high corn.

"I'm here," said Anton.

He was standing two rows to her left, grinning. He had laid a blanket out in the dirt, and he produced a small bottle from his shirt pocket.

"Brandy?" he asked. "I got it from my uncle."

"You mean you stole it," she said.

"Yes, that's what I mean."

Anton watched the smile of Magda's face settle into its grooves. Her smile was her finest feature, and he tried to invent new ways to make her let it out. As Anton crossed through the rows, he was careful not to break any of the stalks. When he reached the spot where Magda stood, he took a long drink of the bottle and handed it to her.

"No, thank you," she said.

Magda looked up and down the row. She couldn't see to the end of it in either direction as she listened to the nighthawks call and dive. The wind was light, but it was enough to surround them with a clacking of leaves.

Anton took her hand and pulled her through the rows, leading her back to the blanket. Magda stumbled and broke one of the stalks, but Anton caught her. Then he lay down and smelled where his fingers had just touched Magda. He took another pull of the brandy. Because she felt stupid standing above him, she found a place beside him on the blanket, sitting cross-legged.

Anton raised himself up on one elbow and surveyed the narrow strip of sky above them. "I was worried you wouldn't come," he said. "I thought you might send your brother instead."

Magda adjusted her bottom because a stone was digging into it. She tried not to smile at his joke, and when she looked down at him, she noted the pleading in his eyes, how the pinkness made them seem raw, how the skin of his arms seemed to be brightening in the slowly deepening dusk.

Anton got up on one knee so that his eyes were level with Magda's. He paused as if to give her a chance to pull away, to stand up and march back out of the corn. She didn't, and when he leaned over and kissed her, the stubble on his face scratched at Magda's chin. He pressed his mouth so hard against her that she worried he might leave a mark. It burned a little, and she was surprised his tongue could open her mouth so easily.

Then Magda felt the roughness of Anton's hand grazing her breast. No boy had ever touched her like that, and she was struck that such a small, ordinary gesture could move her. She felt the blood rush into her cheeks, and the joints of her body—which until a moment before had been rigid—began to loosen, getting ready to fail. Still, she would not stretch out on the blanket with him. She was afraid of what would happen—of being caught, of giving in with her family close at hand. She pushed him away and listened hard to the darkening air. Her dog was barking on the other side of the hill, as it did every evening at this hour, trying to communicate with the dogs of the town, as if it were crucial for each of them to mark the moment. The wind picked up, and another star popped out.

Magda pulled away and smoothed out the bell of her dress. "My brother will kill you if he finds us here," she said. She made two fists in an effort to stop the shaking in her hands. "He may kill me as well."

"Nobody knows we're here," said Anton, and Magda smelled the brandy in his words.

"That's what the deer is thinking right before my brother kills it," she said, waiting for Anton to explain how she was mistaken. He said nothing, but he refused to look away.

It was Magda who stood up first. She watched as Anton shook out the blanket and began folding it into smaller and smaller rectangles. They couldn't risk exiting the field together, so Magda started to walk back, but Anton corrected her. "It's this way," he said, tucking the blanket under his shirt.

She followed him back through the corn, admiring his neck as it peeked out of his collar. When they got to the edge of the field, Anton tried to kiss her goodbye, but she wouldn't let him. She stepped backward into the corn and told him he should leave. It was almost dark now. Magda waited for him to get safely inside the barn before emerging from the corn herself and following the old path home.

Magda licked at her lip and caught a taste of Anton's brandy. With every step, the stars continued to brighten, and the dogs of her world grew more insistent that their barking be finally heard.

CHAPTER 9:
WHY DO YOU THINK GOD
MADE THE LOCUSTS?

When the crows settled into the cornfield, Anton wouldn't even know they were there unless the day was windless. Then he would hear their low cackling deep in the rows and wonder what it would look like if they all rose up at once. They would do so if he fired the shotgun that stood in the hall closet, but it was imprudent to use a shell in that manner—the field would revert to the way it had been in only a handful of minutes.

Anton picked up some gravel and flung it overhand into the corn. It fell like a small pattering storm among the stalks, and part of the field rose up squawking and flustered. It settled down quickly though, and now and then, he could see the blackness of the crows wandering among the rows.

Anton's father did not care about crows. He had known true depredation, and this wasn't it. Many years ago, before Anton was born, the locusts had come. They arrived as a vast clicking cloud, approaching like smoke from miles away. Anton's father had been caught in it. They nibbled at him, and their legs got stuck in his clothing and in his hair. He had to tie a shirt around his face to keep from inhaling them.

After an hour the swarm passed over, and it was surprising how thoroughly the locusts had disappeared. They followed one another into the sky in search of other farms, other lives to destroy, and they had eaten almost everything. Only the thickest stalks remained standing. Everything else—leaves, bean pods, tomato flowers—all went down the billion gullets of the locusts. There were of course some dead and dying insects strewn across the ground, for the swarm was so large that some of the locusts died from natural causes and simply fell out of the sky. But the healthy locusts had all left, as completely as water drains out of a tub.

Once, Anton and Magda were up in the hayloft of her father's barn. Anton was trying to impress her with his ability to walk across the rafters without losing his balance, but she was more interested in the locusts scourging the landscape miles to the south. They were moving with the wind, but Magda couldn't be sure their farms would remain unvisited.

"Why do you think God made the locusts?" Magda asked.

Anton didn't like to think about such things. Why the locusts were here was really unimportant. Their presence was a fact, and he would have to deal with them regardless of the cosmic plan.

"I could just as easily ask why he made you," he said, teasing. He jumped down and handed her an ear of corn that would have been harvested in a day or two. Magda's father would be angry if he had seen this, but Anton reasoned it was foolish to leave it in the field. The locusts could well arrive before the harvest was brought in.

The wind was blowing steadily to the south, so there was little chance of the swarm backtracking toward their farm. But Magda's father had lit several old tires to ward them off anyway. Perhaps it had worked. The tires were still smoldering, the black soot curling off them and into the evening air. Mr. Puzanov was always cautious in such matters.

"Are you saying I am like locusts?" asked Magda. She accepted the ear, ripping the leaves off in three fistfuls.

Anton answered with a crunching bite of his own corn. It was sweet, and he didn't care that it could have used another day on the stalk. Sometimes the good was better than the perfect, and Anton prided himself on his ability to make these distinctions.

Magda kept watch on the changing shape of the swarm. It was another piece of evidence that God was still willing to interfere in the affairs of men, and this made her uneasy. The locusts were not much different than an angel in that regard, and she thought about the story in the Bible, of Moses sending locusts to free the Israelites. She wondered if she was like an Israelite, and where she was meant to be going.

Magda had become uneasy about many things—locusts and chickens and the watchful eye of her brother. The only reason she had allowed Anton into the barn was that Pasha had gone into town to barter away their honey. She could still hear the distant coughing of her father's tractor, and her mother, of course, would never set foot inside a barn.

Anton stood up in the loft door and breathed in the manure of Magda's chickens and goats. It was a good smell. It meant that things were thriving. He flung his cob toward the pigpen, but it bounced into the dirt a few feet in front of the wire fence. The pigs began squealing and grunting in protest. It was almost dark now, but there was enough light to see a fox slip out from behind the barn and carry off the half-eaten cob.

CHAPTER 10:
JERKED INTO A STATE OF SEMI-LEVITATION

Magda's father was always kind to her. He lifted her up when she needed to reach a jar. He did not tell her to be quiet when she plunked at the old piano, even though it had long since drifted out of tune.

Once, when Magda was walking past the barn after plucking the week's chicken, she saw her father tying up her brother. Pasha's hands floated above his head and followed the rope as her father yanked it over a beam, to the point where Pasha's toes hovered just above the dirty straw.

"You need to learn what's needed," her father said. He said it evenly, without heat, as if it were dinnertime and he was passing a bowl of potatoes across the table. In fact, it was only her brother's in-suck of breath that made Magda look inside the barn as he was jerked into a state of semi-levitation.

Magda held the dripping chicken by the legs, and as she watched her brother, the cat came out of the barn to lick up the drops of blood that had fallen onto the flagstones. Then her father picked up a knotted rope and swung it against her brother's back. He did this twice, and each time Pasha grunted. Magda could see where the welts would soon be rising on his back, turning purple.

As Magda's father reached over to put some slack into the rope, he caught sight of Magda standing in the doorway. He let go of the rope, and her brother fell to the ground. "Mind the cat, Magda," her father said. "Or he'll eat up all our dinner." He might have winked, though Magda couldn't be sure, and her brother stood up and held out his hands, waiting for their father to untie him.

Magda lifted the chicken higher and shooed away the cat. She saw her brother shake hands with her father, but couldn't catch the exchange. Magda didn't wonder about what they had said to each other in that moment of intimate brutality, or about what Pasha must have done to bring down such a punishment. It was life on the farm. It was life with Magda's father.

Magda brought the chicken to her waiting mother, who stood leaning against the kitchen sink as if she were a leftover part after a machine had been put back together.

"How are the chickens today?" her mother asked.

Magda dropped their dinner into the metal basin and told her mother the flock had seemed easy. "The fox that Pasha killed must have been the only one," she said.

Reflexively, Magda looked out the window to the place where the skinned fox was drying on a board, pinned in such a way that its limbs were outstretched, as if attempting an embrace. "Maybe Pasha will let me turn it into a hat," said Magda. This was a joke to make her mother smile. Everyone knew that Pasha would keep the skin for himself. The fox would probably end up lining the collar of his own coat. If he gave the fur away, it would be to one of the town girls he was forever courting. It would make a fine muff. Town girls could make use of such an impractical gift, for they were known to stand around in winter without chopping any wood or breaking the ice from the goat trough to ensure that the animals could drink.

Her mother did not smile. "Did you see your brother taking his beating in the barn?" she asked.

Magda nodded that she had, and watched her mother begin cleavering the chicken into its various components.

"He will not use up your father's shells so quickly the next time," her mother said. She went on to explain that Pasha had taken two shots to bring down the fox. He was shooting from fifty yards, and it was clear to his father that Pasha had hit the fox on the first try. There was the telltale stumble into the corn. But Pasha fired a second shot anyway.

"Can you believe it?" Magda's mother asked. "Your brother is too important to spend his afternoon tracking down this fox?"

When it was clear that Magda did not comprehend, her mother explained that there was a girl in town her brother was after. "He would rather sniff around this girl than do his duty. A shotgun shell is for meat."

Magda could see her mother's point, and she glanced again at the fox drying on the board. She bit her lip and thought of Anton, and wondered what her father would do to her if he discovered she had kissed an albino. She saw that the fox's hind leg was missing and surmised it was likely because of Pasha's second shot.

Even so, there was rarely just one reason for her father's beatings. He liked to wait until there were three or four lapses before taking the trouble to tie up her brother. It was more efficient that way. Two days earlier, Magda had overheard her father telling Pasha to be watchful, to make certain that Anton did not sully her. "It is a duty," her father had said. He went on to explain that Pasha needed to discourage Anton's sense of entitlement. After all, being an albino, Anton could only bring Magda to misery.

"He will not be able to provide for her if the crops begin to fail," her father said. Then he returned to cleaning some tool he would likely be plunging into dirt again before many days had passed.

CHAPTER II:
THE GRASS ON THE WAY TO THE
OUTHOUSE WAS COLD

Every night, Magda said a prayer that God would not find her while she slept. All the stories where God showed up ended badly—with a spasm of measles or cancer, with a plague from above—something, at any rate, to make you wish he had never started looking for you. Magda was comforted by the fact that the people who claimed to have seen God were mostly liars. And why would God visit Magda, a girl from the country, whose only possessions were her hunger and her desire to end it? Happily, the evidence for God's presence was meager indeed. Only the occasional discovery of an angel gave credence to the theory that God was alive and meddling in their lives.

Often, Magda's mind wandered over her day on the farm like a circling hawk, rising higher and straying farther with each turn until the whole countryside came into perspective. The sameness of the landscape was sometimes a comfort; other times it was appalling. Would she really live her entire life here, and only here? What was the city on the horizon like? It was impossible for Magda to picture. If anything, she imagined it as many farmhouses and barns crowded together. She tried to visualize what a brick building would look like, and how it might be possible to rise higher than the trees. But for Magda, the idea of the city was shrouded in brown fog, and as undesirable as this one true image was, she knew also that everything she had ever known bent her in that direction: her family's cows, their supplies of goat cheese and rice, the girls who were taken, and the long lines of trains chugging through the countryside, waiting to be unloaded in some paradise of abundance.

On the other side of the wall, she heard Pasha getting ready for sleep—his own mumbling wish for invisibility and then several minutes of a creaking bed. She would have to stay clear of him tomorrow. The day after Pasha was beaten, he was always mean. He would push Magda out of his way, and if her footing wasn't firm, she would end up on the floor getting kicked and spit upon. It was simpler for everyone if she stayed out of whatever room he entered.

Down the hall, her parents rolled around in their bed. It sounded like a struggle that one of them was always losing, and she had long since learned not to come running when her mother cried out, or when her father grunted as if he was trying to lift a heavy log. Her friend Raisa Vyachev had let her know what was going on, which shocked Magda. She began making a conscious effort not to hear these sounds as she lay in her own bed. She found that sleep came most quickly if she focused on the blue star in her window, the one that blinked because a branch in the wind kept scratching that part of the sky. Eventually she would be waiting for it to reappear, and then she would be awake, with the air inside the window starting to brighten. She liked to lie there until the clouds began to turn orange. Then she would sit up in bed and give thanks that God had not found her in the night.

Magda got up to pee. The grass on the way to the outhouse was cold and heavy with dew, and her breath came out in little puffs in front of her. By the time she finished in the outhouse, the sky had given itself over to the coming day. The morning birds were chattering, and the rooster that often tried to bite her as she entered the chicken yard was crowing in an effort to waken a world that would rather be sleeping and sad.

The morning was Magda's favorite time of day. She heard the Petrovich's rooster answering her own, and the air felt new and unspoiled on her skin. Perhaps it was the birdsong that made it seem like this, for the starlings were already making a racket and shooting out of the eaves in an effort to bring back the bugs and worms that would stifle the begging inside of their nests. Magda understood that the begging would only lessen when the baby birds grew up to be as cunning as their parents, and were forced to find different eaves to build their nests beneath—or when they were driven into the woods away from the farm, or when they were pushed even farther, perhaps as far as Moscodelphia.

Magda caught herself. She wasn't sure a bird could fly to the city, and she didn't like to dream of things unless they were possible.

Magda drew water from the pump and brought the bucket inside. She started a fire in the stove. She cleaned up. She boiled water for tea and waited for the kettle to whistle. Only then did she hear the feet of her family on the boards above her. Magda poured herself some tea made of chicory roots and goldenrod, and then she went back outside. For the rest of the morning, she would do her best to stay out of Pasha's way.

CHAPTER 12:
KNOCKING WAS FOR THE WEAK

Pasha unpinned the cured fox hide and took it over to the workbench. He cut it according to the template he began carrying in his head the moment he felt the second shot leave the barrel. He would turn the fox into a cylinder, a muff, with fur both inside and out—the best parts left showing because the town girls were fashionable. It would be an efficient warmer of dainty hands, and he would give it to Katrina Gorky. She was a year younger, and her red hair reminded him of the pelt he was rearranging.

When he was finished stitching it into shape, he had trouble fitting his own hands inside. This was alright. Katrina was tiny by comparison, and a muff that was too large would fail to be effective. If necessary, he would simply force her hands inside.

The weather had not turned cold yet, so the fur was not as thick as he had hoped. Pasha tucked the muff under his jacket and took it inside the house. He would hide it in his room. He had considered going directly to town and giving it to Katrina, but she would not appreciate it in this weather. He would make a better impression if he was fulfilling a current need. For girls, Pasha believed, the future was too abstract to matter. He was shrewd this way. Plus, if he noticed her using a muff in the days leading up to his gift, he could reconsider his choice. Perhaps another girl just as pretty would have even colder hands.

Pasha slipped the muff under the pillow on his bed. Part of him worried his father would make him give the muff to his own mother or sister—as a further lesson in not using a second shell to kill an animal that wouldn't be eaten. If anyone asked about the now-empty hide board out by the barn, he would say the gift had already been delivered. And when he saw his mother burying her hands in her apron in the middle of January, he would not feel guilty for leaving her unrelieved. Pasha was at the age where nothing else mattered but the hands of Katrina Gorky.

When Pasha woke up and before he went to bed each night, he ran through the catalog of pretty girls he had seen in his life. There was the obvious desire to couple with them, to push himself inside the girl so that some essential brokenness could be transferred. For Pasha, girls were redemptive in this respect, but he was also happy to admire them from a distance. Just gazing at the face of a beautiful woman could sometimes be enough. He had attempted to do so more than once, and each time the girl had turned away or, worse, returned his gaze with scorn. It made Pasha feel like an intruder, and he was beginning to understand that doors would only open for him after he kicked them in—that knocking was for the weak and for the damned.

And then Pasha thought of the albino. Pasha had seen him speaking with Magda, on the threshold of the barn or in the kitchen as she accepted the berries he brought with him. Pasha had seen his sister blush when they were interrupted, and he felt certain that Magda was being indecorous, or soon would be. It was Pasha's duty to put an end to such things, but Anton was larger than Pasha, and he would level his pink gaze upon him until Pasha turned away.

So Pasha was left to ponder the lesser of two punishments: the righteous whipping of his father or the unmeasured pummeling of Anton. It was impossible to make a choice, and so his mind drifted back to the muff beneath his pillow and the girl whose hands he'd push inside. He liked how all the resolutions to this other problem seemed like good ones—whether it was Katrina or another girl—and he never tired of weighing them.

CHAPTER 13:
A SOUND OF PLENTY

After the collectors came through, an obscure emptiness descended upon the families whose houses they had visited. It was a feeling that couldn't be understood until one reached for the bag of January rice and found it missing. A family might watch their tractor loaded onto a cart that took it to a train that sent it to the city—where it couldn't possibly be used, but where it went nonetheless—as a punishment, as a joke, as a misguided belief that anything taken was useful. The collectors, of course, had to collect things, and there was a persistent rumor that their quotas were measured in weight alone.

The trains remained in place for days at a time, dividing the landscape like a cleaver. They went on for miles, and when they were finally full, a horn would sound far away and the train would lurch forward. It took many minutes to reach its cruising speed, which even then would never be "faster than a galloping horse." That was something people in the countryside said. Of course it had been a generation at least since anyone had seen a galloping horse. They had long ago been loaded onto the trains and sent to the city, where they were skinned and divided, the meat apportioned to a class of officials who had trimmed moustaches and were fond of epaulettes.

"Will they eat up all our goats and pigs, the way they ate up our cows and horses?" asked Magda.

Mrs. Puzanov stared into the woods around their farm and allowed that it was possible. "When I was a little girl," she said, "we had something called sheep." She dropped the potato she had peeled into a pot beside the sink. "They had coarse hair all over them. We used it to make sweaters," she said, picking up another potato and knocking a clump of dirt from it.

She explained that there used to be vast flocks of them, but the city was so voracious in its appetites that it wiped out the sheep more quickly than they could reproduce. Instead of shearing them twice a year for the wool, they were slaughtered for their meat and their wool at the same time. Then there were none.

The people of the countryside paid dearly for this. At first the collectors believed the sheep were hidden in the woods or some secret barn, and this belief encouraged reprisals and torched houses. But it was something the ministers must have noted as unsustainable, because the collectors began to treat differently the chickens and pigs and goats. They were not devoured with such complete abandon, and the collectors began to allow the farms of the countryside to keep some animals back. Everyone understood that this gesture was not one of kindness so that the people of the country could subsist. Rather, it was a way to ensure that the people of the city had what they wanted. The collectors would return in six months' time to remove what had fattened in their absence.

"If you ever go to Moscodelphia," Magda's mother said, "you'll be able to eat a fine meal. That's where everything ends up."

Magda took the pot of peeled potatoes from her mother and set it onto the woodstove. Then she scooped the peels into a bucket and brought it to the pigs, which stood at attention when they heard the hinges of the screen door whine open, for this was a sound of plenty.

As Magda approached, the pigs snorted and pushed one another away from the trough, even though there was room enough for each of them. They looked up at her with serious eyes surrounded by the fat that Magda found delicious. The face was her favorite part of the animal; the golden fat was succulent, and the stale elbow of bread she sopped it up with became a delicacy.

When Pasha fed the pigs, he dumped the bucket out in one pile in the center of the trough, causing the pigs to raise a ruckus as they squealed and bit the shoulder of the pig that was better positioned. Magda disliked cruelty of any sort. She made a point of starting at one end of the trough and pouring the contents out evenly.

As she walked back from the pigpen, Magda never failed to contemplate the luxury of Moscodelphia. Everyone must be fat, she thought. They must fall asleep easily. She had heard there were things called refrigerators that kept milk from spoiling. To their great credit, city people had such an abundance of food that it was difficult to eat it all in one sitting. Some of it had to be saved. It would be something to live in such a place, to be able to treasure a bit of food without having to worry that something might eat it while you slept—whether it was your own brother sniffing out the morsel you had laid aside or a rat emerging from the kitchen wall.

CHAPTER 14:
A GIBBERISH OF CLICKS AND MEOWS

Sometimes, after she had had a particularly hungry day, Magda would lie in her bed thinking of the feast of angel meat back in the springtime, and how fortunate they were that God had knocked it out of the sky for them. But it was a single day of gorging oneself in a time that was otherwise lean. She had heard that people in the city were always well fed. After all, that's where the cows had gone, and Magda knew that the collectors came to her region two or three times a year, scouring the land for large animals and pretty daughters. The farm girls were especially apt to be taken, as the fathers of the town girls had money for bribes, and most of the collectors were happy to avoid opening a particular closet if a father proved desperate enough.

When the collectors arrived, word of them spread across the countryside like the smell of rain before a large storm. The warning was unmistakable, and if you didn't hide yourself immediately, you would be caught out in the open, exposed. At such times, it was necessary for Magda to go into the secret cellar of their barn. She would hide there with the sacks of corn that would otherwise be confiscated. It was a tax that Magda's family could not easily pay, and although the collectors were not supposed to leave a family destitute, they were known to take the only sow in the pen if it suited them. Other times, they would let the sow alone, knowing they could come back after its next litter was raised and take even more.

Of course there was always a need for girls, and Magda reasoned that allowing herself to be discovered might be a way for her to make it to the city that everyone in the countryside talked about. Her parents, though, insisted that she hide.

"The men of the city will brutalize you," her mother said. "There is nothing they will not put inside of you."

This was enough to send Magda to the cellar, to hide there without making any noise. That's when she thought about the angel meat and Anton, and Magda knew that he would also be in hiding. True, there was little need for young men in the city, and its citizens, purportedly, did not believe in the magic of the countryside. But Anton was valuable nonetheless. His parents knew that some collectors might be inclined to take a finger or an eye, if not as a charm then as a souvenir. It was something to put on their desk—a conversation piece, a way to impress the officials higher up than themselves.

Such thoughts made Magda wish she were with Anton now, hiding together, encircled and protected by his ivory arms. That would never be allowed, of course. And so they huddled separately in the spaces beneath their barns. The dust motes shook down between the boards as the collectors crossed, taking a census of the animals. When they walked through the house, they would be sure to notice if there were more beds than people standing against the wall. One had to have a plan to convert the extra bedroom into storage. One had to be ready to lie and disappear as soon as the smell of collectors was carried on the wind. If a girl was suspected and did not come out from her hiding place, the collectors might burn the house down. In almost all cases, this would produce the girl as she emerged like a salamander from a burning log.

Down in the secret cellar, Magda's mind could wander beyond chores and hunger. She wondered what purpose the angels served. She had asked her father about them once when he was mucking out the goat pen—whether he had ever found a live one and what they were like.

"They do not speak as we do," he had said. "Their language is a gibberish of clicks and meows." He pushed his shovel into the goat manure as he spoke. "Perhaps it is not even language."

"What did the angel do before you killed it?" she asked.

Her father explained that there was never much time between the discovery of an angel and the murder of one. It was too dangerous not to act quickly. "To be surprised by an angel without your gun is to be killed by an angel," he liked to say. Then he continued filling the wheelbarrow with manure.

Magda turned to her mother, who was walking among the tiny herd of goats, trying to decide which one she would slaughter next. Her mother described the angels as marauders sent by God. She said they would grab a girl and fly off with her into the sky, never to be seen again. "They are no better than the collectors," she said.

"Then why don't we kill the collectors?" Magda asked. "Why are we triumphant before one enemy and cowed before another?"

Her father laughed at that. "No one understands why the angels come, whether they are sent or whether they arrive of their own accord." He knocked a final shovelful of manure into the wheelbarrow. It was heaping and foul. "But God allows us to fight what we see fit. The collectors are different."

He explained that if a collector were killed, a hundred more would descend upon their farm. The family responsible would all be murdered, their home burned, and every morsel in their possession carted off to the city. It was a matter of sending a message. The collectors wanted everyone to act a certain way, and they had an interest in making it so. But God didn't care how people acted. Or, if he did, he hadn't made it clear what he expected. So people killed angels with impunity. In fact, one could say they were blessed for such murders. After all, there was a feast at the end of every angel's life, and the man who shot off the head was given the choicest parts. It was tradition.

Magda kept going over this conversation as she nestled herself more deeply between the sacks of hidden corn. She pondered what God's plan could possibly be, and when she was feeling her most metaphysical, she often concluded that there was no plan, or that God was not in control after all, or that the angels were agents of evil let loose in the world and that God needed our help destroying them.

Then Magda heard the hay being swept away from the secret door and felt the brightness of the light entering the space beneath the boards. At that moment, she was never sure whether she was being discovered or being let out, and there was always a twinge of disappointment as her eyes adjusted and her father's hand reached down, hauling her back to the barn.

CHAPTER 15:
THE WHOLE INDUSTRY OF COLLECTING GIRLS

The girls who surrendered themselves would have to be inspected—for the straightness of their teeth, for the strength of their grips—and then they would be taken to the city, where the sons of officials waited for their brides. The families were paid of course, and the lives of the taken daughters almost always improved. They went from living a rural and impoverished life to one where the city provided everything: heat and clothing and a never-ending supply of food arriving by the trainload from the farthest reaches of the countryside.

Some husbands allowed their new wives to return to their country homes for birthdays and funerals. When they did so, the families marveled at the plumpness of their daughters, their store-bought dresses, their lipsticks and bracelets. They enjoyed the salamis their daughters brought back with them. Such tokens were held in high esteem, and the husbands back in the city enjoyed their time apart without worry of their wives' return, for they knew that the families would not allow their daughters to defect, regardless of how they might beg.

The whole industry of collecting girls had sprung up out of necessity. The women of the city almost always gave birth to boys, and as they came of age, the disparity became pronounced and appalling. Only the rich could afford the few native-born girls there were. The rest had to be sent for—from the countryside, which still produced girls as well as it did chickens and corn.

Magda had known a girl taken by the collectors. Raisa Vyachev had been found crouching inside a small tower of hay bales, with enough room in the center for a chamber pot, a jug of water, and a tiny chair on which Raisa could wait them out. But this time the collectors had brought a dog that could sniff out the signs of menstruation. Raisa was sitting in the middle of the hay bales, bleeding, when she heard the dog barking and pacing, waiting for its master to hand over the chunk of dried cod that was its reward.

Magda overheard Mr. Vyachev retelling the whole ordeal to her own parents as Magda sharpened her hatchet outside the kitchen window. Raisa's family had wept at her discovery, and her father and brothers had been beaten to make them understand they had no recourse. The collector handed Raisa's mother an envelope full of money, and Raisa's hands were tied behind her back before she was loaded into the cart. It was two years before they heard anything from her, and when she came to visit from the city, Magda and her family were invited to the reunion.

Raisa was received like a princess. She had in her bags a dress made of silk, and she had a picture in a frame that her parents put on their mantle. It showed the man, Bartov, with his arm around Raisa as if to keep her from getting away, and they were smiling. He had not accompanied her on this trip because he had business in one of the ministries, and it was difficult to go on such a long journey when one was so important. Most likely, Raisa didn't understand that the men stayed home not just because they knew their wives' families would never prevent their return but also because they liked to visit the brothels, which received a new crop of girls every spring, as if they were early peaches.

Magda thought Raisa looked beautiful. Her bosom had come into its own, and her hair was rich and glossy. The women of the city had special soaps and creams they put into their hair. Raisa's father and brothers kept pressing their noses into her scalp and inhaling the sweetness of it. Raisa gave her mother a vial of the shampoo and explained how to use it. She also handed a vial of the soap to Magda and the other girls who had come to see her return. Magda spent many minutes turning the shampoo over in her hands. It was a small bottle, the contents of which were sapphire blue. When she turned it upside down, a bubble of air traveled slowly upward, like a marble dropped into a jar of honey, but rising instead of sinking.

"There is enough for five washings," Raisa said.

Everyone understood the value of what they had been given, and they waited for a special occasion before using the soap in their hair. By the time Magda was collected, two years later, there was still one washing left.

CHAPTER 16:
THERE WAS ENOUGH FOR TWO PIES

Magda and Anton lay in the woods staring up into the Rorschach pattern of light in the branches. It was a bright day, but the leaves of the oaks and maples were so thick that very little light came through directly. It was a dim green sky above them.

"Tell me what you see," said Anton. He was lying on a blanket that he had spread out beneath them a half hour before. Now his left arm curled around Magda. They were both still naked.

"I don't want to play your games," she said. "We should get dressed." She made a move to rise, but Anton tightened his hold on her.

"Stay for another minute. Nobody knows we are here."

Magda worried that her brother would find them. They were a mile from any farm, deep in a woods that no one traveled through unless it was hunting season. There would be too much work on the farm for anyone to get away, which was also what made their situation dangerous. Magda would be missed. Her brother and her father would both want to know where she had been. If they did not trust her answer, they would watch her more closely, and because she knew she was being reckless, she also understood that she would eventually be caught, that her punishment, in a sense, was already in motion.

"I see a city," she said. "A city so big I can disappear."

Anton laughed. "And where would you live in such a city?"

"In a brick mansion, of course!"

Magda wasn't prone to letting herself be open in this way. She was usually careful and taciturn, but being with Anton made her say impossible things, and she savored the words like a roasted jowl.

"I would have servants," she said. "We would have so much food, we could throw it away."

"Tell me what you really see," he said.

"I did!" said Magda, poking him with her elbow. "Right there," she pointed. "That big patch of light. That's the bedroom window of my house."

Anton couldn't see it. When he looked at the patch of light, he saw the shape of his father's property, the one dark leaf to the side of it being the irrigation pond. He told this to Magda, and she mocked him.

"Your mind is always on your farm," she scolded. "You need to think bigger." It sounded wise as she said this, but they both knew it was just Magda's selfishness coming through. She believed, without justification, that she could do better than work her years away on a farm, only to be buried a hundred yards from the house she was born in.

The day was warm and free of insects, so Magda was able to drift back to the first time she had made love to Anton. She remembered thinking it strange that his skin did not feel different. When she touched his shoulder, she expected her hand to burn, or freeze. If she were to close her eyes, she guessed he would seem like any other boy. But Magda did not close her eyes. She stared into the pinkness of Anton's gaze as he entered her and held her down. She could see the blood working beneath his skin. She saw her handprints where she'd gripped his neck as he galloped into her. It was painful, and as her body wavered between clenching up and surrendering, Anton suddenly pulled away from her and groaned.

They had been in the Petroviches' main barn, and Magda recalled her brief terror as she heard a creaking of wood on the other side of the wall. She had held her breath, but it was just the ox shifting in its stall, taking a few steps reflexively to escape the flies and the heat. It was not her father come to beat her with a strap. It was not her brother come to break Anton's bones against a shovel back.

"You need to go now," Anton had said, and part of Magda wanted to embrace him, to tell him she needed to stay. She knew this was impossible and only showed how naive she was. So she kicked straw over the place on the floor where Anton had finished; she wiped the dust from her bottom and straightened her dress.

The barking of a distant dog drifted over to where they lay in the woods, dozing. An ant was crawling up Magda's shin, and Anton brushed it away.

"What will you say when you return?" asked Anton, pulling on his shirt and brushing away the broken leaves.

"I will tell them I was on the moon," she said.

"Be serious," said Anton. "You know they will ask."

"I will tell them exactly what we planned," she said. "That I was out in the woods gathering berries for a pie." Anton handed her the bucket of berries he had collected earlier, and she poured it into the bucket she herself had gathered. Anton's bucket was fuller than her own. He often complained that she was too selective when picking berries and other fruit. Still, there was enough for two pies, and her brother and her father both loved pies. It was an explanation they would want to believe.

CHAPTER 17:
FIRE AND HONEY

Once, when she was younger, the collectors had arrived, and Magda needed to hide quickly. She went into the secret space under the barn boards with one of the new piglets. It was tiny and warm, but it grew hungry in the dark with Magda, and it could hear its mother bellowing for it from the filth of the pigpen.

"Why is the sow fussing so much?" the collector asked.

No one would answer him because it was clear he already knew why. The sow paced up and down the length of its pen.

Magda snuggled the piglet more tightly. She cooed into its ear, but its squealing only grew. She heard the boots of the collectors going back and forth over the barn floor. She had no choice. She rolled over onto the piglet, slowly, until it suffocated. Magda was surprised by how little effort it took. Then the collectors left to inspect some other part of the farm, and Magda lay with the piglet. She felt the small puddle of warmth from its relaxed bladder. Then the body began to cool.

Later that afternoon, when the collectors were gone, Magda's father cleared the hay bales off the trapdoor and pulled Magda up into the light. She was crying, and he saw the suffocated animal. At first he was angry. The whole point of hiding the pig was to bring it to maturity. Magda had no defense. She had done what she thought was right.

"Of course you did," said her mother when she heard the story, ever practical. "Go change your dress."

When Magda left to go up to her room, her mother reached down and picked the piglet up by the foreleg.

"We'll make the best of it," she said. "You'll have a fine dinner tonight."

Magda's father could not argue with this logic, and later, when Magda came down from her room wearing a fresh dress, her father smiled at her to say he was sorry, to reassure her that he would share with her the choicest parts of this pig she had killed out of necessity.

"Sometimes we have to kill the things that are dear," he said. "You did what I would have done."

At that moment, Magda's mother placed in front of her a plate with one of the rear legs roasted and covered in a glaze of crushed peaches and raw honey. Her father received the other rear leg, and Pasha could not comprehend the meaning of this slight.

"Why am I being given a foreleg?" he asked.

"Because your sister has brought us this fine feast, not you," said Mr. Puzanov.

And that was enough. Magda felt less guilty. She ate the meal her mother had prepared, and she did not dwell on the feasts they would never eat—because the pig would not grow up, because it was spared a life of mud and slops, because there is nothing so tasty as a sin forgiven.

Pasha did not persist in his complaints. He was not so full of slights that he would turn away an unexpected portion of pig. He left the table with a full belly, and he approached Magda as she was cleaning off the plates.

"It's only right that the sow enjoys the fruits of your labors," he said.

Magda pushed him away and tried to slap at his face, but he was too quick in his retreat. She could see Pasha's point. After she was done in the kitchen, she would bring the scraps to the waiting sow, who would devour the scant remains of her own child and never be the wiser. After all, Magda's mother had disguised it with fire and honey and the scent of smoke.

It seemed cruel and ironic to Magda, though she would never have used the latter word. The piglet had simply been consumed, and the leftover parts should not be thrown on the dung pile, where only the wild animals could make use of them.

Later, after Pasha had gone out to the barn and her parents had retired, Magda took the slop bucket and dumped it into the old sow's trough. There was no hesitation.

CHAPTER 18:
THE SPREADING OF THE RUST

Across the countryside, the failure of the soybeans was general. Springtime had turned the plains into bright quadrants of purple flowers as it always did, but when the flowers closed up and began to form into beans, a dull orange rust took over the landscape. Seen from the top of the lookout hill, the rust emanated from a corner of the Puzanov farm and kept on spreading like a slow autumnal flower until every acre of soybean in view had been blighted—except for the beans of the Petrovich farm. No one had ever seen anything like it. The rains were good, the weevils in abeyance, the fields well-manured—and yet the soybeans were failing.

When Magda first noticed the rust, she was struck by the fact that it started in the corner of the field where Anton had first put his hands under her dress. It had been getting dark, and he used his family's ox to shield their kissing. Magda leaned against the animal's shoulders as she shuddered beneath Anton's fingers. Then she slipped back into the woods between their farms, following the trail that wild animals had used before she and Anton had begun their regular meetings.

Everything was made worse because the people of the city had made higher demands on soybeans year after year, and it had become profitable to devote whole farms to their production. Now the failure of a single crop meant the failure of an entire farm.

The father of every family began sleeping with his shotgun by the bed. It was times like these that pushed men to thievery and the settling of old accounts. Each morning, Mr. Petrovich looked out on his acres of soybeans with dismay. They remained unaffected by the rust, and when it was clear he would be able to take his crop to market, he showed Anton how to load the shells, how to cock back the hammer.

"Do not reach for the gun unless you intend to raise it," he told Anton. "Do not raise the gun unless you intend to fire it." It was a simple calculus, and it was not difficult to understand that someone would have to die if the gun was ever brought out.

Anton had no intention of using the gun, but his father insisted that people became backward at a time like this; they remembered their old superstitions, their desire for charms. "They will come for more than a toe if we are not careful," his father said.

Mr. Petrovich regretted that he had not taught Anton the rudiments of the family weapon sooner, but Anton had always been so good with the crops that his father had kept back the chore of hunting for himself. He saw now that he had been selfish.

Anton's father took him behind the barn, where they had a clear view of the surrounding landscape. Almost all of it beyond their last fence was a dim orange, and when the wind came up, there was a light rattling of ruined leaves. Mr. Petrovich and Anton walked to within twenty-five feet of a scarecrow. It wore one of Anton's old jackets, which had long ago grown too small for him. It had a crude head full of straw topped by a hat with a broken brim.

Anton's father was willing to sacrifice three shells to train his son. He showed him how to level the gun, how to hold it firmly so that the kick didn't knock him off-kilter. He showed him how to plant his feet. Anton listened carefully to the instructions and hit the scarecrow's head on the second try. He used the third shell to blast the stave out of the ground. Mr. Petrovich felt this was a small price for the training of his son. The scarecrow had nothing better to do anyway, for the crows that landed in the Petrovich fields were not interested in the soybeans bursting in their pods. In another time it would have seemed a miraculous blessing. In this time it felt like a curse.

Then his father showed Anton how to clean the gun and where it would be kept. Anton's ears were ringing as his father spoke to him, and he wondered if hunters had this problem. Were they made deaf to their quarry's footfall by the very means of securing it? His left ear was still ringing as he drifted off to sleep that night, thinking about the smell of gunpowder and what it would feel like to be shot. And then he thought of Magda and the tiny, almost imperceptible sounds that came out of her as he reached beneath her dress. He understood he would not be able to hear them if she were with him now.

In the morning, the ringing was gone, and Anton didn't even think about the gun until he looked outside and the landscape reminded him of what the world must already be thinking.

He went downstairs and poured his coffee, and when he checked for it, the gun was propped in the hall closet beneath a chorus line of the family's coats and jackets, arranged by season. He went to the front door and looked at the dead soybeans on the Puzanov land. There was some debate among the farmers about whether to plow them under or to set them on fire. Plowing was more work, but burning was risky. After all, those few people with the foresight to also plant corn and eggplant had to be careful they didn't harm their other crops.

It would be many years before anyone tried to grow soybeans again. That was always the way. A bad crop could make a family farm unrecognizable to the ancestors buried in the graves behind the main house. Although there were not always markers, there was always a little fence to hem them in—as if the dead might rise up and shake the fathers in their sleep for letting the farm go wrong.

CHAPTER 19:
HER NECK SNAPPED IN
THE THRASHING OF ITS RACK

Magda sat on the edge of the early autumn swamp. The air was pleasant. It was dusk. She went there sometimes to think about her future. Such a strange idea to turn over in her mind when her future seemed foreordained. She would live on her parents' farm until she was married to a boy from some other farm, at which point her parents would pack up her things and send her to live with the boy. That was the pattern of the girls she knew before her. The only other option was to go to Moscodelphia—either under force of the collectors or of her own volition. Magda could think of only one girl in the second category.

Bogdana Ilyich was ten years older than Magda, and she was scarred across her face where a wild dog had bitten into her before her father could break its back with a shovel. There was no farm boy interested in her, and certainly no boys from town. Her mother had died when she was a little girl, and when her father died, she decided to forgo her inheritance of poverty. Magda remembered her parents talking about the way he had died. It was a minor legend in the countryside. Apparently, he had a heart attack while pulling a wagonload of corn with his tractor, but instead of pulling into the barn, he just kept going, dead and still propped up in the tractor's enclosure, coming to a stop a half mile away when he finally hit a ditch and tipped over. It took an afternoon of searching before Bogdana found him.

So Bogdana set off for Moscodelphia. News of her travels came back to her neighbors: A scarred girl disembarking a train on a slow turn. A scarred girl doing odd jobs in town before disappearing. A scarred girl walking through the fields, headed toward the slowly expanding smudge of smog on the horizon. To Magda, it sounded romantic—the belief that you could take charge of your life and make it better.

Eventually the stories stopped coming back. Or they came back and seemed like stories they had already heard. No one could say if Bogdana ever made it to Moscodelphia, but Magda tried her best to imagine what such a life would be like. It was difficult though. Magda was very much a part of the farm where she was born.

Just then a deer stepped out of the woods. The setting sun was behind Magda, which must have made it harder for her to be seen. The deer walked slowly toward her, switching its tail now and then, stooping to munch the tops of the saplings turning pink at the start of the season. Magda was sitting on a fallen log, and the game trail ran right past her. The animal was impressive. The velvet hung off its antlers in ragged strips. The newly emerged points would never be sharper than they were right now, and the breath came out of the stag in agitated huffs.

Magda had still not moved. At first she was quiet because she wondered how close it would come. Now the deer was only a few feet away, and she stayed quiet because she worried she might be injured. The rut was happening, and the stag would want to clear a patch of woods for the harem it would collect. Just then, Magda unmistakably caught the animal's eye. It took a definitive step in her direction, emitting a low snort.

Just when Magda thought she would have her neck snapped by the deer's thrashing rack, she heard a movement in the air above her shoulder and saw the arrow enter the stag's torso. The look of bafflement on the deer's face must have matched her own. She sat still as it turned to run a few steps and then stagger to its knees, tripped up by the blueberry bushes still dotted with late, deflating berries.

It was Pasha. He had been lying in wait, probably for hours, hoping for the deer to emerge. He showed her the pile of corn he'd laid out. He told her to stop worrying when she said he might have hit her by mistake. He said she should be back home mending the fence around the chicken coop, that she had been neglecting her chores to sneak off with an albino. All these things made Magda wish she was as brave as Bogdana—to disavow the life she was expected to lead; to walk a path toward happiness, even if she could not see it inside the smokiness of the city, hovering like a dream that dissolves as soon as one climbs out of bed to use the outhouse.

This is why Magda hiked the lookout hill beside their farm so often. She needed to see that another world existed beyond the surrounding farms. It was something to hope for, like an apple on a branch so far out you wonder if the bough you're standing on will hold until you can grab it.

CHAPTER 20:
THE DEER WALKED BACKWARDS

The gun that would protect Anton was back at home, standing inside the hall closet among the empty torsos of his family's winter coats. Magda's brother had surprised him in the woods between their farms and removed his little finger with a pair of pruning shears that Pasha had sharpened that morning. As Pasha headed home, he thought he saw the deer walking backward, away from him, disappearing into the scrim of harvested corn. This was proof of the magic the albino possessed. Pasha considered going back and cutting off another finger so that he could have a duplicate charm, but then he thought better of it as he stood in the woods sniffing at the finger. It smelled faintly of roasted chicken, which Anton must have eaten earlier in the day.

Pasha knew that if he took too much at once, the albino would be more likely to get infected and die. "I'll have to go into town and talk to the tanner," he thought. "A man like that would know how to preserve the whole thing."

Of course Anton had guessed all of this already. This was part of being an albino in the countryside. There was an understanding that his fortunes could never rise higher than those of his neighbors. Pasha's soybeans had been blighted, and he needed a new suit or he could not go to the harvest dance. The solution was obvious to everyone.

When Anton first encountered Pasha at the edge of his farm, he offered him a fingernail from his locket, but as he was undoing the clasp, Pasha hit him across the head with a wrench. Anton came to with a rag tied around his hand and with the sound of Magda weeping and cursing her brother. She had found him baking in the sunlight between their farms. Anton had trouble speaking, and she helped him back to his house.

Anton allowed Magda to clean and cauterize the wound. Then she scoured the fallow field for mint and jewelweed and made a poultice to keep off fever.

"Does it feel any better?" she asked.

Anton shook his head. "I can still feel the little toe that Mr. Laconovich took when I was a baby." Magda looked at him incredulously. "At night," he said, "in my bed. I can feel the ache of that toe."

Magda wrapped a second rag around the first, which had a bloodstain leaking through. "The soybean failure is general," she said. "The rust is everywhere, and the pods remain hard and yellow."

Anton understood. The countryside was becoming too dangerous for an albino. His neighbors felt a future hunger growing inside their bellies, and they wondered what they could get for one of Anton's pink eyeballs. Magda wept into his chest. She said she wanted to go with him to Moscodelphia, to start their life together now rather than waiting until she was of age, but Anton would have none of it. How would he care for her when he himself was not sure what awaited him in the city? Finally, when she refused to relent, he told her to pack her bags, that he would be well enough by the end of the week. This was a lie, but he was pleased that she stopped crying.

Magda put a log inside the stove and pumped some water out for their tea. She cleaned up the kitchen and checked his bandage again. From the hall closet, she retrieved the shotgun. She broke it open across her lap to make sure there were two cartridges inside. Then she snapped it back together and laid it beside his tea.

"You'll need to take this with you wherever you go," she said, kissing his forehead and wishing she could cut the throat of her brother.

Meanwhile, on the road back home, Pasha kept believing he saw animals stop in their tracks and shuffle backward away from him. Even a flock of starlings appeared to become suddenly confused and flop to the ground as they tried for the first time to flap their wings in reverse, disorganizing the order they enjoyed as they swooped like blown smoke from tree to tree.

Pasha held on to the finger more tightly, confident in the magic that was spreading out around it.

CHAPTER 21:
SHE MIGHT DO SOMETHING RASH
WITH THE BRANDY

Anton allowed Magda to change his dressing, and she was surprised how easily he climbed the ladder into the loft despite his injured hand. He confessed he had second thoughts and told Magda she would not be coming with him to the city after all. It provoked more tears.

"You're just a girl," Anton said. "The city is no place for a girl."

Magda had heard this before. She pushed Anton's hand out of her lap and wiped her face. "I'm not a little girl," she said. Then she got up and found the brandy in its hiding place between two bales of hay. She took a long drink of it, making Anton worry she might finish the entire bottle. "I know just as much about the city as you do."

Anton waited for her to hand him the bottle, but she only stood, looking out of the loft. She listened as the pigs devoured what had just gone rotten. She listened as the chickens strutted over their yard, pecking up the last of the grain Magda had thrown to them twenty minutes before. She listened as the crows rose up from the blighted fields and headed for their roost. Each evening she watched the crows drift into the east as the night came on, crying as they went with their gurgles and shrieks. The birds would reappear in the morning, coming out of the east, returning as reliably as the sun itself—a glossy blackness that flickered through the trees like many thrown knives.

Anton reached up for Magda's hand, and she took a step out of his reach. She knew he was worried she might do something rash with the brandy: drink it all down at once or pour it into the dirt below. She felt the warmth of it spreading through her torso and took another long drink. Then she handed the bottle to Anton, letting it drop before it was fully in his grasp and watching him scramble to keep it safe. He took a swig and replaced the cap and slid it between the hay bales he was leaning against. When she gave no sign, he pulled himself up and stood beside her.

"When you're older, and the rust has ended, I can come back and take you with me," he said. "But for now, it's safer for you—"

Magda cut off his explanation. She wasn't stupid. She knew that every day the blight spread wider, and that every day he stayed in the countryside was a day he was closer to getting skinned or dismembered. He had confessed to her that his father had only twenty-six cartridges left. How much damage could that do against a town full of men with rocks and machetes and other shotguns?

"You are lying to me," she said. "Don't pretend to my face that your cowardice is an interest in my protection."

Anton hated it when she said things like this. Not only was it true, but it made him feel a smallness he wouldn't have otherwise felt. Magda seemed driven to expose each of his weaknesses, to insist that he conduct himself on a level that no one could realistically sustain.

He took a small step in her direction and scooped up her hand in his good one. She didn't try to get away, and it lay limply in his grasp. This was an old trick. Anton said that her hand was playing possum, that if he wasn't careful it would rise up and claw his eyes at the moment he thought it tamed. It was true, and this made her give in and take the magnanimous step of squeezing his hand in return.

Anton got the brandy back out after that, and they shared it together as they watched a snapping turtle making its way across the orange light on top of her father's irrigation pond. It looked beautiful at that moment, like a little cup of gold. But in five more minutes, when the light had changed, when the browns and olive greens had returned to the water, the pond would become what it always was—a stagnation, a home to ugly turtles.

"Tell me when you are leaving," she said. "Tell me the truth."

CHAPTER 22:
HE SMELLED THE MANURE INSIDE
A PASSING LIVESTOCK CAR

Anton was alone as he set out for the train. He heard a clank as the line of railcars grew suddenly taut. Far off, the engine whistled and groaned as it began to pull, moving the whole line just inches at a time. In fact, Anton was far enough away that he had to stand still to be certain the train was moving, so that he could see the kerosene lamp still burning in someone's kitchen as the dark line of iron cars moved in front of it, the light making itself known at intervals as it appeared in the spaces between the cars. Although Anton couldn't see well in this light, the train was loaded with pigs and corn, traprock and oil—everything the city needed to keep grinding forward like a billion clock gears, the turnings of which were mysterious and frightening.

Anton kept watching the train gather momentum as he shambled toward it. At this rate, the train would still be in sight for another hour, perhaps longer, so there was no danger that Anton would fail to reach it.

When he arrived at the edge of the graveled railbed, the dawn was just beginning to orange the sky behind him. He still couldn't see the end of the train, so he waited for the tanker cars to pass and for the sky to brighten enough so that he could safely climb aboard. As he stood there, he fell under the spell of the methodical clanking of the cars. Every now and then, he smelled the manure inside a passing livestock car or the sweet sap of pine trunks headed for the mill. It was easy to forget himself, and he had the sensation of falling asleep as he stood before the gathering speed.

The air was light now. Anton took a moment to tie his possessions more tightly into his pack. Then he slipped it back over his shoulder and waited for the perfect boxcar. He picked it out and took three quick steps to match the speed of the train. Then he leaped onto the ladder that hung down the back of every car. The iron was cold. He regretted that he was not wearing gloves, and he tried to put all of his weight and confidence into his uninjured hand. He climbed to the top and sat down in the center of the roof, using his pack as a cushion.

Anton was on his way at last, and he took out a box of manufactured cigarettes, which he'd been saving for a special occasion. The ones he rolled himself were better, fresher, but there was something about the dignity of having a filter, the uniformity of the packing. The tobacco was dry and burned very quickly, but he enjoyed the heat in his throat as the landscape began to slip by ever more quickly. He passed many farmhouses, which made him think of his own home. More likely than not, there was a single light burning in an upstairs window by now. He wondered if it was his mother or his father discovering the note he had left, explaining his abandonment.

Anton passed through the town. He passed the parcel of white pines that someone long ago had planted in parallel rows that were just now being harvested. Fifty years? A hundred? Anton wasn't sure how long it had taken the trees to grow, but he had played in that forest as a little boy. The grove was shady, which of course was an attraction for him, but he also liked the spongy feel of the needles beneath his feet. He could lie down in them and take a nap. He remembered the trees as being gigantic. This was a trick of memory—the same one that made him believe for a little while that the leopard frogs of his youth were monstrous. He told his father he remembered them spilling out of his tiny hands, unable to contain them. But then his father reminded him that it was his own hands that had changed. It was the same with the pine forest. Although the trees were undoubtedly bigger than they were fifteen years ago, they seemed to have gotten smaller—because Anton, naturally, had gotten bigger.

He flicked the finished cigarette overboard, intending to hold off eating his provisions for as long as possible. He couldn't be sure where the next food would come from, and he felt sleepy with a sense of accomplishment, though all he had done was walk five miles in the dark and climb an iron ladder. Still, it was the most important decision of his life and it was behind him now. The sky was getting brighter. It would be a long time before he felt something as forgiving as dirt beneath his feet again.

Anton knew it would be difficult to sleep when the sun was fully up, so he lay down and made himself comfortable as best he could. He faced what he believed was the direction of Magda's house. Her bed would be just to the left of that tree, he thought. But already he was uncertain. The track was winding, and the little hill that rose between their farms was too far away to make itself known. The necessity of his fleeing shamed him, and he assumed, with resignation, that he had tasted the last of Magda.

CHAPTER 23:
THEY HAD NO BROTHER WADING
THROUGH THE CORN TOWARD THEM

Anton rode for two days on top of the slow-moving boxcar. When the sun was out, he sat with a blue umbrella aimed at the burning light, the fabric eventually slipping off two of its silver ribs. At night he slept by tying himself to an iron handhold to keep from rolling overboard. The sun-warmed metal retained its heat for a few hours, but soon enough he awoke shivering, and it was then he would raid the small provisions he had brought with him: several old potatoes, a bag of deer jerky, and a single dehydrated apple he would save until everything else had been consumed.

Twice during the journey, Anton had seen other stowaways climb aboard the train in the same manner he himself had used. They scrambled up the ladder, and when they saw Anton huddled beneath his umbrella, they were careful to put more distance between them and him, leaping across the space between the cars to ensure the isolation necessary for such a trip.

Anton had planned to make himself look normal, invisible. He had heard there were special lenses he could put in his eyes to hide their pinkness. There were dyes for the hair and makeup to darken his complexion. He had also heard that the people of Moscodelphia didn't see albinos as magical creatures to be pulled apart for charms, but he couldn't be certain. Surely, someone who believed in such things could arrive there just as he was doing. They might even be on the same train, which stretched for miles in either direction. Until he was certain he was safe, he resolved never to be seen without his broad-brimmed hat, his sleeves rolled all the way down.

Anton jumped off the train when the final railyard was a few miles to the north. He fell in with a group of migrants as soon as he made it to the city's outskirts. They shared what they had. They stole from the same people. They had no interest in albinos. One of his new companions explained it this way: "In the country, where there is no money, people will cut up an albino so they can sell his fingers and toes. But here, there is plenty of money, and it is simpler to steal it. Why have two transactions?"

Anton could not dispute this logic, but he still made a point of disguising himself. He was a criminal after all, and he needed to fit in. The thing that gave him away most clearly was his missing finger. It was either the mark of a thief or the mark of an albino. And if he was ever with another girl and she felt the stump of his finger rake across her breast, he worried she would be repulsed. It didn't matter, though, because Anton still intended to find a way back to Magda—after the blight was over, after he had enough money to bring her to the city where now he scrimped.

Until he could find regular employment, Anton remained in a makeshift camp on the city's outskirts. He noted the girls who came to visit and how they were nothing like Magda. In the dark beyond the fire pit, Anton heard them having relations with the men. Magda had always been quiet, her mouth pressed against his ear as he listened for her gasps and muted cries. But these girls were loud, full-throated. They did not care if they were discovered. They had no brother wading through the corn toward them with a cudgel in his hand.

Afterward, when Anton went to sleep inside the lean-to he'd constructed of scrap metal and broken trees, he felt something like guilt for having listened so intently. He was bothered by how easily his body could forget about Magda, despite his promises. But then the practical voice in Anton's head had never been muzzled. He may die tomorrow after all. He would likely never see Magda again.

After a few weeks, Anton found work in a delivery service. It was among the lowest jobs in the city, and it was suited for men just arriving from the countryside because it paid so poorly and because the owners were cruel.

Seeing the stump of Anton's finger, his employer had said, "I see you know already that some people are willing to do anything." Anton nodded and studied the map of the city on the opposite wall, which stretched the entire length like a loose and poorly woven yarn blanket. "I'm one of those people," said Anton.

CHAPTER 24:
HE WAS STUNG OF COURSE,
BUT ONLY HERE AND THERE

Anton's life became a life of packages, and he saw in time that there were ways of tapping into the wealth of those who had required his service. He learned about tipping, the voluntary surrender of money that did not need to be surrendered. It was astounding to Anton, especially because everyone who accepted his packages was a stranger.

Sometimes the tip would arrive in the form of something other than money. The man would open the box in front of Anton and reach in to break him off a piece of whatever was being trafficked: pastries, tea from the countryside, marijuana. The last was his favorite. He went up to the roof of his apartment complex to smoke—not to avoid being arrested but to avoid having to share—and he began to understand the men who tipped him this way. It was how they made sure the package always made it to the right address.

In time, Anton looked forward to being asked to deliver something illegal or indecorous, for he understood that he would come to share in the bounty—not equally of course, but some portion of the contraband would likely become his own. Anton had asked the other delivery men if it was permissible to request money instead.

"It would be safer that way, no?"

They all agreed it would be safer, but it was also bad manners. It was understood that any moneyed portion would be of less value than the broken-off portion could bring.

When Anton was high, he would stand up on the ledge of his building and walk around the roof as a kind of game for his neighbors, who shrieked that he would lose his balance and plunge into the market stalls eight stories below. It would mean certain death, but Anton had an infallible steadiness about him, even with the missing toe. Maybe even *because* of the missing toe.

Anton was a man of comic gestures. He collected money and little gifts for his cavorting around the brick perimeter of the rooms they all lived in. Sometimes he would somersault or stand on his hands. But always, he was careful to lean in a little bit. He couldn't bear the idea of strangers going through his pockets as he lay in a heap among the smashed gourds and ant-filled bags of sugar.

Back on the farm he had often performed such feats. He would walk across a rafter with nothing but tractor parts and plow blades to catch him. On cloudy days he would climb to the top of the split oak to steal honey from the giant combs protected from the rain in the leftmost part of the tree's fissure. He was stung of course, but only here and there. He moved with such deliberate care that the bees never realized they were under siege. They walked across his face, and his breathing was even. There was no danger of sucking one into his nostril as it strode across his lips searching for the defiler of their hive.

"Anton," his new neighbors would say, "show us again how you can roll backward over yourself without falling to your death. Give us the honey of your defiance."

And so he passed the hat or, more likely, placed it in the center of the roof, where he could keep an eye on it. Even his closest friends in the city could not be relied on to refrain from taking that which was clearly not theirs. It was a bit of a game—of trying to judge the honesty of those who could only pretend to have his interests foremost in their minds.

Other times, Anton would sit quietly on the roof, a layer of thick smog perhaps twenty feet above him, rolling along like a contour map of some other land. He did not wish to visit it, and he was glad the smog was beyond his reach. If he had to touch it, to walk through it, his spirit might break. Sometimes the weather pushed the smog even lower. When it was in the streets and Anton was delivering packages, he became winded as he marched up the stairs, searching for the number on the door that awaited him.

Regardless of its altitude, the smog was almost always present, and it was comforting for Anton to believe that no one, no matter how powerful, no matter what floor his ministry office was on, was able to travel beyond the smog, to see the stars and the unimpeded moon, or the blue of the daytime sky in all its magnificent tedium.

CHAPTER 25:
THE OX COULD LEAN AGAINST
THE FENCE OF ITS CORRAL AND BE FREE

After Anton left, Magda became more philosophical. She felt tormented by the choices she had been making—often, it seemed, with scant evidence to back them up. For instance, she could kill the white chicken or the black chicken. It wouldn't matter to her mother which. The feathers of each were just as difficult to remove. The birds were the same size, the same age. And yet Magda made the choice on a weekly basis without hesitation or ambivalence—it was always clear to Magda which of the chickens should die next. She gathered up the chosen bird and took it behind the barn.

The same was true of everything. When Magda woke in the morning, she could smile at her mother as she made her breakfast, or she could sulk sleepily while staring at the knot in the table beside her spoon.

Or when she was out in the field, walking among the rows of nighttime corn, she could focus on the crusting of stars above her or on the brushing of the leaves against her arms. Neither choice would have much of an effect on the basic trajectory of her life, which at that moment was toward her own bedroom and a blanket that needed washing. Even if she looped back toward the woods, she would eventually be headed toward her own room. She was a moon in orbit of her father's farm.

Sometimes Magda would hear an animal out in the woods behind the cornfield. It was a raccoon or a deer most likely. Even if it were something more menacing—a lynx or a wolf—she knew that the animal would run before she herself would have to. The wild animals were too intelligent to stay near people for long. After all, Magda thought, they must see her chickens and goats and be amazed by the regular slaughter they endured. The chickens could fly over the fence of the chicken yard if they wished, but they were content to have their eggs stolen from beneath them. They didn't even peck at the thieving hand.

And the ox. What must it be thinking? By far, it was the strongest animal in the countryside, domestic or wild. If it chose to, the ox could lean against the fence of its corral and be free. The only thing that could really stop it from exercising its will was a shotgun blast, but no one would kill such a precious animal before its time. The value of its meat was less than the value of its labor. Gasoline for the tractor was hard to come by; engine parts broke and went unreplaced for whole seasons. But the ox was always there—ready to be yoked and whipped and made to gouge line after line into the tired soil that Magda was now walking over, in a forest of corn the ox would never taste.

Yes, the animals of the woods were sure to give the farm a wide berth. Now and then, they might sneak in to eat a chicken, but it was understood that a hunger in the woods was safer than a full belly on the farm. To enter the farm was to tempt Magda's brother to level his shotgun on them, and if the pellets merely grazed the animal, it didn't matter. Pasha would follow the trail of its blood—even if it took all day, which it never did. The animal would slowly exhaust itself as her brother pursued it. Often, the last thing the animal saw was Pasha's cudgel coming down on its head as it lay in the dirt panting, somehow believing that it was invisible, that the coat that had saved it up until that moment would do so once again.

It was on walks like this that Magda's mind returned to Moscodelphia. Perhaps she would climb onto one of the slow-moving trains as it threaded the countryside back to the city. Or perhaps, when the collectors were next at the farm, she would cough from her place beneath the boards, allowing herself to be hauled upward into her future. Magda wished desperately to be reunited with Anton, even though she was wise enough to know how unlikely this was. Anton may have succumbed to infection on his journey, been discovered by men who meant him harm, or simply gotten lost down one of city's labyrinthine alleys.

To Magda's relief, her sense of grief and desire refused to diminish with each passing week. It was as if the lozenge of winter ice on her father's irrigation pond remained undissolved, even as another spring approached with its miracle of mud and flowers.

PART

2

CHAPTER 26:
YOU MUST KEEP YOUR VOICE LIKE MUSIC

Josef Baranov lived a comfortable life in the suburbs. His father was high up in one of the ministries, and his mother doted on him, concocting puddings and sweeping the floor behind him.

When Josef was seven, his class went on a farm visit. It was not a real farm like the ones out in the countryside. This farm was for display, to teach the young boys and girls the rudiments of agriculture and animal husbandry, and to show them the essential backwardness of the people who lived by such means. His teacher, Mrs. Plotsky, was always taking them on field trips. One week they called on a river barge; the next week they toured a ball bearing factory.

The children in Josef's class laughed at the women walking around in their sack-like dresses and wimples. Mrs. Plotsky had to keep reminding them to stop climbing the deteriorating haystacks. Someone had arranged them into pyramids many weeks before, and now they were collapsing on themselves in the thick industrial rain that drifted in from Moscodelphia.

"Today we will butcher a goat," said an old woman. She was a docent on their tour, and she was made to look as if she had just come from the countryside. However, the whiteness of the checks in her gingham dress made it clear this could not be so.

The children watched her walk over to a pen, where a dozen black goats climbed on rocks and chewed at the block of hay someone had broken apart in the center of their little yard. She selected a slow-footed goat that appeared to be afflicted with a kind of mange along its flanks. Before slipping a rope around its neck, she fed it the top of an old carrot as a treat, which she pulled from one of the voluminous pockets in her dress. The children followed as she led the goat out of the pen. Josef tried to pet the animal as it passed, but Mrs. Plotsky slapped at his hand and told him it was dirty.

"A goat like this can feed a family in the country for many days," said the docent. It is one of their most valuable possessions.

Everyone ended up at the abattoir—a small outhouse of a building with only three walls and a roof. It had a slanted table inside set up next to a pump so that the water could sluice away the blood and offal as the goat was taken apart.

"You must keep your voice like music," she said. "All animals can sense danger, even a sick old goat like this one." She led the goat inside, tied her end of the rope to a post, and took down a long blade that was hanging from a rafter. Although the meat would be tough and wormy, she explained how the country people subsisted.

"They live by selling the good goats to the people of Moscodelphia," she said. "They have learned to make do with what is left to them."

Josef began to feel sick as he realized what he was about to watch. The goat was the same color as his mother's cat, Alice, and he thought how terrible it would be to see her led to her destruction with a rope around her neck. Josef worried he would make his mother sad when he told her about his day, as she combed his hair with her long red nails while he took his nightly pudding.

The old woman made a kissing noise, as if she had another treat, and the goat looked up into her eyes. Then she drew the blade quickly across the animal's throat. It bucked and made a muffled bleating, but already the blood was pouring out. Josef tried not to look away, and the woman stepped back quickly.

"In the country, you need to let the animal find its own way to die. It can be dangerous to stay too close." She proceeded to tell the children how the animal might kick, how a large one, like a cow, might even kill you. "It's important that the others don't see," she said. She meant the goats.

In less than a minute, the goat lay in a heap as if it were a jacket mislaid by one of the children. With the help of Mrs. Plotsky, the docent began handing out plastic smocks. Then she took down a hatchet and handed it to Josef.

"Here, young man, you can help me get the head off."

Josef was thinking of Alice, and focused on the need to keep from urinating. He took a few anemic, one-handed swings at the goat's neck. The other children crowded in, as if they too might be given a try, and some of them sighed in exasperation when it was clear they would not.

"Fine work," said the docent, taking the hatchet back.

Then the old woman removed the head with three skillful whacks. Josef could hear the crackling of the spine and ligaments as she put her boot on the shoulder and twisted the goat head free. She handed the head to Josef, holding it by the horns, and asked him to pass it around. This ploy served to occupy the children as another docent appeared, helping the old woman hoist the goat onto the table.

"Well, that's enough for today," she said. "There is another class waiting, and I know you have other things to see before the bus takes you back." She explained that she and her assistant would cut the goat into portions, how they would scoop out the organs and leave them for the pigs. She smiled encouragingly, wiping her hands on an old rag, and produced a handful of maple candies from the bottom of her deepest pocket.

"These candies are from the country," she said. "They come from the sap of a tree like that one." She was pointing at a half-dead maple tree with initials carved all over its trunk. The children took scant notice but clamored around the old woman, grabbing at the candy. Josef stood off to the side, striving to obliterate the connection between Alice and the goat.

"You did a good job, little man," the docent told him. "If you come back again, maybe you can cut the throat." She said this with a wink and handed Josef two candies, putting a bloody finger up to her lips to indicate the secret.

Josef walked off with the others. They were on their way to see how a chicken laid an egg. He put a candy in his mouth and made a game of making it last as long as possible. His favorite part of any candy was when he wasn't sure if it had completely dissolved or not, when it might be nothing more than his own saliva sweetened upon his tongue.

He slipped the second candy inside his pocket. He would save it for his mother, and she would be proud of him as he told her the story of his day, and of how he had been chosen, from among so many, to help sever the old goat's head.

CHAPTER 27:
WHEN THERE IS ENOUGH OF SOMETHING TO MAKE ONE PERSON HAPPY

Isabelle cartwheeled over the soft carpet of grass that was her back lawn. There were no dandelions because her father regularly treated the yard, and as she lay in the grass afterward, she sometimes smelled the acrid afterthought of the poison. She stared up at the cloud patterns drifting over her. It felt personal, and she never tired of watching the silver jets slide by. Sometimes they would be followed by white contrails that gradually expanded to become clouds themselves. She wondered if this was how all clouds formed.

"Who flies in the airplanes up there?" she asked her mother, who was sitting in a patch of shade, sipping cherry-flavored water through a straw.

"Rich people," she said. "Important people."

A neighbor's automatic sprinkler was ticking in another yard. A child was laughing somewhere right on the edge of hearing.

"Have you ever been up in a plane?" Isabelle asked.

"Of course," her mother said. "Many times."

Isabelle rolled over on the grass to see her mother's responses more directly.

"Where did you go?"

Her mother explained that Isabelle's father would take her to far-off cities when he needed to conduct business. She told Isabelle how she would look out the window and try to see her own house. She told her that no matter how large the city she was flying above, it never made any noise.

"Once I even flew over the ocean. It was many hours before we saw the land again."

Isabelle understood the ocean. She had been there with her family. She had tasted the salt of it, but heeded her mother when she told her it would make her sick. "Be moderate in all you do," her mother was fond of saying.

"Will you take me flying someday?" Isabelle asked.

Her mother put her drink down on the wooden table beside her chair. It had a large overturned conch in the center of it, balanced on its spines and full of dirt. A single white flower climbed out of it. She felt her daughter studying her expression.

"It's hard to say," her mother replied. "It depends on your father—on whether he makes enough money to take us."

"Maybe he could just take me," said Isabelle. She was only ten, but she understood the concept of money. She knew there was more nuance than just rich and poor. In everything there were degrees. Some bowls of ice cream had one scoop; others had four.

"You would leave me on the runway waving goodbye?" asked her mother in mock offense.

Isabelle understood she was joking, but felt compelled to clarify. "There is no need for everyone to suffer when there is enough of something to make one person happy," she said. Then she rolled over onto her back again and resumed her cloud gazing. Another jet was coming into view. The contrail it created rapidly disappeared so that when it had finally crossed the sky above her yard, there was no trace of it left.

Isabelle's mother picked up her drink, then put it back down without taking a sip. She was pleased with the wisdom of her little girl, and of how she had the sense to hide the machinations behind her comments. She took a moment to assess her upturned face. Isabelle never betrayed more than she had to—a trait that would serve her well in life. When her mother sent her to the market, she never returned with a pear that was overripe. She never bought more than the meal required. She was certain to find a good husband.

Later, after her mother went inside the house, Isabelle crawled over to the conch and plucked up the flower. She inserted it into the lapel of her dress and began wandering about the yard. She knew her mother would be cross if she saw what she had done, but the flower would not have lasted another day, and Isabelle could think of no good reason to refuse what the world had offered.

CHAPTER 28:
THE CREATURE THAT EMERGED
HAD BEEN MORE BEAUTIFUL

Josef became fascinated by the ant lions that lived in the sand along the sunny side of his parents' garage. Each summer, there were a dozen small craters in the blond sand finer than sugar, and he liked to watch the red ants that had made a small highway along the foundation of the garage. Every now and then, an ant would slide down the wall of a crater, and this small disturbance would induce the ant lion—hidden in the sand at the bottom of the crater—to begin flicking its head, throwing sand up at the surprised ant. It was like throwing marbles at a man trying to run up the stairs; the ant slid down to the bottom of the pit, where the jaws of the ant lion would seize the insect and pull it beneath the sand.

It wasn't long before Josef was pushing ants into the pit to study the ant lion's technique. When he finally excavated one of the craters, he was surprised to see how simply the animal was constructed. It was just a fat abdomen attached to a pair of outsized curving jaws, and it was covered with fine hairs. Josef surmised that these allowed the creature to detect the stumbling steps of an ant trying to climb out of the crater.

Josef had always wanted a pet of his own, but his parents craved simplicity within their household, and since his mother's cat, Alice, was already there, a bird or a mouse was out of the question. So was a dog. So was a gerbil. But Josef reasoned that his parents would never begrudge him an ant lion. He would keep it on the dresser next to the picture of his mother, and he would feed it only with ants he found inside the house; and so he believed this secret pet would not become a burden.

Josef took one of the small baby food jars his father used to sort nails and screws. Josef's father was not handy, and it was unlikely a jar would be missed; Josef combined two kinds of screws in one jar and took the other for himself. He filled it with sand and dropped an ant lion in. He enjoyed watching the swirling creation of the crater. Then, every morning before school, he found an ant in the kitchen and dropped it in. Sometimes he fed the ant lion when he returned home as well, or he shook the jar to flatten out the crater, forcing the insect to rebuild the pit while Josef sat at his desk and pretended to memorize his multiplication table.

One morning, Josef peered into the jar and saw the crater was missing. When he emptied the jar, he found that the ant lion had transformed itself into a sand-covered ball. It was a cocoon. This was a shock to Josef. He hadn't thought the thing he loved would transform into something else. But because it was common knowledge that anything emerging from a cocoon would be more beautiful than whatever entered, Josef checked the jar each morning with happy anticipation.

Then, one afternoon when he returned from school, long after Josef had stopped expecting to find anything inside the jar, he was surprised to discover a large insect climbing the glass walls. It looked something like a dragonfly, and he liked peering at the world through the pattern of its translucent wings. When his mother found him with the jar, she made him get rid of it. She watched from the kitchen window as Josef unscrewed the cap and saw the lazy flight of the insect heading for the high branches behind their house.

The creature that emerged had been more beautiful than the one Josef had started with, and he was stung that he wasn't allowed to keep it in his room.

CHAPTER 29:
THERE WERE NOT ONLY COINS IN THE BOX BENEATH HER BED

Isabelle rolled the oven away from the wall to clean the dust that had accumulated since last spring. There, gleaming in the dirt, was a small bronze penny. Isabelle was sly. She didn't mention the coin. She merely bent down and began wiping up the floor. Before she got up, she tucked the penny into her pocket and continued with her chores after pushing the oven back where it belonged.

It was not a coin her parents would miss. She was sure it was her father who must have dropped it. He was careless of everything small and valuable. She had seen him once cut down an arborvitae tree from their yard, even though Isabelle had remarked on the nest of robins chirping from the interior. When she begged him to stop, he slapped her and sent her inside, but she continued watching from an upstairs window. When the tree finally fell down, she saw him walk up to what had been the tallest portion of the tree and stomp on something.

When he came back inside the house, Isabelle was sullen, so he lied.

"Don't worry, Isabelle," he said. "The birds have flown away. They will build another nest someplace else."

Because Isabelle understood lying and because she knew her father wouldn't stand for a tree that was out of proportion to the house it grew against, she accepted his answer and did not let on about what she had seen. It would become her most valuable trait—the ability to carry on in the face of deceit from the people who loved her most.

Upstairs in her room, she took the penny out of her pocket and examined it under the desk light. It was minted three years before she herself had been born, so there was no sentiment she could attach to the coin. It was merely a year and a silhouette in profile of a man she could not name. But she recognized the outline of the Ministry of Opulence on the reverse side. It was no different from the others in her coin box, except that this one was inexplicably shiny.

"What makes a penny lose its shine?" she had asked her mother once.

"Filth," she said without looking up from her dinner. "The constant touching of strangers' fingertips devalues everything." She cut a neat triangle of beef and used it as a prop to lecture Isabelle.

"This is how you can tell a whore from a good girl," she declared. "Whores are dirty. They lose their shine from so many common men pawing at their treasures."

Isabelle was just a young girl during this conversation, but nothing seemed outside her understanding. She absorbed the lesson. She moved on.

There were not only coins in the box beneath her bed. This is where she hid everything that might someday be of use, everything she wished to hold back. She had overheard her parents talking about the necessity of a private life, and she took the idea to heart. If she found a coin or a marble or the wing of a butterfly, she made a place for it inside the box. The butterfly wings, naturally, had a hard time lasting at first. But she found ways to get around the fallibility of the world's most fragile and beautiful secrets. She placed them in a smaller box inside the larger one. She resisted the urge to rattle the contents.

Later in life, Isabelle would always say that the sound of a rattling box was the sound of secrets being destroyed.

CHAPTER 30: A WARNING FOR THE SIMMERING HIVE

Isabelle listened to her parents bickering in the kitchen. Her mother was angry because her father had left the lid off the sugar bowl. Now it was full of ants.

"Give it to me," her father said.

He walked over to the sink, spooned the first centimeter of sugar into the drain, and turned the faucet on as the garbage disposal ground away at what was essentially running water. He handed the bowl back to his wife, but she walked over to the trash can and dumped the entire contents, dropping the bowl into the sink with enough force that Isabelle thought it might have chipped.

"I'm not stirring filth into my coffee," she said. Then she left the room.

Her father stared out the window above the sink. The trees were swaying in the breeze. It was finally spring, which was why the ants had arrived in such numbers. He listened to his wife's footsteps clomping the floor above him and decided it was useless to try to mollify her. He picked up his briefcase and left for work.

Isabelle got up from the couch where she had been reading and found several dozen ants milling around on the kitchen table, searching. She picked up a tissue and began smashing them. They were black and tiny, not much bigger than the sugar grains they were hoping to carry away. She followed the line of ants down the table leg going in both directions, killing them as she went. The trail led to a small gap at the base of the back door, and the ants continued to come in through that opening. There was no telling how many ants living in the dirt outside had already received the signal, or how long they might continue with their current orders. But Isabelle had school. She could not stand there all morning smashing the ants as they entered.

Isabelle considered the problem for a moment. She reached into the trash can and pulled out a handful of sugar, which she left in a small pile in the dirt beside the back door. Then she sprinkled a trail to where she saw the ants rising out of the ground. In less than a minute, this was enough to reprogram the entire colony, and the small mound of refined sugar was soon black with a new purpose. Isabelle then took her mother's perfume from the powder room and squirted the gap in the door where the ants had entered, reasoning that this new scent would override whatever trail they had once been following.

Isabelle was one of those girls who believed that all problems had solutions. Many people would describe such a person as optimistic, but in Isabelle the trait seemed more like cunning. Before she left for school, she made a point of opening the back door and stomping on the sugar pile, crushing the ants even though they had ceased to enter the house. It was a kind of punishment, a warning for the simmering hive that lived beneath her feet, everywhere and unseen.

It was episodes like this that caused Isabelle's parents to both praise and fear her. They had learned to dread when their goals and Isabelle's were not aligned. They knew that if Isabelle cared deeply enough, she would begin arranging the world around them to ensure not just that she would get what she wanted, but that her parents would hurry to make it so. It was an odd sensation she gave them—feeling proud as they were being manipulated. It made them feel that they had raised her right, that she would rise in the world and thrive.

When Isabelle's mother came back downstairs, she thanked Isabelle for cleaning up the ants.

"It smells pretty in here," she said.

Isabelle could tell that her mother thought she had taken a liking to one of her favorite perfumes, and she did not try to correct her.

CHAPTER 31:
IT WAS PRACTICE FOR WHAT CAME NEXT

"I want to live in the heart of Moscodelphia," declared Isabelle following a visit to her father's offices. She was sixteen. "I want to live in the hum of everything."

Her mother disagreed. "The city is nice for a while," she said. "But here in the suburbs you have the best of everything. Just look."

She was gesturing to the window, where Moscodelphia's skyline jutted here and there out of the dense brown smog. They were only twenty miles out, but because they lived on the western side of the city, the air was blue above them. The prevailing winds kept the poisons to the east, and because of this fact of the weather, their suburb was considered desirable and prosperous. To the east the suburbs were less so—Moscodelphia's pollution stretched many miles beyond the city, like kicked-up mud in the current of a slow-moving stream.

Isabelle agreed that the clean air was a benefit. But she had been up in the skyscrapers. She had seen her father at work and been impressed by the people who feared him. At home, she had thought of him as henpecked. But in the city, in his ministry epaulettes and beside his obedient adjutant, he seemed like a powerful animal, barely restrained, as he put to order the world outside his tower.

"Father likes it in the city," Isabelle countered. She took a sip of the tea that had gone a little cold, but she didn't feel like telling the maid to reheat it for her. *If I were in the city,* she thought, *the servant would have known to reheat the tea without my asking. Or, better, she would have brought me a fresh cup and wiped up the tabletop where the stirring spoon had rested.*

"Your father doesn't have any choice," said her mother.

This was true of course. Isabelle's father was high up in the Ministry of Opulence—a subminister. If the minister himself were to die or get removed, it might be her own father who ruled from the top of the blackened spire full of windows that had to be cleaned on a weekly basis.

Isabelle grew bored of the conversation. She did not wish to debate her mother about free will or the relative merits of suburbs and cities. She only knew that she wanted to have a large role in life, the same way she had gotten a large role in the school plays over the years. The stature of her name made her a part of every production, but her willingness to actually invoke the name of her father assured her of the lead. She was always Jocasta or Lady Macbeth. As in life, she was not content to be a mere ornament. She took the role she wanted, and she commanded the audience's attention. It was practice for what came next.

CHAPTER 32:
THEN SHE THREW IT SIDEARMED INTO THE SUMAC

"I'll meet you at the ghost road," said Josef. He meant the crumbling asphalt under the overpass that jumped the train tracks. Years ago, before Josef was born, the trains were shorter and less numerous, and the people of the suburbs would simply wait for the train to pass before continuing onward. But at a certain point, an overpass became necessary. Otherwise, the people would start to feel divided, as though they lived in a country separated by the iron walls of a slow-moving train. It was possible to wait half an afternoon for a single train to trundle by. Plus, the people who lived in the suburbs had money, and they had no intention of putting off their shopping while a train clicked by through the middle of town.

Josef's father told him that when he was a boy, people would jump onto the trains, scramble up the cold iron of the ladder, and descend the ladder on the opposite side. Then they'd jump off, perhaps a hundred feet farther up the tracks. It was something you did if you needed to see a girl. Every now and then, of course, someone was too cocky or too drunk and slipped under the polished wheels. The trains never stopped moving. No one on the train even knew disaster had struck, and the snipped-off arms and legs would lie between the rails, unable to be retrieved. The trains were so long, it was impossible to tell whether the engine was in the front pulling or in the back pushing. Often, the engineer was the only person onboard, and the train might stretch for more than a mile.

Josef's friends had climbed the trains in the same manner—on a dare, on a whim—but Josef never did so. He thought it was foolish given that an overpass was right there in the middle of town. He explained how easy it was to ride one's bicycle to the overpass. It was twenty minutes away, and Josef's arguments were sound, but everyone knew he was a coward. It was common knowledge that cowards were skilled in the ways of argument and reason, for it was fear that made them studious.

His own mother, on the other hand, traced his hesitation toward life to the bright red coil of their kitchen stove. Josef had tried to pick it up when he was just a toddler, and he never quite got over the injury—how something so beautiful could cause him such pain. It left him with thick scars along the tips of his fingers.

The ghost road was almost not a road at all anymore. If not for the overpass above it, you might think it was something else altogether. None of the asphalt was intact. It had all crumbled to fist-size bits and smaller. It had detached itself from the original roadbed and been kicked apart or washed away into the adjacent gully. Thistles and dandelions pushed out of it. Sumacs formed a prehistoric-looking grove. This is where Josef came to smoke his cigarettes or look at pornographic magazines. He had stashed them in the angle formed between the overpass and the ground. Sometimes the rats got into his treasure, but usually everything stayed clean and dry.

"What took you so long?" said Isabelle. She was smoking one of his cigarettes, and Josef could see she had been flipping through his ancient magazines. Such magazines were no longer produced, of course, and any that existed had been passed down through the decades. It was a world where pornography had outlasted novels and scripture.

"I had to wait until my mother went into her room," he said. "I didn't want her to see where I was going." He picked up the box of cigarettes from the concrete berm and lit one. Then he slipped the box into his shirt pocket.

"I suppose you will need a new hiding place now," she smiled.

Josef stared at her, admiring the tiny mouth as it spoke and how skillfully she had applied her lipstick. He would have called the dark pinkness of it "alluring" if that was a word he knew.

Isabelle flicked the cigarette into the underbrush without bothering to stub it out. She added: "If you're not careful, I may smoke up all your cigarettes."

Josef did not understand and asked if she would like another. Isabelle declined and picked up a chunk of asphalt. She broke a small piece off to give it a better shape. Then she threw it sidearmed into the sumac. They heard it whipping through the leaves, and a small brown bird shot out of the branches, rising into the sky with a little scream.

"I did not have to come here," she said. "If I wanted, I could have taken everything and left before you arrived."

Josef tried to build a wall of smoke between himself and Isabelle. He had been nervous to see her, and now Isabelle seemed angry, or some other emotion he was not familiar with.

Isabelle stepped through the smoke and put her hand on his shoulder as she spoke to him. "I do not want to do that," she said.

Josef should have kissed her then, but he had no sense of occasion. Instead, he asked her about their algebra homework and made several other deflecting comments as Isabelle tried to talk about what was in his magazines and what he was hoping she would do to him. But Josef was a disappointment. He was unable to take up the bait she had laid before him. Eventually she got bored with the failed seduction and rode away on her bicycle, leaving Josef to return the cigarettes and magazines to their hiding place. Because he did not wish to offend her, he left them in the same cranny as before—in case she returned, fearing that she might level the charge of cheapness against him.

When Josef rode back several days later, all his cigarettes were gone, his magazines scattered in the oily rain. He found the small pile of finished butts, half of which were stained with the pink of Isabelle's lipstick. Beside them, drooping over an asphalt clod, was the condom that Isabelle and some other boy must have needed.

CHAPTER 33:
THE WORLD FELT LIKE A JEWELRY BOX

When he was seventeen, Josef began attending the academy, where it was one humiliation after another. The boys were faster and stronger. They took the girls he liked behind the gymnasium, and afterward there were tears. The worst part was that the other boys knew how Josef had come to be among them. His family was rich. His uncle was the Minister of Victory. All doors fell open before his name. This led unswervingly to a lack of mercy. But even these boys at the academy knew there were limits. If Josef decided to denounce them, there would be repercussions—if not for them, then for their fathers, toiling in some government basement, hoping for their children to thrive.

Josef had always loved Isabelle. She was slender and full-breasted, and she did not speak to him with open derision, despite his anemic encounter with her at the ghost road, despite the fact that he had never had the courage to arrange another meeting. All through his academy years, Isabelle had been with one boy or another, each of them hated by Josef. He watched from the side of the gymnasium as she slow-danced with a boy whose hands roamed freely up and down the spangles of her dress. He could not comprehend her lack of resistance. She even seemed to encourage the behavior. Other times, Josef watched as a boy walked Isabelle back to her dormitory. He saw how there was no hesitation, how she opened the door and invited him inside.

It was circumstances such as these that bent Josef toward poetry. He believed that committing his humiliations to paper would somehow lead to their rectification. His muse was a fictionalized version of Isabelle. True, he praised her dark hair and the scent of the air as she passed through it, but it was fiction in the sense that she eventually gave in to the flowery entreaties, the noble pleas. She eventually made him her king.

At a certain point, Josef began to leave his poems, anonymously, for Isabelle to find—slipped into her notebook or left on her desk before the headmaster brought the class to order. Unfortunately, Josef was a terrible poet. He believed that strong emotions led, by necessity, to strong lines. Every bad poet who had ever ruined paper made the same unforgivable mistake. The true poets, though, learned their lesson, pruning away their biographical selves in the service of language. To the true poet, language was mystery; it crawled down through the centuries freighted with meanings beyond the writing man. This was not the case with Josef, though, and Isabelle feigned ignorance as to who could be leaving her this maudlin propaganda.

After a dance or a rally, when Josef found Isabelle at the cafeteria—bleary-eyed and waiting for her fried egg in the food line—he would try to catch her attention. The most he could hope for was a weak smile, a grudging acknowledgment that she had drunk too much, that she remembered his being at the dance, even if only vaguely. In a naive impulse toward camaraderie, Josef would feign having a headache as well. It was one of several things he did that kept her out of reach.

In truth, Josef also drank vodka at these dances, often to excess, but the fogginess of his own hangover cleared at the sight of Isabelle waiting for her egg, which he experienced as a light breeze from which he did not shield his face. It was in this sense that Josef could be taken as a romantic. He believed in the power of women, the power of beauty. Just being in their presence improved a person, even if the improvement had to do with something as nebulous as mood.

It was toward the end of his time at the academy when Josef finally realized the power of his last name. He went to his professor to ask about a low grade in accounting, and the grade was changed before he had left the office. The professor made a point of having Josef watch as he erased the low number from the gradebook and put in one that was considerably higher. Another time, Josef mentioned that his steak was too well done; the manager of the cafeteria brought him another steak, this time larger, and cooked the way he had hoped. The girls, too, acted differently now. Josef had grown out of his pimples and greasy hair. He was someone who could be useful to them in a way that other boys could not.

Perhaps the power had been there all along and Josef had failed to appreciate it. But no matter, the deference was clear. The line he found himself in moved faster. People got out of his way as if he were a truck moving steadily down a street. Toward the end of the semester, he conducted a test. As the forsythias were just letting go of their yellow petals, transforming into ordinary green bushes, he walked over to Isabelle's table in the cafeteria.

"Isabelle," he said. "Why don't we go for a ride on the gondola tonight?" The academy was built on an old ski resort. No one skied anymore of course. The deep snows had stopped decades earlier. But the gondola continued as a kind of entertainment for the upperclassmen. On Saturday nights, it was cranked into operation, and the students would take it to the top of the small hill at the center of the old resort. It was considered romantic. Couples would cozy up to each other in the gondola and marvel at the world below them. There was often kissing. Then they would walk the three miles down the winding trail that led to the edge of their campus, where they learned about the importance of centralized control and collective farming.

As he had hoped, Isabelle accepted his offer, and Josef told her the time he would pick her up. The boy with whom Isabelle was sitting said nothing, and Josef was astounded by his own boldness. He went back to his dormitory and ate one of the chocolates his mother had sent him for Christmas at the end of the previous year. Suddenly, the world felt like a jewelry box from which he had broken the lock. He spent a lot of time replaying Isabelle's smile and the other boy's sullenness. It was surprising how little effort this victory had taken, and he was dumbfounded by his previous timidity. It was as though he had realized the doorstop he'd been using was actually a rare artifact—a meteorite or the femur of some dinosaur. Josef felt giddy. He ate a second chocolate, leaving the foil crumpled on his desk. The maid would clear it away before he returned that evening.

PART

3

CHAPTER 34:
SHE SAW HER FATHER PICK UP
A SHOVEL AND HEAD TO THE BARN

When the collectors came back the following year, Magda didn't bother to hide. She didn't have to mull over whether she should start coughing from beneath her straw-covered boards. The call went out that the collectors were arriving, and Magda simply continued with her chores. She was found out in the open, behind the barn, speaking to a chicken's head as its body flapped against a wall, surprised by the wideness of the barn. She did not resist when they approached. She would go to Moscodelphia under the conditions at hand.

Magda allowed her wrists to be bound, and she watched her parents receive their payment. Some parents made a show of leaving the money on the ground or spitting on it. Magda's did not. Her father folded the envelope into his breast pocket and took a step closer to his wife. Magda sat in the cart with a bushel of corn and a cage with three chickens crammed into it. Pasha skulked in the barn and refused to catch Magda's gaze, which was full of acid. Magda waited to be taken to the train depot in town, where she would hope for a window seat so that she could watch the landscape civilize as the train carried her closer to the city where Anton had fled.

When the wagon started to move—pulled by two mules—Magda looked forward and stared at the back of the head of the man who had captured her. He had scabs on his nearly bald scalp, and one of them was weeping where he occasionally reached up to pick at it after slapping the reins onto the animals' backs. She couldn't tell if it was gratitude or revulsion that kept her so focused. A crow flapped out of the trees as the cart pulled onto the main road to town, and Magda looked back at the farm she had always known. It got smaller. She saw her father pick up a shovel and head to the barn, but her mother kept staring in her direction. Magda did not try to wave back with her bound hands. When they made the next turn, the farm would be invisible, quite likely for the rest of her days. Magda seemed to be getting exactly what she wanted. Still, she watched the acres of head-high corn spread out behind her and tried to memorize the rustling of the leaves as a breeze brushed over the fields.

When they pulled into town, they stopped in the main square. A second girl was loaded into the wagon with Magda, along with a pile of goat leather the people of Moscodelphia would likely turn into shoes and belts and the wide-brimmed hats that Magda would soon find on the head of almost every man she met. The second girl was younger than Magda. She had brown hair and a dress that fit better than anything Magda had ever worn. She determined that her name was Eliza, and her parents were wailing in the background. Magda could see the bloody face of the man who must be her father. He had been struck by the collectors. She saw the envelope of money lying on the ground where he had dropped it; her mother was held back by another man, who explained that the girl would have to be beaten if everyone present did not comply.

When the cart began moving again, Magda spoke to the girl. "My name is Magda," she said. "I've been waiting for this for years."

The girl did not look at Magda. She was a town girl, and she believed her station in life made conversation unnecessary. Magda, after all, came from a farm, and this was the lowest rung on the ladder of the world. Magda understood the insult, and she resented the nerve of a younger girl invoking the social order at a time when it had all but disappeared. They were not town girl and farm girl. They were captives, prisoners, things to be beaten or fondled. Magda had a vague sense of what might happen to them when they reached their destination.

She thought of Anton and the hopelessness of finding him so far away and in a city so vast. It was the first time in her life that she had truly felt this way. She was embarking on a great adventure, and the boy she loved would likely remain invisible. Her only consolation was that at least she was moving in the right direction. Anton had taken the same tracks toward the city. She would make inquiries. She would keep her eye peeled bright. That was something Pasha sometimes said: "keeping an eye peeled bright." He used it to describe the watchfulness needed to find the animal that would feed them all as he ranged through the swamps and woods beyond their farm.

After another minute of listening to Eliza's soft blubbering and finding her undeserving of the dress she wore, Magda leaned over and made sure she caught her eye.

"They will put things inside of you," she said. "You will have to enjoy it."

CHAPTER 35:
LITTLE PIECES OF GLASS

Mr. Puzanov walked into the bedroom where his wife was already curled up on top of the sheets. It was hot and the windows were open, but the curtains hung limply in the humid air. He placed the candle on the nightstand and undressed, staring at his wife's back, which was damp with sweat.

When he had stripped, he caught sight of himself in the mirror and felt pained by his flabby belly. It was not weighed down by the fat of gluttony but by the fat of age. He had been something years ago, when he'd first met Magda's mother. Now he was an old broken-down farmer—the kind of man he used to laugh about when he was a boy, when he was interested only in money and girls and the freedom of whiskey. If he wanted to have his wife right now, he could do so. If she resisted, he would overcome her. But glimpsing himself made him understand why she had not turned over to stare at him. She was pretending to sleep. The fact that he could not hear her breathing gave her away.

He blew out the candle and counted only up to three before the orange ember of the wick went black. Then there were just the stars in the window for light, though he couldn't see those yet because the candle flame still floated around on his retina. He crawled into the bed beside his wife and felt her shift away from him.

Mr. Puzanov remembered the day Magda had been born, how she looked like a bloody, squirming crab as the midwife held her up so that both of them could see. Then she cut the cord and cleaned the baby up and placed her at the breast of his wife. Magda was hungry. She began to suckle right away.

Later on, he looked into Magda's eyes. They were large and black and seemed to be drinking in everything around her. At the time, he thought that what immediately followed were the difficult days—the diapers, the growing appetite, the need to be near his wife. He felt that Magda was his true rival, for Pasha had never demanded so much attention from his wife. Pasha followed him around the farm as soon as he was able, and ran to the window whenever he heard his father's commotion outside.

With Magda it was different. She seemed not to mind being in his presence, but given the choice of her father or her mother, she would always choose her mother. He assumed it must be this way with all daughters.

"Are you awake?" he asked.

His wife did not stir, so he stared into the darkness above her shoulder. The stars were visible in the window now, but just barely. The air outside was too full of leafy trees and humidity for them to be of consequence. He remembered telling Magda about the stars—that they were little pieces of glass shining because the sun was reflecting on them from the other side of the world.

Suddenly he jumped in place. He had been falling asleep, dreaming of Magda, tiny in his arms while the midwife cleaned up the birthing room, and Magda had tumbled off his lap, hitting the floor with a smack. It was something he had feared for a long time—the loss of his daughter because of his own inattention, his own weariness. The world would devour his daughter if it could. That's what he found himself believing all those years ago when she arrived in the room smelling of blood and anguish.

Now, after all that vigilance, the loss of his daughter had come to pass.

CHAPTER 36:
INCAPABLE OF MAINTAINING
A PROPER FENCE

That night, Pasha took his dinner in his room. He had heaped his plate full of what would have been Magda's portion, and he did not wish to see the eyes of his mother staring into him. She was practical. She would understand. And yet her gaze was something he would rather not endure.

When Pasha finished, he placed the dirty plate on the table beside his bed and lay back. Somehow, the bed seemed larger, more able to accommodate. He felt the albino's finger touching his neck. The chain it dangled from was too short, preventing him from lifting the finger up for inspection. He could smell it though—a hint of rot. Fortunately, the smells of the farm easily competed against those of Anton's finger, allowing Pasha to carry it with him wherever he went, ensuring that he received whatever luck it might impart.

The charm was already working. His sister had been taken away, and Pasha hadn't had to do anything to make it happen. He merely witnessed the pleading and the tears and saw, once again, how ineffectual such tactics were. The collectors took her without remorse, just as if she were a sack of milled corn.

Pasha had been right to cut off the albino's finger. Before, it had seemed selfish. Now he could see he would have been a fool not to, and he knew that it was right to carry it around his neck as it cured. To leave it in a drawer might tempt a rat. Or if his father discovered it, he might take it for himself. It would only be right. A charm left unattended is a charm without an owner. It was the same logic that applied to anything. If a neighbor's pig wandered onto one's property because the neighbor was incapable of maintaining a proper fence, it was only right that the pig be killed and eaten by whoever found it. A farmer has no claim to an animal he can't control. There would even be shame in letting the pig continue to wander, for that would be an invitation to the wolves. Better to sleep with a full belly, Pasha reasoned. Better to show your neighbor how to make a stronger fence.

The moon was out on Pasha's side of the house. It came in through the filmy curtains and bounced off the buttery residue of Pasha's dinner plate. He took his finger and ran it around the rim, savoring the meal to its smallest increment. It was something he had resolved to get better at.

Then, because he could not avoid the thought forever, Pasha thought of Magda rolling away in the back of a bumpy cart. She had been the favorite of her parents—if only because she was younger, if only because her girl-ness made her weak and in need of protection. He liked the idea that he would no longer have to watch over her. Her honor meant nothing to him now. Besides, she had squandered it all on the albino, who had most likely been killed in some other part of the starving countryside. Pasha thought how stupid Anton was. His leaving suggested that he believed there was an end to hunger, that if he traveled far enough, he could elude whatever he was fleeing. It was delusional.

Now Pasha's sister was gone too, and Pasha would eat better. He would not listen if his mother tried to give him Magda's chores. It would be unreasonable to act as though luck had not arrived.

CHAPTER 37:
EVEN HER HUSBAND CALLED HER "MOTHER"

Magda's mother's name was Eleanor. It had been many years since anyone had called her that. Always she was "Mother" or "Mrs. Puzanov." Even her husband, if he called her anything at all, called her "Mother."

Now her daughter had been taken from her, and strangely she found herself wondering if she would ever hear her own name on someone else's lips again. She could say it to herself, but that would be bad luck. It would bring down calamities. At the very least, if she were overheard, she would be thought crazy or self-absorbed.

She went to the window of her daughter's room and looked out at the darkening farm. Her husband and her son would be returning soon. Probably they were nearby tinkering with something in the last light, or loafing in the dirt, having a cigarette. There was a kerosene lamp burning in the hall where she had left it, and as the sky darkened, her face became plainer in the glass. In another ten minutes, her own face would be more prominent than the distant trees and rows of corn.

"Eleanor," she whispered. It was startling to hear it. She hadn't thought it would sound different in her own voice, but perhaps that was natural. When she was a girl, she had a friend who liked to sing—Norah Kaminsky. Norah sounded terrible. She couldn't carry a tune, and there was no portion of the attempted song that was pleasing. And yet Norah never tired of singing, of believing she was skilled. Eleanor remembered thinking at the time that this must be because we never hear ourselves as others hear us.

The songs and the words travel up our throats and reverberate through the bone and fat of our heads, muffling the true sound of our own voices.

Some boy that she and Norah had known had a recording device that ran on batteries. He was mean, and he invited Norah to sing to the turning spools of brown tape. Then he played back the song for everyone, and Norah heard for the first time what she really sounded like. At first she would not believe. She thought it was a trick, but the boy pointed out that he and Eleanor were on the tape too, and they sounded the same as ever. The boy made a move to play back the song again, but Norah claimed she was tired.

The following day, when Norah and Eleanor met again, they pretended that the previous day did not exist. Eleanor was surprised at how effective this tactic was at erasing an uncomfortable memory. Still, she never heard Norah sing again.

How strange, she now thought, to feel deprived of something so unpleasant. She knew it was possible though. She knew women whose husbands had died, husbands whose snoring they had complained of bitterly. Then, after their husbands' death, when they were faced with the first quiet night they'd had in years, they were unable to drift off. It was too quiet, too relaxing. The silence only emphasized their essential aloneness in the bedroom, which was really just a pile of rags against the cold, a single candle in the towering dark.

"Eleanor," she said to the glass again. It was now completely dark outside save for the crimson bunting behind the trees. "Eleanor."

She felt like those widows finally freed of their husbands' snoring. Magda had always been a burden to Eleanor. She was strange and full of inconsequential worries. Now she was gone, and she would not have to put up with her. She would not have to bother with wedding arrangements and dowries and all the other things that can drain a household of whatever momentum it may have achieved.

Eleanor heard the door to the kitchen open, and the heavy boots of Pasha and her husband came in. She became self-conscious. She wondered if they had observed her staring out into the night, and whether they could have guessed that she was really staring into her own face—counting the lines around her eyes and lips, noting the pockmarks, the dark hairs sprouting from her chin, which had grown more numerous despite her willingness to pull them several nights a week in an effort to keep her girlhood close at hand. It was a waste of time, she determined. She smoothed down the sides of her skirt and her apron. She adjusted some hairs that had slipped out of her bun, tucking them neatly behind her ears. Downstairs, they were opening cabinets. It would not be long until they wondered where she was and why their dinner was not prepared. It would not be good to keep them waiting.

She took a last look around Magda's room, practically invisible now, despite the kerosene lamp burning in the hallway. Magda's keepsake box was on the dresser. Eleanor had looked inside it once. She found there a shard of rosy quartz, a dragonfly's wing, a scarlet feather from a cardinal, a few dried flower heads ready to crumble if anyone tried to pick them up. It was an odd collection. There was no evidence of a boy inside—no lock of hair, no button from his shirt, no love note folded like a swan against the prying world. She failed to notice Anton's fingernail because the flowers had shaken their way to the state of loose tea, and she had not thought to poke through them like someone poking at the ash of a burned-down home, searching for coins and forks.

"Mother?" her husband called up the stairs. "Are you there?"

Of course he sounded aggravated. Of course he did not use her name. Of course she answered and went downstairs and began to break apart the evening's cabbage, which would carry them through to morning.

CHAPTER 38:
A TRAIL OF DEAD GIRLS
ALONG THE TRAIN TRACKS

As the day progressed, Moscodelphia grew larger in the train window that Magda refused to give up. Some of the girls had to stand or sit in the aisles, and Magda resolved to hold her water as long as she could. It was clear she would not be allowed to sit in the same seat twice. Outside, the monotonous poverty of the countryside repeated itself: a checkerboard of blighted crops, the occasional goat high in a wild pear tree, the carts inside of barns waiting to be hitched up to something and filled, men smoking in a rag of shade.

Magda thought of her family gathered around the table, grinding a block of salt into the night's stew and talking about what had happened to her. Many times, she had heard her parents speaking of the collectors as they prepared the evening meal. Sometimes it sounded like her father was wishing the collectors would penetrate more deeply into the countryside. Having a daughter taken off his hands would make things easier. She was of a marriageable age, and he mused about what they might buy with the money they would get. Her mother's response to such talk—heard through the mouse-filled walls of Magda's bedroom—was unsentimental. She said that they must hide Magda out of duty, that the chickens depended on the deftness of her hands.

Magda felt a small sneeze tickling her nose. She focused again on the landscape drifting beside her and realized that she had entered the brown smudge she had so often seen from the lookout hill. The sky above the train had rusted slightly, while the sky behind them remained bright. The air smelled bad, but the change had come on so slowly that she wasn't aware of its foulness unless she concentrated on it.

Another train was visible now, traveling alongside her own but just on the horizon. It made her think there were many such trains pointing at the city like the spokes of a wheel, each train full of girls or corn or whatever the city demanded. There were houses everywhere now, achieving a greater and greater density. When there was no more space for even a tiny lawn, the houses began to grow higher, one story on top of another, until suddenly Magda couldn't see very far at all. The deepening smog intensified a sense of claustrophobia. When a space opened up in the wall of buildings, she could see many large buildings in the distance, reaching into the clouds. They were so large that she didn't even think of them as buildings at first, but rather as a more blocky part of the landscape. She had heard of mountains, and she wondered for a while if that was what she was seeing. Later, she would learn that these were the ministry buildings—the center of political power that had commanded her train to approach. Magda shifted in her seat and felt an aching urge to relieve herself.

Up in the sky, she saw what she assumed were angels streaking through the air and gleaming with silvery light. They were very high up, and she wondered why there were so many more angels above the city than above the countryside. She thought it must have something to do with the city being full of God's chosen people. She heard other girls pointing them out and making the same surmise.

Occasionally, Magda heard a single shot or a rattle of machine gun fire, and if she were looking in the right place, she would see a girl fall over in the dirt. Then a voice on the intercom reminded the girls that they had been paid for and would not be allowed to leave under any circumstances.

The girls in front of Magda discussed their situation. They had overheard some other girls saying they would leap from the train when they went to relieve themselves at the buckets. If there was a turn or a junction, the train would have to slow, and this was the only safe moment to disembark. Apparently, though, they did not count on the men standing guard on top of the train cars, whose only job was to shoot the girls who tried to run away. They were good at what they did. At night, they would lock everything down, and the girls were not allowed to use the buckets. It was the only way.

The soldiers had warned the girls about escaping. It did not help anyone's cause to leave a trail of dead girls along the train tracks. But some of the girls had heard stories about what awaited them, and they did not wish to become prostitutes for the soldiery. They did not wish to be violated in painful and disfiguring ways, leaving them childless and unhappy.

Throughout the journey, the men with the guns enjoyed themselves. The girls closest to the train car vestibule were most likely to be picked, simply because it was so hard for the soldiers to see more deeply inside the car. And of course the girls were vulnerable when they had to use the buckets. There was even a persistent whisper that some of the girls, the ugly ones, had simply been pushed out of the train or been shot for sport, while the prettier girls were defiled and made to return to their seats. Magda had not expected any of this, and she thought how pleasant it would be if she were back at home, hiding beneath the barn floor—the sack of corn forming a kind of pillow as she listened to the rhythmic tramp of the collectors' boots.

Still, there was a sense of anticipation. As the train pushed through the thickening smoke of civilization, Magda stared into the crowds and lighted windows, hoping to spot Anton. He was somewhere inside of this smoggy metropolis, and she felt closer to him now than she had in months. She would find him. She would keep her eye peeled bright.

CHAPTER 39:
THEN WE CAN COMMENCE
TO PROPERLY STARVING

Pasha enjoyed not having to wait for the outhouse. He enjoyed not having to pass his sister the boiled potatoes. Still, when he retired for the evening after a long day of following the ox or harvesting corn, he was surprised to find her scent lingering in the upper part of the house, even though her door was closed, even though he had not bathed. It persisted for two weeks, and then one day, he walked past her room and did not smell her laundry or the special soaps she sometimes used. The eviction was complete.

His mother took Magda's leaving the hardest. This was surprising even to Magda's mother, for she had long evoked the kind of stoicism that might lead someone to accuse her of being cold. Now their mother sat at the breakfast table stirring a single drop of honey into the scalding tea that Magda used to gather for the whole family. It was mostly buds of red and white clover, lobelia, yarrow, goldenrod—whatever the fallow field gave up to them. Sometimes Magda would bring a basket with her into the surrounding swamps and would return with the heads of pink and yellow flowers that almost no one ever saw. They bloomed for only a week, and she had to travel across mud to find them. They looked all the more striking when she laid them out to dry because of the drabness of the landscape from which they came. It was odd to see such a concentration of color and variety. Of course they were all faded and brittle by the time the tea was made. Magda's mother loved to crunch an intact clover bloom into her tea strainer, forcing it to give up the last bit of fragrance before the boiling water brought it briefly back to suppleness.

"Is there enough water left in the pot?" Pasha asked.

His mother nodded and blew into the darkening cup in front of her. But when Pasha picked up the pot, he could feel there was not enough. He took the dipper and refilled the pot, placing it onto the stove in what he thought would be the hottest portion, the spot that would get him out of the kitchen most quickly.

"Stay out of her room," his mother said without looking up.

Pasha turned and regarded his mother. She looked defeated, like something that had been let out of a trap but was too weak to escape.

"I haven't been in her room," Pasha said. "I have no interest in her trinkets and rags."

His mother blew into her cup again, dispersing the steam. She did not look up at him, which was her way of accusing him a second time. Pasha was about to defend himself, to enumerate the reasons he would have no use for anything that might be found among Magda's effects, but then he heard his father descending the stairs.

"We'll clear the last acre of corn today," his father said as he ducked under the lintel. "Then we can commence to properly starving." It was a joke, but his wife continued to stare into her cup where a stray petal from a flower Magda had picked was still revolving.

Pasha turned back to his own pot, which was starting to rumble. He placed his cup on the counter, filled the strainer, and stepped through the back door to use the outhouse.

CHAPTER 40:
A DISTURBANCE IN THE TOPMOST TASSELS

Out in the corn, away from his father, Pasha walked down a row, yanking the ears from their stalks. It was late enough in the season that if they weren't ripe now, they wouldn't ever be. The rains had stopped, and frost would be the next weather to arrive. Pasha did this work cheerfully, despite the yellow eye of the sun staring into him, despite the soreness in his hands. He would be at it all day. There was no end visible down the long green rows.

To his left, he could hear his father working in the opposite direction. He had long since outpaced Pasha and was working methodically. He was so quick that Pasha had suspected him of skipping over some of the ears—that they each carried in them a different idea of what was ready, what was pickable. Yet on those occasions when Pasha had checked his father's rows, he saw nothing to suggest he was being sloppy. If anything, his father was willing to expend energy to take down even the meager ears. If Pasha had walked the same row, he would have left some of them on the stalk, telling himself they could yet ripen, even though he knew he would not walk down that row again before it was plowed back under.

Pasha and his father started the field on the northern edge together, a dozen rows between them. It was a matter of professional interest who would reach the halfway mark first, just six rows over. It used to always be Pasha, but now his father took great delight in shaming his son, in finishing his rows and setting down in the shade of their only oak. Mr.

Puzanov rolled a cigarette and watched his son moving through the corn. From where his father lay, Pasha was just a disturbance in the topmost tassels. If the wind was right and Pasha smelled the smoke of the cigarette, he knew he was beaten. The smell might have induced a different man to speed up, but Pasha slowed down. He dreaded coming into the final turn to find his father asleep with his hat upon his face—or at least pretending to sleep.

In the old days, if Pasha dragged his bag through the field, his father would grow angry. "The corn will bruise," he would say. "Do you need me to go get your sister?" Remembering this taunt filled Pasha with a pang of regret, for he thought of Magda and what might be happening to her now. The corn was mostly for the goats at this point. They had to lay up enough for the winter to keep the milk from going dry. Pasha did not care for the milk, but he had a great fondness for the wheels of cheese his sister and mother put up in the pantry. He loved breaking off the first handful many weeks later and placing it into a rag he slipped inside his coat pocket. It was a snack he allowed himself against his mother's wishes. She disapproved because, for her, cheese was the farm's most valuable commodity. It was better than the goat itself. Pasha didn't care, and he didn't mind if the center was sometimes sour and viscous. He licked his fingers. He ate his cheese in peace.

It would be a while before anyone was eating cheese again. Pasha hoisted the bag higher onto his shoulder and stepped out of the corn, affecting the swagger of a job well done. He didn't care that his father was watching him through the weave of his hat as he feigned sleep. He felt the albino's finger tapping against his chest and believed his luck was turning.

CHAPTER 41:
AN HOURGLASS OF PINK TAFFETA

Moscodelphia had risen up from the plains gradually. As Magda traveled toward it, there would be glimpses from the train window when there were suddenly no hills or trees or disintegrating barns to stop her from seeing it. It was a gray city, and from far enough away it looked like a storm building in the distance. But as she got closer and the buildings became discernible and she could see that some of them rose into the thick blanket of smog, she realized there was very little turbulence, that part of the reason it looked like a storm was the lack of any wind to clear it all out.

The city eventually resolved into a chaos of stasis—buildings pushed together like a child's blocks, streets that dead-ended by surprise over and over until she had the impression that she was traveling in a maze from which she could not escape.

Magda would soon learn that this city, like all cities, was divided into classes. Of course the lowest caste consisted of the derelicts and criminals, and the city made a point of exterminating them on sight. The most populous class was the workers, who lived in the squat apartment buildings that lined the streets. They worked in the factories along the river, making plastic couches and cement tables, or in the many power plants where men shoveled coal all day into furnaces to make the electricity the city demanded. Above the workers were a class of officials. They populated the tall ministry buildings like a hive of delicate insects. They lived in set-apart houses on the outer rims of the public parks, in the shadows of the ministries. And then there were the leaders, the oligarchs, the rulers—the most mysterious of the classes. They lived, it was said, at the very tops of the ministerial buildings. They traveled about the city by helicopter and motorcade. Soldiers escorted them, and it was considered impolite, even dangerous, to look into the dark windows behind which they rode. It could arouse the suspicion of the government minders who were everywhere in the city, checking to make sure that order was kept and that the factories were efficient. If there were another class, a class above the rulers, no one could say. They would be so powerful that they would likely be invisible, living perhaps in dirigibles that floated high above the smog in the quivering blue of creation.

When Magda's train finally came to a stop in the railyard, she and the other girls were marched off and taken to a large locker room full of showers and dressing tables. The man who led them there told them they would need to make themselves presentable.

Later, Magda believed she had never looked so pretty. She wore proper lipstick, and the dress she had selected was an old pink prom dress. They were popular and in fashion, and she felt giddy with the primping attention that was given her. Before stepping into the lights to be viewed, she examined herself before a full-length mirror. She had never seen such a thing, and she felt like she was seeing herself accurately for the first time. She looked like an hourglass of pink taffeta, and it was the best color to show off her skin, which had just come out of the only hot shower she had ever taken.

Magda and the other girls were walked out into a large gymnasium filled with smoke and laughter and the clinking of bottles. They were lined up against a wall. It had many horizontal lines running across it to mark off their heights, and each girl held a sign that showed her age and weight, and the sector from which she was taken. Magda's placard read "Sector 26." The girls were made to turn around, to reach for the ceiling, to smile. One by one they said their names down the long line of girls by way of introduction, and then the bidding began. Out of twenty-five girls, Magda had been selected twelfth, which she took as an honor, if only because the girls who remained against the wall instantly treated her with scorn.

Magda had stayed with the same girl since they'd gotten off the train. She didn't bother to learn her name, but they showered together. They picked out their dresses together. They helped each other with their hair and makeup. The other girl had tired brown eyes. She was older than Magda and regarded the whole process with a good deal more menace than Magda imagined.

"You never know who will get you," the other girl said. "He may want to stick it in your bottom every night, and it'll be your job to let him."

This information had unsettled Magda, and she walked with dread toward the voice of the man who had purchased her.

"I am Josef Baranov," he said, taking her by the elbow and leading her to a table in the back of the gymnasium. Magda noted the strange scars on the tips of his fingers. He had a pockmarked face and a clever smile. He wore the jacket of a junior official. She did not understand the insignia above his breast pocket—a yellow star at the tip of a tall building, as if the light had been extruded from it, like juice from a grape. Other men had the same type of jacket, and they were the ones who had made off with the first twelve girls. Men with other jackets and other insignias continued to bid and shout lewdly at the remaining girls, a couple of whom had begun to cry. Magda watched as Josef signed some papers then folded the receipt.

Magda scanned the room as Josef finished up. She saw the girl she had showered with trying to stay composed as the man who had purchased her told her to sit in a chair and keep quiet. He was a big man. He did not try to hide his cruelty. Then Josef was telling Magda to follow him, and Magda turned away before the other girl caught her eye. They moved to exit the building, but a photographer stopped them and asked them to stand against a wall. He told them to smile and then there was a blinding flash, the spot of which stayed with Magda as she was led outside, trying to blink it from her vision.

Magda found herself with Josef in the back of a chauffeured car, which whisked them through the canyon-like streets of Moscodelphia. Sometimes there were gunshots and people fleeing an unseen pursuer. Once there was a man hanging from a streetlamp, a fire truck ladder extended beside him—to either take him down or hoist him higher.

"Don't worry," said Josef. "The glass is bulletproof. No one will stop this car."

Magda had not thought she was in danger. She assumed that whatever was happening outside the car was intentional and choreographed. It had not occurred to her that the murderousness might touch them without permission.

"Where are we going?" she asked. She looked at the side of Josef's head as she asked him this, and she saw that he did not avert his gaze from the road in front of him when he answered.

"We are going to see our new home," he said. "It won't be long."

It was only this last part that disturbed Magda. The people she saw outside the window appeared desperate and untrustworthy. If she were asked to get out and walk, she would beg to stay inside the car.

The driver made a sharp turn to the right, and suddenly the demeanor of the city changed. The streets became steadily cleaner and less frenetic. They drove through two checkpoints where papers were produced and stamped, and then they were driving down a street with trees. Theirs was the only car on the road now. Back at the gymnasium, when she was undressing, an attendant had taken each item as she removed it and thrown it into an incinerator. Magda shifted in her seat, feeling the straps of her dress cut into her shoulder. She wondered if this is what she would wear each day as the wife of Josef Baranov.

CHAPTER 42:
SHE WONDERED WHAT COLOR FLOWERS THE BUSHES WOULD EVENTUALLY BEAR

The house was modest, but it had a yard. That's what set it apart from the otherwise tenement-filled streetscapes they had driven through. They were in a section of Moscodelphia devoted to the official class—the men who wore ties and worked in the various ministries that towered above the cigarette-strewn pavement. There were dozens of stand-alone houses, and some of the buildings around them were so high that the smog prevented one from knowing exactly how far they reached.

The driver opened the door for them, and then Josef led Magda by the elbow up three concrete steps. They entered the house together, and the foyer had a sterile newness to it—the smell of recently applied paint to cover the scuffs and stains of the previous tenants. As they walked about inspecting, their heels echoed against the still undecorated walls. Outside, they heard the car that brought them there pulling away.

"I think this will do," said Josef. "Don't you agree?"

Magda nodded, and Josef went on to tell her that this was his first time in the house, that they were reserved for married officials. Josef made it clear that unmarried people weren't welcome here at all. He had an acquaintance once—Alexander—whom he had not seen in years because he'd advanced so much more quickly in the ministry and thus had the chance to marry sooner. For all Josef knew, they might be neighbors now.

Magda stood beside the front window, and Josef told her to open the curtains. The yard was fenced in and small, but there were some bushes in each corner and a low hunched tree that looked like a maple in the center of the yard. It was practically fall now, and everything had an air of premature exhaustion. The day was cool and drizzling. She wondered what color flowers the bushes would eventually bear, but the sternness of Josef's profile scanning the rooms made her think better of wondering aloud. She would wait for her answer after the spring arrived the following year.

Josef stepped behind her and put his hands on her shoulders. It was a gesture of affection, but there was force in it.

"I am pleased with how the bidding went today," he said.

Magda allowed his hands to linger and thought about whether she also was pleased. Josef was more handsome than not and, apparently, a good provider. She liked his jaw. He did not seem brutish, as she had been warned some men could be. Magda was certain she had heard Josef bidding on most of the eleven girls who walked off before Magda, and yet he seemed earnest at this moment, if not tender.

Josef left her side and walked to the kitchen. It was small and neat, and the refrigerator contained vegetables and fruit, a large bowl of potatoes, and something Magda had never seen before: two slabs of beef.

"We will have a feast," said Josef, smiling. He held the door open for Magda to see, and she stepped over cautiously. She worried it might be some sort of trap, and tried to imagine how she could escape it if that ended up being true. She looked inside and felt the cold air gathering around her feet.

"Shall I prepare this food for you?" she asked.

"Of course," he said. Then he walked alone through the rest of the house, getting the lay of it, studying what was his.

Magda began opening and closing drawers. Everything seemed to have been provided for them, and Magda was especially struck by the fact that all their utensils matched. Back on the farm, the knives and forks and spoons were a hodgepodge of styles and sizes. In fact, there were just two forks that matched exactly, and this was remarked upon by everyone who ate at their table. "They must be twins," her father would joke, and everyone would enjoy the strange coincidence.

Now there were six of everything—all of them gleaming and nested into each other, as if no other mouth had ever closed itself around them, as if the oatmeal might surprise the spoon. When Josef came back into the kitchen, Magda remarked on the utensils. She was beaming, but Josef said only that he liked his meat with salt.

Magda opened two more cabinet doors before finding the block of salt with a small metal grater beside it. She poured a little vinegar over the meat, which is how her mother would have prepared the goat steaks they sometimes ate. Then she filed away at the salt block's sharpest edge, coating the meat with fine gray flakes.

Josef had removed his jacket and tie by now and hung them on the coat stand by the door. He had found a bottle of wedding wine and poured himself a glass and was relaxing in the big chair by the front window. He was halfway through his first serving when Magda interrupted him.

"My husband," she said, "forgive me. But I don't know how to make fire in this kitchen."

At first Josef was confused. Then he remembered that his new wife was from the countryside, that she was backward and would have to be told even the simplest things. Josef put aside his glass and strode into the kitchen. He showed Magda how to work the dials of the oven. He showed her how the coils turned red and must not be touched under any circumstance. He was happily surprised that she understood the concepts of temperature and numbers. Then he went back to his wine, keeping one eye on Magda but pleased with his selection.

CHAPTER 43:
THE LUXURIES THE CITY OFFERED
SERVED ONLY TO PRODUCE ANXIETY

Magda looked up from the soapy basin of dishes and saw Mrs. Constanti-nopolis staring at her through her own kitchen window. It was a common occurrence, and Magda had stopped waving long ago. Mrs. Constantinop-olis never acknowledged the gesture or looked away, and Magda felt she must be violating some Moscodelphian custom wherein people pretended not to be staring into their neighbors' windows even after they had been caught doing so. Either that, or Mrs. Constantinopolis had very bad eyes.

Regardless, Magda touched her hair to make sure it wasn't wild, and she was careful to work without frowning. Mrs. Constantinopolis had remarked more than once how girls from the country were ill-suited to life in the city. Because such girls were simple, the luxuries the city offered served only to produce anxiety. That was her theory anyway. Magda reached into the basin, found a dish, wiped it, and rinsed it under the running tap.

When she looked out the window again, Mrs. Constantinopolis was gone. Magda saw her neighbor's bathroom light go on, and Mrs. Constan-tinopolis went in and sat down. Magda could see only the top of her head, but it was clear she was on the toilet. The layout of their home was the same as Magda's. When Magda realized people could see into her own bathroom, she put up curtains, but Mrs. Constantinopolis either didn't care or hadn't realized what it might be like for Magda staring at the back of her house. Even an outhouse has a door, Magda reasoned.

When Magda looked up again, Mrs. Constantinopolis was still sitting down, and she drew conclusions. It was strange. When she had lived in the country, she hadn't really thought about what someone could see through a lighted window at night. There weren't any neighbors close enough to worry about it, and anyone prowling around the farm risked being mistaken for a bear and shot. Here, there were so many windows that their sheer number seemed a deterrent. Certainly Josef had no great concern. When she first put up curtains in the bedroom, he had chastised her for spending so much money on something that had no practical value. Still, it seemed to be customary among the official class, and so he relented, but he continued to think the bathroom curtain was an extravagance.

"The only people who can see are Mical and his wife," he said. "And only the tops of our heads," he added, taking a spoonful of the stew Magda made every Monday night, which she cobbled together from the leftovers of the previous few nights. This was true, but Magda had been able to prevail upon Josef. She had made the request in the early days of their marriage, when he was still in a mood to make concessions to his new wife, because he himself was not sure about the proper conduct in such a circumstance. He didn't wish to ask what others thought, for it would mean that he was out of his element, but a review of the neighborhood's windows showed that most of them had curtains.

CHAPTER 44:
MAKE SURE IT HITS THE ROCKS

It had been a long time since anyone in Moscodelphia had seen the stars. At best, when the moon was full and the smog not heavy, the light could fight its way to the ground and force a weak shadow from the denuded apple trees that lined the boulevard beside the river. When they were first married, Magda and Josef used to walk there, and there were still song-birds in the air. Now the river was sulfurous and slow moving, and no one wished to walk along its banks.

Starlight was more or less a figment. You would have to travel far from the city to see anything like it, for the air that fitted over the city was like a dome of illuminated gray smoke.

"Give me your hand," Josef had said back in the old days, and they would walk together beside the river, watching the air go dark between the buildings. "Make a wish," he would say, handing her a bright penny. It was Josef's one extravagance. To throw money into the river, even so small an amount, seemed wasteful to him. But Magda appreciated the gesture. The first time she tried, the penny fell short, and they heard the single metallic ping as it hit one of the granite boulders beneath them. "I'm sure it bounced in," said Josef, because she was looking at him to give her another penny, another chance to wish for something happy and prosperous.

Magda wished always for the same thing: starlight, clean air, the scent of animals drifting in through the windows. And every time she wished it, she couldn't believe this was her wish. She had spent her entire life hoping to escape the countryside, to experience the curious and incomplete darkness that now rose up around her. When she was younger, she wanted only to shed her old life like a bandage and find herself healed by the excitement of money and style and comfortable shoes. Why had she wished for these shoes? It seemed like somebody else's wish now, and Magda often felt that she was not the same person she once was.

And why, she wondered, did she not wish for Anton? When she had first arrived in the city, he was all that she could think about when she was alone with her chores and Josef was at work. She surveyed the crowds as she ran her errands, believing she would find him. But her years in Moscodelphia acted as a balm, and it became harder and harder to remember the touch of Anton's fingers reaching beneath her dress, or the taste of his lips as they'd shared a bit of brandy. The longer she lived in the city, the smaller and more sensible her aspirations became.

"I threw my mother's cat, Alice, from a bridge like this," said Josef. Magda stopped and looked at him. His face was dark, but she could tell it was something he had been wanting to say to her, though it had only just occurred to him. The cat had been sick, his mother distraught. His father had handed him the sack and told him to throw it off the bridge that crossed the river that ran through their lavish suburb. "Make sure it hits the rocks," he had said. It was a terrible command, but one Josef carried out because it was necessary. The cat's mouth and anus had both been bleeding. It could barely walk. This is what happened when a pet had to be put down in the suburbs. It was a common practice. When he was very young, Josef would play along the riverbanks, and he would find the skeletons of cats and dogs bleaching on the gray boulders beside the water.

Magda listened to the story and marveled at its excess. To her it sounded like a waste of a perfectly good sack, but she knew she should keep this to herself. She remembered watching Pasha drown whole litters of kittens because the rats were under control, and having too many cats on the farm would only make them wild and sneaky. They might start stealing the chicks as they wobbled about the yard. The farm she grew up on—every farm, really—was a cruel and practical place. There was no room for sentimentality in one's relationship with animals. True, even Pasha didn't look forward to drowning the kittens in a bucket, but it was very quick, and nothing was wasted. While people never ate cats because the meat was tough and flavor-less, the pigs ate them greedily when the kittens were mixed in with their slops. Magda wanted to be sensitive to her new husband's revelation.

"Did the cat die quickly?" she asked.

It did not—even though Josef had thrown it down hard, even though it had hit the rocks directly, twenty feet below. He told her that he could see the cat still moving inside the sack. He had thought about climbing down to it, but the banks were steep and muddy and he was wearing his good pants. His mother would be cross if he came home dirty. He tried to finish the job by dropping large stones onto the sack, but he kept missing. After ten minutes, there was no movement coming from the sack anyway, and he could see where blood had seeped into the cloth.

When Josef returned home, his father gave him a little whiskey and a bright penny. The next morning, Josef was awakened by the sound of laughter. He found his mother holding the new kitten like a baby. She wouldn't put it down, and he remembered thinking that a terrible mask of sadness had been torn from her face. Josef took private pleasure in this. Of course he could not tell his mother what had actually happened, but he came to believe in his later years that she probably understood. His father, after all, had been talking about putting the cat down for days. When the cat was suddenly replaced with a new kitten climbing her living room drapes, what else could she have surmised?

Josef was nine at the time.

CHAPTER 45:
WHY HAVE YOU KILLED MY TURTLE?

Magda remembered the first time she was with Josef. This was before the present thickness of the smog, and a half-moon was shining down, turning the window a bright gray beside his pillow.

"Tell me something from your girlhood," he had said. "Something that nobody else can know."

It was a lover's request, and Josef had never asked Magda something like this before. Of course she worried that it might be a trap—that he would use her answer as a reason to punish her, to show how she had strayed from the better path. Still, a dozen memories rose up, each one urging her tongue to speak it, to make it real, to relieve herself of having to carry it alone, without respite or encouragement.

She wanted to tell him about her younger brother, Benjamin; how he had slowly been consumed with fever and jaundice. The doctor had no name for it, and each day he grew smaller and less emphatic. Listening to him try to speak was like trying to read an old wet newspaper with the candle too far away. Magda dreamed once that Benjamin floated out the window because he had grown so light and the wind had kicked him up. It terrified Magda, forcing her out of her own cold bed in the middle of the night and into the room of her younger brother, only to find him present and alive, but somehow tinier than he had been just six hours before when Magda kissed him goodnight. Magda had never told anyone that. Not even Benjamin.

And for a moment, she considered telling Josef about the fallow field—how every couple of years, it was moved one plot farther to the right around her parents' house, as if that field were a slow hand of wildness revolving around the clock of the family farm. It was her favorite plot of land because the butterflies tended to exist only above that rectangle of rocky weeds jammed with goldenrod and clover and wild mint. This was the field from which their tea would come. It was a place she could lie down in the center of and credibly disappear—unless of course someone had walked up to the lookout point. One day as she lay in the center of all those bee-filled weeds, studying the easterly drift of the clouds, she saw Anton staring down at her. He had his umbrella open, and he was smoking; the wind took his smoke in the same direction as the clouds, despite his exhalations to the west.

Instead, she told Josef about the snapping turtle that had crawled out of the irrigation pond on their farm. It was covered in slime and had a fat, powerful neck. She had found it on the path to the well, and she was afraid of it. She had seen it swimming in the pond, which is why she herself would not swim there anymore. To find it on the path like that inspired her. She saw her chance. She could pick up the shovel leaning against the well stones and chop its head off. It would never get close to her. And that is what she did. There was a hissing of air when she pulled the shovel back—and a terrible stink. And then the voice of her father called out: "Magda! Why have you killed my turtle?" She did not understand, and there was a great disappointment that descended upon her. Her father picked up the turtle by the tail and left it on the back porch for her mother, who pried apart the shell and scooped the eggs into a large bowl. They ate the lot of them that night because they would not keep, and Magda's father smoked the meat of the turtle into a tough jerky. The following morning, her father would not look up at Magda as she walked by with her bucket on the way to feed the pigs.

"This was the first of the many disappointments I caused my father," she said.

"I don't believe you," said Josef. He was teasing. "What girl could be so brave as to chop the head off a turtle?"

She knew it sounded far-fetched, and she doubted she would have the presence of mind to act the same way now. If she were back on the farm and that same turtle showed up, she would find a reason to not need water. She would let it lay its eggs in the sandy shore and then watch it disappear into the ponds and swamps that rimmed their farm. Like everything else, it would be a matter of waiting.

"That turtle ruined the pond for me," she said. "I saw it eat a baby duck once as it paddled in a line of ducklings behind its mother." She explained that she had loved the pond when she was very young. She had learned to swim there, and when she went underwater and opened her eyes, she saw fat, slow-eyed sunfish fanning the sand among the weeds.

Josef was impressed. He pulled her closer. He wanted her to know that he hadn't meant to tease her so badly.

"And after the turtle was dead," he said, "you returned to the pond? It became yours to swim in once again?"

Magda was ashamed to admit that this was not the case. It didn't matter that she had killed the thing that frightened her. The idea of the turtle—its mineral eyes, the leeches suckered all over its shell—kept her away from the thing she loved.

As Josef lay dozing in the darkness of the room, he realized there was no siren in the air around them anywhere, even when he listened into the farthest reaches of the city. It was an oddness. He decided at that moment he would take Magda to swim in the sea. Then he fell into sleep like a stone that was dropped off a pier, landing without a sound in the gas-filled mud beside the pilings.

CHAPTER 46:
HER SKIN HAD DRIVEN HIM TO POETRY

Josef was surprised at how satisfied he had become with Magda. She was a comfort to him, and she knew when to keep quiet. Some evenings he would see her waiting in the lighted doorway, watching for his approach from the Ministry of Opulence. When she spotted him, she would at last fill his water glass with ice. It was the final task before the meal was ready, for she knew Josef detested warm water. Even worse was water where the ice had melted and only begun to warm. A glass of water like that told Josef that his wife was out of step, that she did not understand the rhythm of their life together.

In the very beginning of their marriage, Josef often thought of Isabelle and what it would be like to have married her instead. He could not stop thinking of the olive smoothness of her shoulders, the vibrations of her throat as she laughed when he was kissing her. Her skin had driven him to poetry, and the memory of it distorted his perception of everything else he touched. When he married Magda, he thought it would be a marriage of convenience. He needed a wife to rise in the ministry, and a woman from the countryside could fulfill that need. Many of his colleagues had gotten such brides, and he recognized that not everyone could be Mical Constantinopolis, with a wife who was city-born and who had already given him a son.

"When we have our child," Josef said, "we will be able to apply for a better house." He knew this was wishful thinking. Mical Constantinopolis still lived in the same house despite having a son. But he also knew that the better houses always went to men who were expected to rise in the ministry. Josef thought Mical's unchanging residence spoke better of his own chances for advancement. Someday, he thought, Mical would be taking orders from him.

Magda, for her part, wanted nothing more than to provide the child that Josef craved. They had regular relations, and Magda drank special teas she ordered from the countryside. They were supposed to improve fertility, but the mandrakes and sweet flag of which they consisted were never fresh enough. The teas they produced were not aromatic, and Magda suspected they were ordinary leaves crushed up into something approaching dust so that the ruse would go undetected.

When she finally conceived after more than a year of trying, she held off telling Josef until she had gone two months without bleeding. "I am finally with child," she told him, and Josef almost cried as he hugged her belly and spoke to the child hidden beneath Magda's housecoat.

But when Magda woke up the next morning, she had a dull aching in her pelvis, and there were several drops of blood mixed in with her urine after she used the toilet. She knew everything in an instant, but she did not tell Josef. At that moment, he was in the kitchen, attempting to make a breakfast of fried eggs and bacon, and his joy terrified her. She kept the secret to herself for as long as she could. It was important to be sure.

Josef grew dark when he learned what had happened. He asked why she hadn't been more careful. He asked her to remember the thing she must have done. When he grew tired of listening to her tears, he left the house and drank wine in one of the restaurants. He thought of Isabelle and her beautiful skin. Then he patted at his pockets in hopes of finding a pen.

CHAPTER 47:
IT WOULD SMELL THE BACON MORE

Pasha was happy when he woke to the ground covered lightly in snow. The grass was still sticking through in the yard, and there were uncovered patches under the pines. Behind the trees the sky was lightening, and the windows were not creaking. The morning would be windless.

This would be Pasha's chance to find the fox that had been trying to get at his chickens. Every night for a week, the coop had erupted in commotion as they smelled the fox approaching or heard him testing the wire of their enclosure. Although the fox had so far failed to kill one of the hens, Pasha knew it would happen soon if he didn't take action. If the animal was willing to risk entering the farm at night, it must be desperate. It would eventually succeed.

It was cold out, and there would be little work on the farm. His mother and father would take the opportunity to sleep in late, though he knew they must be listening to him even now, trying to judge his movements down in the kitchen. Pasha put on both of his coats and grabbed the two steel traps they used mostly for gophers. Then he went out to the chicken yard to see what the tracks would tell him. The chickens were not yet up and out of their coop, but he could see that the fox had never gotten inside the fence. He saw how it paced twice around the entire enclosure looking for a weakness, even though it must have performed the same inspection on its other visits to the pen. In a couple of places, Pasha saw where the fox had sat back on its haunches, sniffing at the feathery, dung-filled air. Then the tracks headed off between the barn and the outhouse, in the direction of the woods.

The tracks were neat and unhurried, so Pasha went back and grabbed a biscuit and a strip of old bacon and put them in his pocket. He decided he would follow the tracks until he found where the animal had denned. Then he'd lay the traps and return the next day.

The trail was easy to follow, though the fox took Pasha through prickers and thick bushes that made it impossible for him to move with any secrecy. It didn't matter. Pasha was not attempting surprise. In fact, he hoped the fox was just ahead of his footfall. It would force the fox into a hole more quickly, a hole the fox might not be familiar with. A second entrance would be less likely, and Pasha would not have to walk all morning.

But the fox's trail continued unhurried through the woods, being careful to keep the farmhouses as far away as possible. Then the tracks changed. He saw where the animal had stopped to think. The tracks briefly disappeared, and it took Pasha a moment to see where they began again. A dozen feet away, he saw where the fox had landed. There was a disturbance in the snow, a small bit of blood where it must have come upon a rabbit or a rat. It was clear the fox had dined on the spot rather than carrying it back to the den. That meant the den must still be far, and Pasha steeled himself.

Farther on, Pasha saw where another fox had crossed the trail perpendicular to the one he was following. It was only the other fox that had paused to sniff at the paw prints, so there had been no midnight meeting. Pasha continued, and the trail began to loop more wildly. This was a good sign. It told Pasha that the fox was near its den, that it was exploring a familiar hunting ground. Then Pasha came to the intersection of fox trails where he had been an hour before. He recognized his own footprints and grumbled that he'd wasted an hour. It was not two foxes but one, and he could have saved himself some trouble by following the other trail. Of course he could never know that without staying the course he'd taken.

A half hour later, the tracks terminated at a low, rocky hillside. It was full of potential lairs, and Pasha saw where the fox prints entered a suitable hole and did not come out. He had found the den. Pasha sat down on a stone beside the entrance and began to eat his biscuit and his bacon. He didn't mind when the crumbs fell to the ground at his feet, because this is where he'd be laying his traps. The bacon was very greasy, and he smeared it across the pan before he opened the jaws and staked the trap into place. It was a meager inducement, but he was certain the animal sleeping in the hole before him would take notice. In a lean time such as this, caution can cost your life. The fox would have to investigate. And while it would surely smell Pasha on the newly laid traps, it would smell the bacon more.

CHAPTER 48:
EVERYTHING ELSE IN THE WORLD FELT MUTED

The following day, Pasha did not hurry to check on the traps. He took his breakfast at his leisure, and he made time to finish chores that could have been put off for another day. He cleaned out the chicken coop. He brought the pigs their slops. In fact, most of his morning was spent fashioning a new wooden handle for the pump beside the barn. In a few weeks, the iron handle, while effective, would almost be untouchable. The purity of the cold would slip easily between the weave of Pasha's yarn mittens. Besides, arriving at the traps too early meant only that the fox might still be alive. He was hoping that the jaws would have come down on its neck or skull when it leaned in to learn about the bacon wafting up from the trap's metal pan. But another outcome was also possible, that the fox would have tested the trap with its paw.

When that happened, it was a matter of waiting out the fox or clubbing it to death. Neither option was ideal. If Pasha let the traps linger for too long, the fox would expire from exhaustion, but it might also be eaten by some other opportunist—a roving coyote or bobcat. If it was cold enough, another fox might even be the one to finish it off—maybe one of its brothers. Finding the fox still living in the trap jaws meant a clubbing. But that could damage the coat, and there was always the chance the fox might hook you with its fangs. Bites were serious. A tiny animal could bring a large one down with sickness.

Pasha was eating a lunch of biscuits and wild leeks when his father commented on the missing traps.

"You have another girl you are trying to impress?" he asked.

His father was smirking beneath his beard, but it was visible mostly in his eyes.

"What the trap catches will determine the girl," said Pasha.

Mr. Puzanov sat down in the chair beside his son, and a board in the floor made a low squeak beneath him. "Well, let's hope you get something better than possum."

The two of them laughed about some of the possum girls in town, how they weren't much better than farm girls, really. Then Pasha opened the hall closet and took down his satchel and his club. The weight of the club was pleasing to him. It was the same pleasure he felt when fishing and the pole bent down farther than he'd anticipated. There was a density, a solidity that said good things were coming. The club was a single piece of oak two feet long and thick as an arm but tapering where his fist would hold it. The knot at the opposite end had two fat nails protruding, but only on one side, so that in any situation Pasha had a choice of puncturing the skull or cracking it apart.

Pasha made it to the lair more quickly than the day before. It took only an hour to arrive. There had been another light dusting of snow, and the landscape looked untrammeled. As he approached the spot where the traps were laid, he crouched down in the holly branches to see what might be waiting. There was no commotion, no sense that animals had found his fox. The snow was white. The blackness of the lair was plain.

Pasha approached further, and there, from a slightly different vantage, he saw the humped-up fur of the fox. Its redness was shocking, for the sky was overcast, and everything else in the world felt muted, depleted. When he got closer, he could see that the death had been a quick one. The fox had nosed into the pan and the jaws had come down around its neck. Pasha bent in closer. The eyes were lightless. From the look of things, it had probably set off the trap not long after Pasha had laid it. There was a dusting of snow along its fur. He pulled the jaws away from the fox and let it fall to the ground. Already it was stiffening. This was good. It meant the fleas would have left the carcass by now. He stuffed the fox inside his satchel.

The second trap was unactivated, so Pasha pushed a stick into it, feeling the metallic snap travel up his arm through the cracked wood. He unstaked the two traps and headed home. He enjoyed the feel of them and the fox bouncing lightly against his back.

When he returned to the farm, there would be enough light left to dress and skin the fox. It was an excellent specimen. The coldness was such that its coat was at maximum richness. There could be no better time for the fox to succumb to the wish to end its hunger. Nothing comes easily in weather like this, he thought. The fox must have sensed the danger of the trap even as the animal fell under its bacony spell.

Pasha arranged the town girls in his mind in order of best to worst. Surely, he thought, Bettina could do with a fox fur hat. Her yellow hair would form a striking contrast to the fur of the murdered fox. He groaned as he imagined Bettina thanking him with her skilled and tiny hands.

CHAPTER 49:
SHE DIPPED HER FINGERS IN AGAIN

Magda had heard of the ocean after she came to the city, but it seemed exotic and remote and never to be touched—like the air inside a painting—so she never pressed Josef for more information. Now she was on her way to it.

At first the train ride to the sea was lively and Magda had many questions. She wanted to know if the water was truly salty. She wanted to know about leviathans and starfish and whether the moon rose out of it dripping. But the journey would take a full six hours, and the tedium of sitting in the same place eventually took over. When Magda woke up, she was surprised to find the window full of pine trees and blue sky.

"Where did the smog go?" she asked, squinting.

Josef was oblivious. He was working on some papers and had failed to notice they had escaped the air of the city.

"The sky above the sea is always painful," he said.

When it became clear that Josef had nothing further to add, Magda concentrated on the pine trees stretching out on either side of the train. The sameness of the landscape frightened her. She wondered how she would find her way out if she were suddenly lost among those trees. But the rhythm of the train was seductive, and Magda dozed off again.

Then there was a jolt and a surge of deceleration, and Magda woke to passengers rising and gathering their bags. The train tracks had ended in a resort town at the edge of the ocean. Josef took up their basket and guided

Magda away from the crowds, who were all heading toward a line of lack-luster casinos, where they would be served an afternoon of watered-down whiskey and rigged games.

Josef led his wife over a grassy dune topped by an ancient hurricane fence with bits of trash stuck all over it. Magda smelled the sea before she saw it. The wind was driving over the dunes and turning her hair wild. It reminded her of lying in the fallow field while the weeds swayed crazily around her, staring up at Anton as he stood on the lookout rock above her family's farm, where there was nothing to impede the wind's travels.

And then the sea was there—a gray flatness that stretched farther than she could imagine, and the part that was touching the shore kept rising and rolling to a froth of dull thunder. She held Josef's hand more tightly. The gulls were screaming. A man dove into the surf and came up glistening.

Josef put down the basket and told her to take off her shoes. He pulled her to the sea, and she stood in the waves and felt the sand eroding from under her as the water rushed back from where it came. It left her wobbly, and she worried she would lose her footing and be swept away into that gray infinity. The sensation was not displeasing.

Magda dipped her fingers into the water and tasted them, and it reminded her of tears. She dipped her fingers in a second time to be certain of where she was.

The ocean greeted Magda as it did everyone for the first time—as a demonstration that you could go no farther without drowning. Josef pointed out the large ships on the horizon, and at first Magda did not believe him. She thought they were buildings. But when she looked up again after trying to find pretty shells, the ships were someplace else. Some of them had even disappeared, and Josef explained about the curvature of the Earth, which only made Magda laugh.

"On the other side of the water, farther than we can see, is more land," he said.

"Now I am sure you are joking," she said, a little insulted that she would be teased this way for having grown up in the country.

Josef took her hand and looked into her eyes with great seriousness. "It does exist," he said. "And we are at war with the people who live there." He explained that the ships they saw disappearing over the horizon were taking men and bullets to the battle. He explained that the war was almost over.

"Why have I never heard of this war?" she asked.

It was a sensible question, but Josef redirected her attention to the crabs hiding in the stones of the jetty. It was simpler not to answer, and Magda was happy to follow the conversation wherever he led it. Not far away, a gull was ripping the insides out of a crab while the other gulls circled, screaming, looking for their moment to steal what scraps were left.

"Why don't they just find their own crabs?" she said. "They must be lazy."

Josef nodded. It looked like it would be easy to reach down and grab one of the scuttling blue shells before it disappeared into a crevice of the jetty, but he knew how difficult it really was. He had visited this beach more than once during his boyhood, and his mother had told him to catch as many crabs as he could. Five minutes later, Josef had returned to her crying because the crabs had pinched him. There was even a little blood. Now Josef saw several crabs waiting for the next wash of waves to arrive, their claws raised expectantly. He pointed them out to Magda.

"Why don't you try to grab one?" he said.

She handed Josef the shells she had been gathering and picked out the crab she would capture first. It had been a strange day. If Josef could be believed, then the Earth was round and mostly made of water. And that water tasted like tears. And there were wars and continents she had never heard of. And as the crab bit into her hand, she realized there would be stars when the sky went dark above them.

Magda hadn't seen stars since she was taken from the farm, and she had to shake her hand twice before the crab let go. Then she saw Josef laughing.

CHAPTER 50:
THE SMELL OF A LARGE MEAL
LEFT OVER IN THE KITCHEN

Pasha came home drunk. If there had been no moon, he would have had trouble finding the farm, for he had cut through the large woods that divided the farmland from the townland. He had spent the evening with Rosilyn, the town girl who ended up getting the fox fur hat. She had allowed herself to be enjoyed, and Pasha drank more of her father's brandy than he should have. Afterward, when her father discovered the missing liquor and then the drunken Pasha, he chased him out of the house, threatening to shoot him. Rosilyn's father had hurled the empty brandy bottle as Pasha fled, and it had grazed the side of his head. He wasn't hurt badly, but it was evidence that the man was serious. Pasha decided to cut through the woods rather than risk walking home on the roads.

Deep among the trees, Pasha kept tripping and falling to his knees, and once he stayed down for half an hour so he could vomit and clear his head. He was lucky the night was warm, for he'd left his jacket at Rosilyn's house, and he doubted he would see it again. The jacket wasn't a good one, but it would have to be replaced, and the thought of having to spend money pained him.

Pasha heard the animals moving around. He wondered how many had seen him before, and whether his scent was known. The moon was bright and high above him, but it failed to illuminate the source of the breaking twigs. It was just as well. He sat up with his back against a boulder and sniffed his fingers. She was still there—like the smell of a large meal left over in the kitchen.

The moon made the woods unfamiliar, even though he had hunted there many times. The quality of dimness and extravagance subdued him. He could not trust his eyes in a light like this.

When he finally made it home, the house was dark, but the stairs were where he expected them to be. He climbed to the second floor by leaning against the wall and pulling himself upward by means of the railing, but he turned into his sister's room by mistake. He fell into the bed fully clothed.

In the morning, he became aware of his headache before he registered the intense sunlight falling all over his face. The curtains were open. He felt sick and confused. For a moment, Pasha thought he was still at Rosilyn's, and he jumped up with a start, thinking he might have to defend himself. He looked down on the pillowcase. It was smeared with blood from where the bottle had caught him in the temple.

Pasha rubbed deeply at his eyes and realized that he was in his sister's bed. He got up and swatted the blanket into order. He burped. He tasted the brandy again.

CHAPTER 51:
TELL ME ABOUT THE LAST TIME
YOU HAD RISEN ABOVE THE SMOG

"What is it like," Magda asked Josef one evening, "when you go to the top of the ministry building and get above the smog?"

Josef put down the magnifying glass he was using to complete his puzzle. He had been working on it all week. The pieces were spread across a card table in the living room, and he had already assembled the edges. Two pieces were missing, though, for there were no more flat pieces on the table; he was sure of it. When Josef had complained about the missing pieces, it reminded Magda of her younger brother, Benjamin. Before he had died, Benjamin had the habit of hiding a puzzle piece somewhere in the house as Magda worked to put the picture together. Then, days later, as Magda was pressing in the last piece in her possession, her brother would emerge from the shadows, triumphantly inserting the final piece—which for the last hour he had been holding in his sweaty palm, making the cardboard damp. It had infuriated Magda to the point where she felt guilty thinking about it now. It seemed a petty thing to hold onto, given that her brother had wasted away, slowly and painfully. In fact, Magda had been working on a puzzle at the time of Benjamin's death. There was a missing piece, and Magda was never certain if her brother had hidden it or if the puzzle was simply incomplete. After the burial, Magda had made a search of her brother's room before dismantling the puzzle and putting it back in its box.

But the missing pieces in Josef's puzzle either had been left out at the factory or, because this was a used puzzle, had been lost for many years. As far as anyone knew, there were no more puzzle factories. All the puzzles that existed in Moscodelphia came from an earlier time, like the prom gown Magda was made to wear on the day of her bidding. Thus, the cityscape of Paris that Josef was working on was no longer accurate. The Eiffel Tower had been torn down long ago and used to make freight trains, even before Josef was born.

"I have not been to the upper floors recently," Josef said.

"Well, then, the last time," said Magda. "Tell me about the last time you had risen above the smog."

Josef put his hands on the unassembled pieces as if he were performing a séance and was about to raise the table up by means of magic or chicanery. "That would have been at the Founders Day Luncheon."

The luncheon had taken place several months earlier. It was the day when everyone at the level of junior subminister and above gathered in the dining hall on the ninety-eighth floor. In the old days, the focus had been on the food brought in from all corners of the world—something concrete to make everyone understand what they were here for: a bounty of prawns, the miracle of a crisp and unbruised apple. Nowadays, since the smog had been hovering for decades above Moscodelphia, the biggest draw of the luncheon was the chance to take in the unadulterated sunshine of the upper floors. Some people thought the blueness of the sky was a trick of the windows, a tint applied to make the world seem more joyous. The ministers joked that if they could do that, they would apply it to all the windows of the city. The subministers wanted to open them, to stick their heads out, to breathe in a whipping wind of cleanliness that had not even a hint of sulfur.

"Mical Constantinopolis got drunk on vodka and fell into a display of sliced peppers," he said, laughing to himself and reaching for the magnifying glass.

"What color were they?" asked Magda. "The peppers?"

Josef wiped the fat lens on the tail of his untucked shirt. "All colors," he said. "It was amazing: green, orange, red." He held the lens up to the light to test it. "This year, the red peppers were still crunchy." Josef reminded Magda that he had brought her some of the red peppers; he had carried them back inside his coat pocket. He said that everyone had a great laugh at Mical's stupidity.

"They were delicious," she agreed. She ran the tap and poured a little water into the basil plant she kept on the kitchen windowsill. "I would like to go up there someday, to see what the air is like. It sounds like the farm I grew up on."

Josef felt a twinge of envy whenever Magda spoke of the farm. Because he had been born on the outskirts of the city, in the affluent suburbs, he had often known clear days, but he believed these to be his privilege alone. The suburbs were for the well-to-do, and the clear air of his childhood was something he prized. He had a hard time believing that lowly people from the countryside could enjoy such a sky with anything approaching regularity. He wanted to believe his access to the cerulean was a perk he shared only with his peers when he took part in the annual lunch on the ninety-eighth floor of the Ministry of Opulence.

CHAPTER 52:
THE THUMB-WORN IMAGE OF A SAINT

The day was like any other. Magda's mother got up, made her water, and began her chores. When she ate her morning egg, it tasted a little of dirt, and she knew that hen must be almost depleted. As she carried her plate to the counter, she felt the lump in her armpit throbbing. She tried to judge whether it was worse today than yesterday and couldn't be sure. This was a fool's way of measuring progress. It gave her hope. When she considered the lump in comparison to last week or last month, the worsening was unmistakable. She had first noticed it not long after Magda had been taken from them. Mrs. Puzanov was dying.

The family could not afford a doctor, but the doctor was no good for curing things like this anyway. The pain was still local. She could go whole hours without remembering it. She was eager to carry on with whatever the day presented.

After she fed her husband and her son, and after they left to fish in the river on the other side of town, she sat on the top step of their crumbling porch and enjoyed her coffee and her cigarette. She would tend to the chickens and goats later. They had been Magda's responsibility, and they fell to Mrs. Puzanov after her daughter was taken. The work was monotonous, like all work, but she enjoyed it nonetheless. She liked how the chickens surrounded her as she sprinkled feed over the yard, giving them something to do while she filled their trough and stole their eggs.

She saw the hen that had laid the dirt-tasting egg. It was a red one that had been around for a few years. It was time for her to go. No need to have her clogging up a nesting box with dirty eggs. It wouldn't be long before they became inedible or ran out altogether. She told herself she'd come back for the hen later. She would make a feast of her if Pasha and her husband did not return with enough fish. She laughed a little at the thought, because suddenly she understood that the hen would see another day. In previous years at this time, her husband had never failed to extract a full basket of fish from the river.

When Mrs. Puzanov died, she wanted to be buried instead of burned. She had written a note to this effect and left it among her jewelry, where she knew it would be found. Her treasure consisted of a single ring that no longer fit her and three silver chains, from one of which dangled the thumb-worn image of a saint in bas-relief. Burning a body was an extravagance, and a burden for the living.

After dinner, she would ask her husband to start digging her grave. She had never been much for ceremony, but she did not want to be dumped directly into the cold earth—and the thought of having dirt all over her face was more upsetting to her than even the idea of dying. She would insist on a coffin, and she would make sure Pasha got it built before she actually needed it. She would make him take her measurements before he left the table.

CHAPTER 53:
IT WAS CALLED THE NAUGATONIC

In the autumn, Magda would look up and listen for the high formations of migrating geese heading south. It was something that gave her hope—the annual ability to fly away from the place that held you. And though she could hear their voices, she never caught sight of the shape-shifting Vs that seemed to know exactly where they were going, if only because they did so year after year. She remembered them from her girlhood.

Magda wondered what awaited the geese—probably warmth and food, the same things all of us would expect at the end of a long and purposeful journey. She could not imagine putting forth such effort only to have hunger and cold. If there was one thing Magda was certain of, it was that animals weren't fools, that the natural world knew what it was doing. When a squirrel leapt from one branch to another, it never missed. A river didn't have second thoughts about where it was headed.

When Magda was a girl, she lay in the fallow field, listening to their chorus of escape. It sounded optimistic, like the world was getting better with each wingbeat. She turned the oxeye daisy around between her fingers and felt how easily the contours of her back settled into the dirt beneath her. It was a ground that accommodated. It would be hard to leave. The geese seemed magical to her, foreign. She felt herself more closely aligned with the flowers that surrounded her. They were rooted. Certainly, they had their own migrations—when the autumn deepened and the blossoms turned into fluff. A strong wind could set the feathery seeds in motion, but how far could they really go? If they landed in the soybean fields, they would be plowed under the following year. Their best hope, really, was to stay where they were, to drop into soil only inches from where the parent plant grew. Magda was a daisy. Magda was goldenrod. Magda was the trillium that climbed out of the mud each year in the swamp beyond her farm.

Now Magda was grown and she would sit on her back porch in Moscodelphia, listening for the din of geese each autumn. Amazingly, she sometimes heard them. The clamor of the city would stop for a while, or, more likely, she would hear them before the city got properly started, in the early morning. Of course she couldn't see them. The smog was thick and forbidding, and the geese might not even recognize her home as part of a city. She was invisible to them. Only the spires of the tallest ministry buildings were able to pierce the smog. It might even look like a lake to them—a lake enshrouded in morning mist and spilling over the adjacent countryside.

Magda was often a fool, so she believed there might be a way for her to take to the air, to leave the life that had tired her, just as she had left the farm. There were the silvery planes that skidded across the sky like angels. And Josef had shown her the ocean and told her about the continents. Just that fact alone made her think anything might be possible. She had grown up knowing only her farm and a dim discoloration on the horizon, but clearly there was more. The unseen world seduced her.

"Will you show me your maps of the known territories?" she asked her husband not long after she had tasted the ocean.

Josef took down a large book and opened it on the coffee table. He showed her the maps of the world, and Magda was amazed by the amount of blue.

"The water of the oceans is deep, yes? You cannot wade across it?"

Josef smiled at the question.

"The ocean is deeper than the mountains are high," he said. "It is dangerous to find yourself in the middle of it. No one can help you there."

On every map, she wanted Josef to show their location, and she was both troubled and delighted to find that not every map had a place for their home. For Magda it meant that the world was large, that there were possibilities. Once, she asked Josef to show her where her family farm had been. Grudgingly, he produced a map that was far from Moscodelphia. He pointed to the train tracks radiating out like spokes from a wheel. He pointed out a river that was near her farm. On the map it was called the Naugatonic. But on the farm they knew it simply as the Big River. This too was a pleasing discovery—that something could have two names and still be one thing. It reminded her of married women.

"I hope this doesn't mean you want to visit the farm," said Josef.

He began packing up the maps. He became gruff.

"Of course not," she said. And this was true. Magda had no desire to return to her farm, to lord over the town girls her ministerial sophistication. A trip back to the countryside would mean a carrying of presents, a series of difficult conversations and sadness. It had been years since she felt the impulse to go there. After all, Anton was the most important thing from her previous life, and returning to her farm would only place him farther away.

At another time, she would ask Josef where the geese went when they traveled south. She felt sure he would know. For now, she would listen for the high honking of the geese and be content that they were headed somewhere else, perhaps even beyond the places depicted on the maps. She wondered if it was possible for a bird to fly across the ocean. She liked that the world was both as simple and as difficult as the maps made it seem.

Magda began clearing the dishes. She watched where Josef stored the maps so that she might touch them outside his presence.

CHAPTER 54:
THE RECTANGLES OF PURPLE FLOWERS

The day after he buried his wife, Mr. Puzanov climbed the hill beside the farm and saw the brown smudge of Moscodelphia on the horizon. He thought of Magda. She had made it to the city, its imagined glamor and plenty, and for this she must be happy. He kicked a pebble over the lip of the trail. Of course he couldn't be sure that she had actually made it there. She had sent no word. He and his wife had to assume that she'd gotten there and been married off, that some benevolent force had taken her by the hand.

It had been years since Magda had left, and her father surveyed the surrounding farms, the clutter of the town. It had looked the same when he was a boy. The farm had been in his family for generations. He knew this mostly from the markers in the graveyard beside the irrigation pond. His own father had said little of his parents and of how they had come to be here, but the marker stones told a story of Puzanovs with steadily older dates until the stones were smooth, and it was hard to tell if some of them were marker stones at all.

Now his wife was in the ground too. He could see the low mound of disturbed earth that covered her. He still needed to place her stone. A man in town was chiseling the letters into a small slab of marble. He would make the short journey in a few days to check on it. For now the farm demanded he stay here. He was growing soybeans again, as were many of his neighbors, and the rectangular fields of purple flowers stretched for miles. It was clear that the people were forgetting that they should not trust everything to a single crop.

When the people his own age were all dead, the countryside would be free to fill completely with fools once again. The younger men like Pasha would not correctly remember the mistakes of their fathers. They would think of themselves as smarter.

Mr. Puzanov pulled a cigarette from his pocket and lit it. It was store-bought. He hadn't had one since Magda had been collected, and he enjoyed the dark and fragrant heat at the back of his throat. He exhaled and watched his breath carry and disintegrate on the meager wind, and it was nice to not have flecks of loose tobacco on his tongue afterward. It would be Pasha's turn next. He would inherit the farm, and Mr. Puzanov would have to depend on his son to dig the grave and leave the marker so that Pasha's children would know something of where they came from.

He worried that Pasha was a fool. So far he had not found a wife. He was too particular, too insistent on the kind of beauty that could only be found in town. But Pasha himself was not a town person. He didn't have the money or the clothing or the worldliness to fit in there. The old man didn't have any of that either, but he at least understood his limitations. Without children, Pasha would have difficulty running the farm himself. He may have to sell off plots. He may have to hire hands. Either way, the farm would diminish. There would be a constant temptation to sell the land to someone in town so that more fancy houses could be built for the tinkers and merchants, the people who did not have to rely on barter, who had money at the ready for whatever need arose.

Mr. Puzanov finished his cigarette and started the long walk down the hill. He wondered if Magda sometimes looked in his direction from the top of one of the buildings, searching for a clear blue patch on the horizon. He hoped she did sometimes. He'd probably be dead before she ever returned.

When Magda's father got back to the house, he went straight into Magda's room and opened the top drawer of her dresser, pulling out one of her old shirts from the bottom of the stack. He pressed his face into it, but of course he could no longer smell his daughter.

CHAPTER 55:
THE PURRING INCREASED

Josef lost patience with Magda after the third miscarriage. He understood that she would not give him a child, let alone a son. He would not advance beyond the subminister level. He could see that now.

"We have everything we need," said Magda.

Josef handed her the tea and stood over her, counting the squares in the pattern of the wallpaper.

"My requirements exceed your own," he said. "When I brought you here, I had expectations."

Josef left the room to let Magda rest and cry. The cat came out from under the bed and leapt to Magda's side, purring as it tried to nuzzle under Magda's left hand so that she would scratch it. The cat was full of a pleasing selfishness.

Magda listened to Josef clanking the pots and plates in the kitchen as he cleaned up after their dinner. It was generous of Josef to let her rest, and yet she felt rebuked—as if he couldn't bear to be in the same room as this woman who had failed him again. She hoped that he stayed out of the wine until he was finished. It would not do to have him drop a plate on the kitchen floor. He would become angry. She suspected he would leave such a mess for her, and she would have to be careful to wear her slippers until she had swept it up properly.

The cat continued to arch its back and twitch its tail as Magda's hand roved over it. The purring increased, and the cat squinted in pleasure.

"Such a simple life," Magda said to the air. "A baby would change every-thing. I might not be able to scratch you every night."

Down the hall, the faucet cut off and the last cabinet closed. Magda heard Josef place the wine jug on the counter. She heard the cracking of the cap as he twisted the new bottle open. It was a matter of waiting, of staying out of his way.

A moment later, Josef began walking down the hall toward the bedroom, and the cat stopped rubbing up against Magda. It opened its green eyes wide.

"The kitchen is clean," he said. "I am going to stay up and watch some-thing."

His footsteps receded, and she heard the monitor click on, then the collage of sound as he scrolled to the place he wanted—a story about police, where everyone bad was punished.

The cat became more insistent now. It pressed up against Magda's hand more forcefully, and Magda did her best to give the cat pleasure. It was almost instinctual. Then, without warning, the cat turned and scratched Magda's hand. Two of its claws hooked into her, and the cat leaped off the bed as Magda shook her hand free.

Magda could see two tiny drops of blood forming where the claws had caught her. She was not sure why the cat had reacted that way. She never was. But the cat, like Josef, followed the scent of what it needed until it was satisfied. Then it went immediately on to the next wish—a nap, a dinner, a tending to its claws on the bedpost that Magda had covered with a swatch of old carpeting.

When the cat came round again—an hour later or the next morning—Magda would scratch it. She would do whatever was required to hear the deep purring beneath her hand.

PART 4

CHAPTER 56:
HE ENVIED HOW THE CHOCOLATES
KEPT KNOCKING AGAINST HER HIP

Despite all of Magda's searching, it was Anton who found her first. She was across the market turning the peaches over in her hand, checking for bruises. He watched her lift one to her nose then place it in her basket. She moved over to the apples, surveyed the table, and decided without touching them that they were past their prime. Then she turned briefly in Anton's direction. She wore dark glasses and a head scarf to protect her hair from the misting of rain that morning. There was something about the way she chose her fruit, how she selected the very best of whatever was laid before her. There was also the curl of her red mouth. He remembered how it smiled. This woman's mouth was not smiling, but he could see how her face could accommodate the expression. He was certain it was Magda, and he followed her through the market at a distance.

At first Anton had no intention of making himself known. How could he? He had ruined her. He had fled to the city and left Magda to wonder what had become of him. There was no message to soften the blow. He had promised to take her with him and then, for her own good, had left without her. Despite what she believed, he knew she was suited to life on the family farm.

But as he followed her through the market, watching her lift a necklace with two fingers so that the light could hit the cut glass more flatteringly, he felt he would have to speak to her. Within a minute's time, he had decided he would touch her shoulder; he would make her turn around; he would say her name like the breaking of a spell. Then Magda would have to do something. He wasn't sure what. He only knew that, first, he must touch her shoulder.

A man came up beside Magda, and she leaned in to let him kiss her cheek. Anton understood the lukewarm greeting—this was her husband. He saw the ring on her finger now. He saw how she adjusted her stride to his. A small gray bird zipped through the air behind Magda and darted over to the bouquets of flowers. Anton began to doubt himself. He had seen the man she settled for. He looked wealthy. His clothes were clean, and he had the kind of mustache that suggested he had the means to clip and prune. They could afford to while away a morning browsing at the market. Magda had a life that many would envy.

Anton's own position seemed shabby by comparison, and he laughed at himself for thinking that a woman with such a life might have anything to do with him, a man who drove a van, a man who left odd packages all over the city, a man who had grown gaunt, a man who had betrayed this woman sixteen years earlier.

Suddenly, Anton remembered his hand truck full of boxes. He turned and they were still there. He was lucky. Had he allowed the boxes to be stolen or damaged, he would be fired at the least—quite possibly worse. It depended on what was in the packages, who had sent them, and who would end up not receiving them. Their value could not be known, so he treated everything as if it were gold. Anton took another look at Magda pushing down the aisle and heading for the life he assumed she had chosen. She was entering the vegetable section. It seemed like she would be there awhile.

Anton returned to his hand truck and felt the boxes reach equilibrium in his grip as he tilted the handles back. He took the packages in the opposite direction, to a small and ancient elevator that was broken the last time he had tried it. This time it was working, and when he came back down just minutes later, Magda was still in the market, having some chocolates put into a bag. He took the hand truck back to his van and decided to follow her home.

First he called his service and told them the van wouldn't start. Then he locked it up and threaded into the crowd unencumbered. He heard her voice disengaging from conversation with one of the merchants and decided this was his moment. He bumped into her, forcing her handbag to spill onto the ground. As he helped retrieve all the contents, he saw the address on her identification card and committed it to memory. Then, as he handed it back to her, she saw the paleness of his skin, the stump of his finger, and he smiled. Behind him, Anton could sense her husband.

"Magda," he called out, pushing Anton out of the way, but Magda touched a hand to Josef's elbow.

"It's alright, Josef" she said. "This man was helping me pick up the things I dropped."

Josef turned to Anton and looked him up and down. He did not like to see his wife accosted by someone from the lower classes, and because he had never seen an albino at close range before, he seemed taken aback, like he had to be careful of touching him. To Anton, Josef looked like a man who would become a cuckold—if he wasn't one already.

"At your service, Madam," Anton said, making a small bow. When he looked up again, he saw Magda retreating to her plush and separate life, the little bag of her purchases hanging from a strap, and he envied how the chocolates kept knocking against her hip. Then she stopped and turned around to see if Anton was still watching. He was, and he saw her mouth curl into its old shape. Anton kept staring even after she turned away. He felt the river of his life redirected into a channel of new and broken stone, which he set about grinding down, smoothing it over, turning it all to sand he would force by inches down to the slumbering sea.

CHAPTER 57:
SHE PLACED THE NAIL UPON HER TONGUE

Anton did not need to write down Magda's address in order to remember it. He had already placed her house in the detailed map of Moscodelphia he carried in his head. In fact, it was only two weeks previous that he had been on her street, delivering to one of her neighbors a small but heavy box that made no sound when he shook it. Magda's yard was bordered by a weak line of lavender bushes that would perish as soon as the gardener forgot to water them. Her house had a chimney, but he had never seen it smoking. This was encouraging, for that would be the mark of true luxury. Only officials at the highest echelons could afford to import wood from the countryside and then burn it in their living rooms as their guests milled about, admiring the flames as a kind of short-lived arrangement of flowers.

He tried to remember if he had ever seen some evidence of Magda—her face in the window, her voice on the breeze. He could locate no such detail, but he remembered there was a dog on the street—a mean one.

Anton found an old box and filled it mostly with packing materials. In the center he inserted a small vial containing a single fingernail clipping. He added a note that contained instructions. It would be too dangerous for him to enter Magda's house or to talk for more than a moment on the porch. The wife of an official is never truly alone, and Anton would have to contend with the fact of her neighbors. He knew their sort. They would not peer from behind their curtains, embarrassed at the idea of being caught watching. They would step boldly onto their porches to assert the privilege of their station as soon as they sensed something was amiss. This was the trade-off. If he arrived after dark, Josef would be there, and Anton would be deprived of seeing her true reaction to the gesture. And Josef would surely remember Anton from the market, putting an end to everything just as it was beginning. But if Anton arrived during the day, Magda would almost certainly be alone.

The note told Magda to attend the symphony in three nights' time. The crowd that gathered on the evening streets would sufficiently cloak his presence. He might be able to catch her eye, to hear her voice, to brush up against her as he passed through the crowd in search of a reason to pause.

Anton parked his van in front of Magda's house. He had two boxes with him, in case her husband surprised him by being home. He got out and walked up to the door and heard his boot heel scuff against the misaligned flagstones. It was the same sound his boots would make in any other part of the city—from the poorest tenements to the wall-encircled mansions. The only thing that had any effect was the weather. Rain or snow could change the way one sounded in the world, but even then it was the same for everyone. Anton was pleased by this fact.

When he delivered the box, he knew at once that Magda had not lost any of her shrewdness. As he guessed, her husband was not home, and the transaction was conducted with efficiency. But her fingers brushed over his own as she accepted the package. There was a small but unmistakable pressure before her hands withdrew. She did not look him in the eye. She merely turned, and Anton walked back to the van, trying to protect his fingers from the wind so that when he was alone behind his rolled-up windows, he could inhale the scent of Magda from where she had touched him.

For Magda's part, after Anton drove away, she opened the box immediately. She read the note and burned it, already calculating how she would arrive at the music hall and what she would wear. She took out the glass vial and held it up to the light like a jeweler appraising a new stone. She removed the stopper and knocked the nail into her palm. Before Anton had fled to Moscodelphia, he had given her a charm like this one, even though she did not believe in such things. Still, she regretted that she had left it behind in her keepsake box when she had been taken. But that afternoon, with the proof of Anton finally manifest again, she placed the nail upon her tongue and tasted whatever she could. For the next hour, she ground away at the nail as she disposed of the box, as she took a jar of pepper from the back of the kitchen shelf and moved it forward. If Josef asked about the box in the trash, she would tell him it had contained the pepper he was shaking over his stew at that moment. She would show him the new jar. Then, to be doubly safe, she dumped the remains of the night's dinner preparations on top of the box, knowing that Josef would be loath to pick it up.

The next hours were strange for Anton. His deliveries kept taking him farther and farther from Magda's neighborhood. It was a slow and plodding route, and yet he seemed to be rushing toward her, like something dropped and bouncing down a hill, gathering speed, heedless of its own destruction.

CHAPTER 58:
PASHA HAD TO REMIND THE OX
IT MUST TURN AROUND

The year his father died, Pasha learned how hard it was to keep a farm running. The tractor could not be revived after the long winter, and Pasha had to use the ox to pull the single-harrowed plow through the settled dirt of last year's corn. Pasha could not afford to hire hands, so he allowed half the farm to go fallow. This would make the following year's plowing still more difficult.

Pasha was old now. He was thirty-four. It was unlikely that he would ever have a wife. There were no unmarried women his age in town. Even the ugly and the stupid had all been selected by this point. The young girls, of course, wanted nothing to do with him. Why would the parents of a pretty girl arrange for her to die in poverty when she could have her pick of so many men?

Pasha only went into town now for necessities—for salt and sugar and flour. If he killed a fox, he ate the unpalatable meat. He stitched the coat into something he himself could wear as he hunted in the frozen swamps, following the trail of deer that had fattened on the corn he could not completely harvest.

Pasha considered it a fair trade. The deer had made off with his corn, and now he made off with part of the herd. Shotgun shells were expensive, and Pasha's eyesight had been getting worse. He didn't have a trap big enough to hold a deer, and he didn't like traps anyway. Often he would return to them only to find some other animal had eaten what was his. He was left with a withered leg still stuck in the trap, while the snow around it was covered in blood and fur. Or he would come back and find the animal still alive. It was sickening to have to club a large animal to death. He could always shoot it, but then why had he bothered to set a trap?

The Petrovich farm had fallen into disuse. The albino had never returned from wherever he had fled, and the parents had eventually died. The whole farm was going fallow. Eventually, someone from town would seize the land and build a better house on it. Pasha himself had already scavenged what he could. The ox he now urged ahead of him was the same one the albino used to beat so mercilessly. The ox might last another year, and then Pasha would walk it into town so that he could have it properly butchered, returning home with a pocketful of coins and an armload of bloody steaks.

After the season's first row, Pasha had to remind the ox it must turn around. And then Pasha had to explain, by means of the whip, that it must pull the harrow through the soil all morning. It was exhausting for both of them. Pasha felt like he'd been having a loud argument by the time they finished. He was vibrating with the words he had shouted, and his arm was sore from whipping.

When they were done plowing, Pasha left the animal to browse in the field he would plow tomorrow. The ox replenished itself on the sweet weeds that had yet to flower. Pasha watched it walk over to the silver ribbon of the brook and drink until it was completely sated. Then the ox lumbered back to its meal of weeds, occasionally walking over to a new spot where, presumably, it saw a leaf it liked. It would take hours to fill its belly, and Pasha was confident the ox would not try to leave the fallow field.

Then Pasha walked into the house to see what could be done to prevent his own starvation.

CHAPTER 59:
IT BOUNCED OFF ANTON'S SHOULDER

Wearing a beige scarf, Magda left the music hall and walked to the alley where they had agreed to meet. She saw Anton's delivery van parked at the corner. It was a cool night, and he was delivering grapes to the wealthy apartments of the district. The grapes were a delicacy, though Magda still found this hard to believe, for the grapes in Anton's charge were halfway to becoming raisins. It had been a long time since anyone had eaten plump grapes in the city. In the woods around her farm, Magda had often gathered purple fistfuls of them. She always picked more than she could easily carry, and she would have to be careful not to crush them during the short walk home as she cradled the fruit in her apron. Nowadays, the journey from the countryside was transformative, and some fruit like strawberries wouldn't even be loaded onto the trains. The lack of refrigeration cars made it impractical. When Magda had first come to the city, she had tried these imported grapes but could not develop a taste for them.

Magda saw that Anton was already waiting for her, beside a dumpster. She followed the glow of his cigarette in the exaggerated blackness that flourished between the two buildings, which climbed perhaps ten stories high on either side. It was a good place—no one would enter such an alley unless their need was great.

Over the years, Magda had learned to regard things coolly, as if she were watching them happen to someone else from behind the mirror of an interrogation room. It was an objectivity, a discernment, and it had never felt stronger than it did right now, as Anton slid the stump of his missing finger along the edge of her brassiere strap.

"Someone will find us," she whispered. But Anton only crushed his face into hers more forcefully. It made Magda stand up straighter so that he could press still more of his body against her own, through her clothes, in an alley between dark buildings. She tried to stay conscious of the occasional car passing on either end of the alley, and then she felt the stump of the same finger riding up her thigh beneath her dress.

Magda tried to give herself over to the moment, but her mind always worked on more than one level. And when her life was blazing brightest, when her heart began banging around like a bird inside a shoebox, she only retreated higher into the tower of herself. There she could regard the world as it happened to her. She could watch the woman hitching up her dress and not worry—except in a very theoretical way—about how quickly Josef would kill them both if he found them like this. The publicity of their embrace would be unforgivable. He would interpret it as treason.

When a window opened a few stories above them, Magda and Anton grew more quiet. There was no stopping now, and Magda was fully detached. She watched herself make sure she was standing fully in the shadows, and she saw the man above them, oblivious, ash his cigarette out the window, how the small gray flakes lit up as they passed a lighted window below him, floating down like bits of dirty snow.

Anton had gathered her dress in a fist above her waist. His breath was bad as he kissed her neck, and she worried about the cleanliness of his fingers as he pushed them inside her. She did not try to stop him, though, and despite her best effort to maintain control of what her body did, she began to feel a shuddering, increasing the silence that spread around them like oil from a sinking ship.

And then the arm above them flicked the cigarette into the alley. Magda studied the arc of it—how slowly it revolved, how the coal seemed to brighten slightly as if the air were inhaling it, how almost nothing but filter was left. She stood there watching it come toward them as if it had been aimed. It bounced off Anton's shoulder, and she saw him step sideways onto the minor coal, crushing it out. The two of them were panting hard now. It was the only sound besides their blood, which seemed to course through their bodies like a tipped-over bottle of wine.

Then Anton waited for Magda to look up at him so he could read in her eyes the answer to his body's question.

CHAPTER 60:
SHE COULD SMELL THE WINE ON HIM

The toads began falling that night. Magda had come home late, and she was washing her hands at the kitchen sink with the water on low when something slammed into the window, making her upset the pile of pots in the drying rack. They clattered to the floor, and a light came on in the bedroom down the hall.

"It's just me, Josef," she said. "I dropped a pot."

But Josef came out anyway. His hair was wild, and his belly fell out of his pajama top.

"Where have you been?" he asked.

Magda recounted the lie she had memorized—that she had gone to hear a symphony, that she had left him a note.

Josef walked over to where she was pointing. Under the empty vase in the center of the table was a paper confirming all she had said. He picked it up and read it carefully. He still seemed bewildered. She could smell the wine on him.

"What was the symphony?" he asked.

Magda told him, and he took a step toward her.

"Did you like it?"

"Very much," she said, biting her lip and stooping to pick up the steel pot she had used for the evening's stew.

Josef put the note back under the vase, went to the sink, and drank a glass of water while staring into the dark rectangle of the window. Magda watched him and could see the light of the neighbor's house within Josef's reflection. She wondered what he was looking at, but then he put the glass down and made his way back to the bedroom. She stood in the kitchen, still holding the pot, and watched the bedroom go dark at the end of the hall.

The next day, Magda got up early and found the dead toad on the back porch. She saw the dirty smack-mark of it against the window, and couldn't understand how it might have happened. The night had been windless; a low roof stuck out above the window. The toad could only have been flung. She scanned the mud of the back yard to see if there were footprints.

The toad had burst like the overripe eggplant she had dropped on the kitchen floor one night when she was making Josef's dinner, and the ants were making the most of it, burrowing deeper and deeper into its split belly. Magda could see the irony of it. Ordinarily the toad would be eating the ants, and now the ants devoured the toad. The world felt upside down for a moment, like she might tumble upward into the sky and disappear if she didn't keep hold of the railing.

Magda remembered a fat toad that would show up every night to feed on the side of her father's barn. He kept a lantern lit there as he broke down the tools or cleaned some piece of equipment. The light attracted moths, which the toad gobbled up as they looped too close to the ground. He also ate the carpenter ants that came out of the barn wall all year long—a steady stream of black maleficent soldiers on the way to someplace better. The toad would get its fill within ten minutes and then spend an hour digesting, waiting for the wriggling inside its belly to stop. It looked peaceful as it sat there watching a praying mantis walk along the ocher barn, snatching up beetles and moths that couldn't resist the flickering light cast by her father's lantern.

The toad on her back porch was clearly a message, Magda thought, and it had something to do with Anton. But who would do this? Even if Mrs. Constantinopolis had known what Magda had done, she was not the type of person to throw a toad at a window. Mrs. Constantinopolis reminded

Magda of the country women who believed that toads were curses incarnate. She would never pick one up, let alone traipse through the mud to hurl it at a back window. Such a message would be too obscure for Mrs. Constantinopolis. No, if she wanted to reveal her neighbor's affair, she would simply denounce Magda before her husband and leave it at that.

Magda knew, though, that her secret could not have been found out. Mrs. Constantinopolis would never go to a symphony—she could not bear to mingle with strangers—and Magda was certain her meeting with Anton had been conducted in secrecy.

Magda left the toad where it lay. There was no reason to hide this strangeness from her husband, and because the morning had yet to fully arrive, she returned to bed. Josef was deeply unconscious, and she did not worry about waking him and having to contend with his wishes. She got under the covers and turned her back to him, keeping her face away from his own so that she might avoid the reeking breath that otherwise would keep her awake. She lay there trying to concentrate on the stump of Anton's finger, and how she had shuddered as if she were a young girl discovering men at last.

Later, when the sun was fully up and she was making Josef's breakfast, she saw that more than just the one toad had fallen in the night. There were several in the yard and on the roofs of the neighbors' houses, but she kept this observation to herself.

CHAPTER 61:
BUT THEY HAVE STEAK HERE

It was two weeks into their affair before Magda visited Anton at his apartment. She told Josef she would be making a day of the museums, and he waved her off, happy to have work that would keep him from her side. Anton's apartment was dirtier than she expected, and the walls were thin and drafty. She could hear a neighbor washing dishes as they made love. Afterward, she recounted, as she often did, the moment of her capture, when her life tipped irretrievably into its next phase.

"When the collectors tied me up," Magda said. "I was terrified. But by the time the cart started to move down the driveway, I felt happy. I was headed in your direction."

Magda rolled over to look at Anton. She explained herself, that she thought it would be a simple matter of arriving in the city and then escaping into Anton's arms as soon as she spotted him. He was an albino after all. He would stand out even in a crowd.

"And then you got here and realized your mistake," Anton said.

It was true. The city was larger than Magda had imagined. On the final day of approach, it filled the entire horizon, sprawling over the landscape seemingly without design. Not only that, but it rose higher into the air than any hill she had ever seen. The tops of the buildings disappeared into the smog that seemed to be escaping from every vent and tunnel of the city.

"I was a young fool," Magda said. "But how could I not be? How could I have guessed what was waiting here?"

Anton agreed. He had had the same disillusioning experience. While there was little danger of his starving in Moscodelphia, it was not the land of plenty he had thought it would be. In many respects, the food was worse than what was in the countryside. But there was a greater variety of it, and a more reliable supply. The choices were simple ones. He could grow fat on food that was always on the verge of going rancid, or he could wither in the countryside because there weren't enough fresh eggs.

"But they have steak here," Magda said. "That was something we never had in the country, unless somebody's ox died." As she spoke, she saw a toad fall past the bedroom window, which opened on a weedy courtyard. The toads were falling often enough that no one in the city remarked them anymore. They were merely a nuisance.

In Moscodelphia there was steak for the rich—for the class of officials. When she had asked Josef about it, he said there were herds to the north and west of the city, that the land was better for grazing there, and that's where the cattle came from. Years ago, when Josef took her home from the ocean, they had seen a herd of cattle in the distance, sliding over the landscape like a brown stain. There were no barns in sight, though, and Josef told her they were allowed to roam freely. Then the ranchers would cull them, often by helicopter, shooting down on the herd indiscriminately as the cattle galloped over the steppes. When enough animals had fallen, the rancher radioed in the coordinates, and the trucks drove out to retrieve the carcasses. They did this mostly in winter so that the weather acted as a refrigerator until the men from the trucks could arrive on the scene. Sometimes they found coyotes or vultures fussing with a carcass. It didn't matter, though. The bulk of the animal would be intact. The cow was taken to a rendering plant in the bed of an open truck, and it was not uncommon for the animal to be frozen all the way through by the time it arrived.

Magda acknowledged the ingenuity. Spoiled meat was always a problem on the farm. Her family could not refrigerate, so they either ate it all in one sitting or had to go to the trouble of drying it and curing it. In the countryside, no one had enough salt to preserve meat. There was only enough for flavoring. It was one of the countryside's few luxuries, and back then she would not have believed it if someone told her where the salt came from. She had never heard of the ocean. She did not understand that salt was part of the water, that you could get to it merely by letting the water evaporate and scraping up the mineralized crust.

Sometimes there was sand in the salt they used. Now she understood why.

CHAPTER 62:
A MAN WITH BUSINESS ABOVE THE CLOUDS

For all of Isabelle's intelligence and striving, she eventually wound up in the same subministerial enclave as Josef. She had seen him walking among the ministry buildings not long after she herself had moved to the city. She was the wife of a vice minister. Her beauty and her being natural born, not a woman imported from the countryside, made her valuable. But she was merely a wife, attached to the city by virtue of her husband's power.

Now that she was married, the cunning with which she had navigated every previous social encounter seemed to dissipate. The bottle was empty. The mountain was climbed. She fell back on her husband's plans because she hadn't thought this many steps into the future. She conceived a child quickly—a son named Fyodor—and when she went to market, the women parted for her as she slid the carriage through the crowd. Her son was small and handsome. Even in his toddlerhood, he was well-behaved.

From a distance, Josef looked powerful and confident. He still had the habit of pointing his chin upward as he surveyed the landscape in front of him, and he took the first few steps in his new direction with his chin jutting out. It looked both brave and foolish. She watched him conversing with several men who were clearly beneath his station. Then he sat down on the lip of the Great Fountain.

Isabelle positioned herself so that a column was between the two of them. She watched as he opened his briefcase and kept it in his lap like a large lunchbox. She saw him unwrap and eat a pickle. She watched as he broke a small wedge of cheese in two and slowly chewed while tearing a roll into scraps.

The bread must have been fresh. It did not disintegrate into a thousand crumbs. *He must be doing well for himself,* she thought.

Then she watched him check his watch and open a small notebook on top of his briefcase. He seemed to be staring at the fountain in the reflection of the building opposite him.

I hope he is still not writing poems, she said to herself.

She recalled how he had given her poems when he was courting her. They were bits of drivel, but his feelings had been hurt when she laughed at his efforts. Perhaps he had continued all these years. After ten minutes of Josef's staring into the notebook and writing nothing, she thought that, clearly, he had not made his mark on the literary world. For Isabelle, action and output were the measure of the man. It was bad enough to be a poet. But to be an unproductive poet was unconscionable.

Then, just at the moment she was thinking she would go over to him, feigning surprise at finding him here, he jotted something down. It couldn't have been more than a sentence. Then he popped open his briefcase and lay the notebook inside. Josef swiveled his head around, stood up, and raised his chin in the direction of the Ministry of Opulence. Twenty stories up, the building disappeared into the smog, and he walked toward the revolving door like a man with business above the clouds.

CHAPTER 63:
THE BERRY THAT HANGS TOO LONG UPON A BRANCH IS PASSED OVER EVEN BY CROWS

For years now, Magda had looked on her husband as a disappointment, despite his plodding rise in officialdom, despite the violence he was able to summon whenever his pride was hurt. The fat belly, the drunken breath, the insistence on order he himself could not maintain—all these things disposed Magda toward fantasy. Then fantasy became wish, and it was at this moment that Anton had upset her handbag in the market.

Her adultery evolved so naturally that there was no shock when it finally arrived, no hesitation at the threshold. She would never have entered such an entanglement when she was younger. She would have looked down on such women and pronounced that they were whores or traitors. Now she was one of them.

"I am going to the symphony," she would say. Josef would be sitting in the living room chair, his shirt unbuttoned, pouring out more wine. He would not dissuade her. He despised the symphony—the swirling unpredictability of the music, the memories a melody could evoke as it rose and fell out of the instruments like a drowned body making its way down a choppy river. No, he would stay home tonight, as she knew he would, and she would wrap around her neck the fox stole that Mrs. Constantinopolis had already guessed was dog, but which she was saving to mention.

Always, Magda put the glass up between herself and the driver. She liked to be alone with her thoughts as she stared at the nighttime city through the tinted, bulletproof windows. The effect was a mellowing, making the city seem less vital, less repugnant. There were small groups of people standing around barrel fires, but never more than five, which would invite a raid. For many years now, it had been illegal to have large gatherings. The men around the barrel would be smart enough to have such meetings behind drawn curtains.

Once, a bullet had struck the window Magda was staring out of. The special glass had kept it back, and it was doubtful there was much intention to it. The driver merely accelerated and ignored the next few traffic signals, pulling up to the music hall as Magda fingered the smooth glass on the other side of the pockmark.

She would exit the car and ascend the steps, stopping beside a column. Watching the chauffeur drive away, she would take out a cigarette and pretend to look for a match. Then she would turn behind her and ask the smoking man for a light. Always, the smoking man was Anton. He would light her cigarette, and Magda's smile would curl again to radiance. The two of them would enjoy the smoke until they heard the applause and the first notes of Bach or Mozart; then they would disappear.

It was that simple. Her happiness hung like a juicy plum she had merely to reach up and pluck.

But all deception longs to be exposed. She had known this from her girlhood and had seen it repeated all her life. The snake on a shelf of stone pretending to be another stone eventually rears up. The lie she told her mother about the maple candy untold itself by the look on her face, the stickiness of her fingers.

On rare occasions, a storm would scrub the sky above Moscodelphia, removing the smog that burned Magda's eyes and induced a steady wheeze. But always, sometimes within hours, the true sky of the city reasserted itself, letting the inhabitants know that this was not a paradise scintillating with wet pavement and pearly drops strung along the bursting azaleas of the main boulevards. No, the city was a place where thirty-five million people toiled and murdered and cried out in grief for where they lived. If one could rise high enough, it would look like a concrete scab.

And so Magda carried her secret around with her like an egg that would soon be broken. She couldn't say how this would happen, of course, but she knew it was folly to hope that it would not. When she told such things to Anton, he had an answer: to run away with him, to live out their last years in happiness. They were already in their thirties, after all, and how long could they expect to live? Being past their primes, shouldn't they seize their happiness and nourish it for the decade they might have left? Magda, because she had grown more cautious than Anton, would counter that they already were, that the hour they might spend in an alley beside a dumpster or in the public bed of a hotel was just such a grasping and a savoring.

"It is wonderful, yes," Anton would agree. "But the berry that hangs too long upon the branch is passed over even by crows."

CHAPTER 64:
A MESSAGE FROM THE COUNTRYSIDE

Moscodelphia was a city where magic evaporated. No one believed in angels. No one hired a sorceress to interpret what the coyotes were saying. And no one ever ate a firebug at midnight to cure a cold.

Back on the farm, Magda used to pull the legs off the firebug first. Then she swallowed the beetle with a glass of salted water while the light on its abdomen was still at full strength. She did this in darkness so that she could watch, in a mirror, the glowing insect move down her throat, absorbing the soreness as it went. And although it always worked, the citizens of Moscodelphia never entertained such a cure. For them the countryside was backward, and Magda could tell it was best to keep her thoughts deep inside her front pocket, where no one could sneak away with them.

Now there were toads falling from the sky, and none of the ministers could properly explain the phenomenon. The toads didn't have magical properties—other than their mysterious origin—but the ministers worried that the people might invent a magical rationale for them. They were falling for a reason, surely, but that reason was anybody's guess, and this spurred the ministers to action.

To Magda it was a message from the countryside. It told her to leave, that everything she had hoped for in Moscodelphia would never come to pass. She was in her thirties—an old lady at this point—and she did not wish to die an old lady, unable to see the sun as toads were falling all over her roof and lawn.

Magda felt strongly that the physics of the world would change when she got beyond Moscodelphia. There was something to be said for stars and clean air and a gurgling stream you could drink from without worry. She remembered the snowfalls that would transform the landscape of the farm to purity. It was a purity that was always there if she chose to look for it. When the snow melted, the purity seeped in and came up later as corn and marigolds. Even the mud season that followed the melting snow was more pristine than Moscodelphia. The mud was just evidence that the world could not easily absorb all that was clean and holy. It was like trying to swallow too much wine at once.

Now Magda had all the wine she wanted, and that was a kind of magic, but not the kind she was able to sustain. If she drank too much of it, she woke with a headache that was incurable here in the city. She had to wait for it to leave of its own accord, which usually happened in the afternoon. If she were in the countryside, on the farm, and woke with a hangover, her course of action was clear. She would gather up a handful of red clover blossoms and willow bark, boiling it into a dark tea. Once she drank it down, the headache would disappear and she could go about her chores. But the only willows in the city were down by the river, barely surviving on the foul water. Their roots crawled over the bank and into the current, which left them stunted. There was no fresh clover either, and the store-bought clover had all the magic leached out of it on the long train ride away from the flowering steppes.

CHAPTER 65:
THE BARREL OF HIS GUN
HAD SOMEHOW WARPED

Pasha felt like a man who had "dropped the day's hours down a narrow well." That was an old saying his father used to chant whenever he found Pasha loafing in the hay while the corn went uncollected. In his boyhood, Pasha had taken it as a rebuke, but now he saw the wisdom of his father's saying, how any farmer engaged in leisure had more than likely left a gate unlatched.

Pasha felt this way because now he had learned how difficult it was to run a farm by himself, but other things were failing too. His eyes, for instance. As he stood in the barn looking south, he used to be able to say with certainty the name of the animal stepping from the woods beside the irrigation pond. Now he couldn't tell if it was a gopher or a wildcat. Only the fox was discernible without doubt, because a red figure slipping over the landscape could never be anything else.

When Pasha leveled his gun at such an animal, he missed his shot more and more often. It didn't matter if he used the shotgun or the rabbit rifle. His bullets missed their mark unless he was practically on top of the animal. For a while, his pride allowed him to wonder if the barrel of his gun had somehow warped.

All of this led to a change in the way Pasha hunted, and he began to see why his father found it necessary to chide him for using an extra shell.

They were simply too costly. No more could Pasha wander the woods in search of game. No longer could he hope to hit a random animal as it entered the farm in desperation. Now if he wanted meat, he would have to wait for it in a tree, or in the blind he built on the edge of the swamp. He disliked the blind because it always meant shivering. Pasha would have to install himself inside it before the dawn, before the ducks had awakened and begun to paddle the muck of the mist-heavy shallows.

Among the indignities was his inability to smoke as he waited. He would have to chew if he wanted to avoid detection, and he missed the easy heat he drew into his lungs, and how he expelled his anticipation in billowing clouds that refused to take a definite shape.

The whole character of the farm had changed. The pigs had long since been carted off to the city, and at a certain point, he'd decided he could not raise both chickens and goats. The goats kept raiding his vegetable garden, and he had the ox to worry about as well. So he feasted for a month on the youngest goats, sucking the fat off their bones and feeling himself strengthen. Then he tied them all together in a line—a dozen of them—and walked them into town to the butcher's shop.

He took the money and found a way to spend it, and within days he regretted his decision, and how it wasn't a decision at all but a move made out of necessity, because he was growing older, because age and diminishment were tormenting him like gnats. He felt he was constantly swatting at the air to keep them at bay, but eventually he would become less vigilant and they would land on him and bite him and suck up the blood he'd been trying to hide. He wouldn't even notice if it were just one gnat, but there were clouds of them. He saw their shape-shifting pillars in the evening sun as he walked along the swamp and listened to the bells of a thousand tiny frogs.

CHAPTER 66:
A WORLD WHERE TOADS WERE NOT FALLING FROM A POISONOUS SKY

"What if you came away with me?" asked Anton, sitting beside the pile of kicked-up sheets at the bottom of the hotel bed. He was watching her dress. "What if we drove deep into the country and lived on a farm?"

Had anyone asked Magda this question sixteen years ago, she would have laughed. When she was a girl, all she wanted to do was escape her family farm. Now the memory of it felt like refuge.

"Where would we get a farm?" she asked. She stepped into her skirt and cinched it around her waist. She slipped into her right shoe and began looking for the left.

"If we go far enough to the north, we can find a place that hasn't been taken yet."

Magda knew this was at least a possibility. She herself had asked Josef what lay beyond the borders of the map on his office wall. Josef had been evasive, but he acknowledged that there was land beyond the control of the ministries. On the map it was referred to as the Outer Territories, and there was no indication of roads or cities or even terrain. Presumably, this is where one would go if she needed to escape her husband or the state, to live in a world where toads were not falling from a poisonous sky.

Anton pulled her shoe out from under the bed and watched her step into it. He was trying to judge the possibility of Magda's agreement. On many levels it was a ludicrous request. He was asking her to leave luxury behind. Josef was a good provider after all, and she was able to avoid most beatings. He was asking her to run away, not just to the countryside but to beyond the countryside—to start a new life with an albino who might be killed for a good luck charm even before they arrived.

"I would take a van," he said. "I would fill it with gasoline cans, and we would travel without stopping."

Magda eyed him as she buttoned her blouse. "You mean you would steal it," she corrected. "If Josef caught up with us, he would kill us both." Then she realized she had misaligned her buttons and began undoing them. "How would you steal a van?"

Anton explained how he could report it broken down in another part of the city, how that would give them enough time to get outside the city limits before anyone began looking for them. Once they were past the city's checkpoints, their success would be more likely.

Magda finished rebuttoning and stepped into his arms. "It is not so easy as you say. Josef would hunt us. It would be expected."

"And yet you are willing to come here, with me, in broad daylight," he challenged. "What do you think Josef would do if he found us here?"

It was a fair question, one to which Magda had no answer. She turned to look at him in the mirror and felt a fog of competing desires rising up.

"Why do you choose to remain unhappy?" Anton asked, touching the bruise along her wrist where Josef must have grabbed her. He asked the question as if it could be answered with words.

Magda stared into the hotel mirror. Anton's eyes were like strange red pennies. They kept Magda from being cruel. His hands were on her shoulders now, and she thought for a moment that his fingers looked like the fringe of epaulettes on Josef's dress jacket. She turned to face him so that she didn't address his reflection.

"You do not understand," she said, placing his hands back upon her shoulders. "I am the wife of an official. There are things I cannot do."

Then she offered him her neck, and he took it, willingly, again.

CHAPTER 67:
IT WAS A BOOK THAT HAD
LONG SINCE CEASED TO BE RELEVANT

Josef stared at his screen and saw the spots floating across the words he had been reading. It seemed they had been there for years—the same ones: the large one in the shape of his desk at the academy; the smaller one just to the right of it, which looked like a goat's head lying in the dirt, or like a piano with the lid propped open. It depended. He tried to fix them in place, to see them directly, but always the spots drifted off—slowly or quickly—refusing to let him study these mysteries he traveled with.

"You must be dreaming, Josef," said Mical Constantinopolis. "Why do you look at your screen so intently?"

Josef turned to Mical, who was smiling, standing with one arm behind his back and the other resting on Josef's cubicle wall.

"No dreams," said Josef. "Just thinking of the work." He took his hands away from the keyboard and pushed back to see Mical more clearly.

"I read what you did with the Exodus text," Mical said. "A very good job. You sounded like God himself."

Josef smiled. It had been an easy task to rearrange the words of Moses so that the toads sounded more like a blessing than a plague. He had the Israelites survive on the toads that covered Egypt. It was surfeit for them. And later, he replaced the manna of their wandering with toads. It is what allowed them to last in the desert for forty years. Still, it felt strange to alter the story that way. He knew from the monthly reports that very few people actually accessed the Bible through their home connections. It was a book that had long since ceased to be relevant.

Of course the Bible was not the only book that had fallen by the wayside. It had become too expensive to keep making books out of paper, so after generations of basement floods and moth infestations and the need for kindling, almost all books had disappeared. Before that happened, though, the Ministry of Opulence had converted many of them to digital files. They were available to the masses, but very few people had the inclination to read them because they were so tired at the end of every day. Josef was the same way. He much preferred to sit in front of a puzzle than to download a long book without any pictures in it.

Josef remembered his own mother's Bible. She would read him the stories as he sat at her feet drawing pictures of flowers and pretty girls. She read to him from Genesis and Exodus and the Gospels where Jesus showed everyone how much better he was. There were pictures in it— lavish color plates that depicted the pleasures of Eden and the agonies of Hell. These pictures frightened Josef when he was a boy. His young mind intuited, rightly, that even Eden was a kind of curse—a way of reminding men how they had possessed, then squandered, everything. It was a heavy book. When he was very young, his legs fell asleep if he laid it in his lap too long.

"Thank you, Mical," he said. "I am pleased you find it useful." He swept his hand across his empty desk as if he were removing a residue of dust.

Mical let go of the cubicle wall and stood behind Josef, forcing Josef to swivel to keep him in his sights. "But you are unhappy? Something is bothering you about the work?"

"Not bothering me. Just wondering, I suppose."

"Tell me," Mical said.

Josef was always wary about opening up to Mical. He worried he would be indiscreet or, worse, that Mical would denounce him. Now that Mical had been promoted above Josef, there was less danger of that, but it was best to be cautious.

"Why bother to rewrite it?" Josef asked. "Wouldn't it have been easier to delete the passage altogether?"

Mical came over to the other side of Josef's desk. He pushed aside a briefcase and sat down with his feet squarely on the floor. "It would have been easier, yes," he conceded. Then he looked at the air above Josef's head. "But we must act carefully. There are those among us who might remember the story of Exodus. If they went to read it and could not find it, they would be able to say with certainty—or at least with more certainty—that the book had been tampered with. Now they will say that they merely misremembered it."

Josef looked doubtful. "But surely there are Bibles that people have hidden. Could they not compare those paper Bibles with the one we provide? Would not the lie be apparent then?"

"What lie?"

Josef rubbed at his hands and looked into Mical's eyes to judge his sincerity. When he did not answer quickly enough, Mical continued.

"Our job is to give the people hope. Allowing them to believe that God was attacking them, punishing them with toads, would undermine their faith in everything we've built."

Josef nodded. He knew that Mical was correct, but this knowledge did not undo the knot of unease that had been tightening in him every day.

"You have done a good thing here, Josef. You must not let your worries get the better of you." Mical reached over and took one of the hard yellow candies from the dish on Josef's shelf. Their taste was bland, although they smelled powerfully of lemons. Josef could hear the foil wrapper coming apart beneath Mical's fingers. Then he caught the scent of citrus. "A very good thing," repeated Mical as he turned and followed the hallway back from where he'd come.

Josef returned to his screen. The spots were still there, coasting across the lambent page, which he would fill with his report on the improving water quality of the river that bisected the park. They were the same spots he had been seeing for years, spots his doctors could not explain.

CHAPTER 68:
WHY WOULD SHE LOVE A THING HER HUSBAND CARED NOTHING ABOUT?

Isabelle laughed when she heard the stories—angels come down from the heavens, their murderousness, their oily meat wafting off the kitchen table.

"These country women are so superstitious," Isabelle said after the waiter had replenished her wine.

Josef blushed. He could not deny the silliness of his wife, and yet hearing her spoken of this way by Isabelle was an affront.

"She has learned to overcome many things since becoming my wife," he said evenly, his fingers wandering around the stem of his glass.

It was a mistake to have lunch with Isabelle. When she had finally made contact with him in the ministry courtyard, he was proud. She had found him in a position of some stature, and he was wearing his best suit. She had studied his lunchtime routine for three days before making herself known. She wanted to look radiant as she wheeled her son's carriage before him. When she suggested they have lunch together that day, Josef was pleased that he could put her off. He had an appointment, and he was glad he did not reshuffle his day for her. She was glad too. It would have been a mark of weakness.

When they agreed on a restaurant later that week, she made plans to leave Fyodor at home. She went to her hairdresser and used some of the expensive perfume her husband could afford to buy her. It was viscous, and she rubbed it into the skin behind her ears. The lily scent would follow her all afternoon.

"You have no children?" she probed.

Josef shook his head. "Magda continues to miscarry. The doctor has said it may not be possible."

"Then the fault is with her," Isabelle said decisively. "As the husband, you have done your part by putting the baby inside her." She took a long sip of her wine. "It is up to the woman after that."

Josef nodded. The logic was undeniable, and yet the calculation behind everything Isabelle said was difficult to hear. He wondered what she hoped to gain from this luncheon.

"What did she say the angel tasted like?" she asked.

Josef told her again of the boiled meat and the oily musk.

"Perhaps it was a swan that somebody fed her," he suggested. "The people in the country are backward. Their poverty can make them see what is not there."

"Yes, a swan," she said. "That's the most likely thing." She took a forkful of steak and chewed it carefully. Josef had paid dearly for this luncheon, and she wanted to savor it. Even at her station in life, Isabelle could not eat steak very often. She crushed the fatty pieces between her molars and let the juices coat each part of her tongue before swallowing.

"You should take her to a magic show sometime," Isabelle teased. "Tell her the magician is an emissary of God. Tell her the handkerchiefs flowing from his sleeve are sacred."

Josef let her laugh. He understood her reasons for the luncheon now. She wished to show him that he had not married her. She wished to show him that his own line was coming to an end. He restrained himself from chastising Isabelle, which, he would realize later, was yet another of his mistakes.

From a young age, Isabelle had shown herself to be intolerant of disloyalty in all its forms. When she found the cat peeing on her pillow, she picked it up and threw it out the window. They were only two stories up, so the cat survived—but it never again allowed Isabelle to touch it, and Isabelle did not miss the cat's company. When she was older, she grabbed a fistful of a girl's hair and forced her to her knees. The girl had been mocking Isabelle's haircut. She was bigger than Isabelle, and because Isabelle had made her cry in front of others, the incident cemented her reputation for ruthlessness and quick action. If girls talked about her haircuts later, they did so fearfully and behind closed doors.

Now that Isabelle was a grown woman and living in the city proper, she could not depend on the history of her terrors being handed down and magnified by the people she wished to control. But she carried herself in a way that put others on notice. To stoke her own enthusiasm, she told herself, often, that she was capable of doing anything to a person who went against her.

When Isabelle asked Josef if she could see a picture of his wife, he opened his wallet and showed her the photograph from their wedding, still radiant in its color once he slipped it from the plastic sleeve. Josef and Magda stood against a white wall with a palm print above their heads, as if someone had leaped up with great effort to slap it. Beside them stood a very green ficus plant, which in retrospect was probably plastic. The photographer had commanded them to smile, and out of fear and relief they obliged.

Isabelle stared closely at the picture. She recognized Magda as a woman she had seen smoking on the symphony steps. She remembered that she stood beside a strange-looking man—a man with ivory skin. It was only for this detail that she was able to summon the memory of Magda. She regarded her face as common and unremarkable, but her proximity to this startling man made her easy to recall. Isabelle remembered thinking they seemed familiar.

"May I keep this?" she asked.

Josef had not expected the request. He looked at Isabelle, waiting for an explanation. When none came, he said, "I'm afraid that's my only copy."

He returned the photograph to its plastic sleeve.

"Why would you want that picture?" he asked. "What good could come of that?"

"Indeed," she said, and began moving the noodles around with her fork, searching for a caper. "You don't look happy, Josef. You look like the ox is driving you and not the other way around."

He wasn't sure if she was repeating some country saying or insulting his wife. He drained his glass and began getting ready to depart.

"I just wish she were as devoted to you as you are to her." She speared something off her plate and forked it into her mouth.

"My wife's devotion is adequate," he said, hoping to cut the subject short. His right hand was rifling his pockets as he spoke, searching for his cigarettes.

"Why do you think she goes to the symphony?" she asked. "Why would she love a thing her husband cared nothing about?"

It was a fair question, but Josef enjoyed his nights without Magda. He could drink as much as he wanted, and he did not have to endure her watching and her sighs. If his wife was having an affair, as he thought Isabelle was implying, that would be bad, but he had no intention of finding out. The energy his public outrage would demand was enough to keep him complacent, assuming the best, assuming his wife had merely fallen out of step with him. It happened in other marriages. Maybe in all of them.

Josef paid their bill and left without further pleasantries.

When he returned home that night, a little drunk because he had gone out with Mical Constantinopolis after work, he became displeased about everything in his life. The lamp was too far away from his easy chair. The windowsill was dusty. When he threw his cold dinner onto the floor, he felt a little better, but Magda's weeping only incited him to strike her.

CHAPTER 69:
SHE WOULD OFFER HIM TEA OR
A LOZENGE OF MAPLE CANDY

"Do you remember when we ate the angel that fell through our barn?" Magda asked.

Anton nodded and pulled her closer, feeling the cold for the first time as they lay upon the sheets.

"I was hoping you'd come over," she said. "I liked you even then."

Anton knew this of course because he was older, and back then, at that age, two years meant a lot. She had seemed like a child to him, though he himself was one.

"What was it like knowing we were all having a feast you couldn't take part in?"

Magda adjusted herself so that she could see his jaw as he answered. She couldn't guess what he would say, and it struck her that most of her questions were not like that. Magda always had a dim or sharp sense of what the answer must be, but she had never considered what it must feel like to go without while those around her feasted.

"I was jealous, naturally," said Anton. "That's why I walked over and looked in your kitchen window while you dined."

Magda wasn't sure if he was joking. She reached up, grabbed his chin, and bent him into her gaze. "You hid outside and watched us eat? You spied on us?"

"Yes, I spied on you."

Magda let go of his chin and pushed it back so that his eyes were pointed at the black ceiling again.

"You all seemed to like it very much," he said. "Such platefuls of meat."

Magda recalled the rail-like body of Anton as he whipped an ox or hoisted a ladder onto his shoulder. He was a stripped-down, powerful muscle of a boy, but he was also on the cusp of starving. They all were. The angel meat had made life easy for a day as their bodies absorbed the nutrients, thankful for the gluttony.

"And now you're the wife of an official," he said. "Filling your face again."

She swatted at him as he laughed and pulled at her. But she knew it was true. Her life had become easy. She had put on weight, a healthy plumpness. Twice she had had to buy new dresses because the zippers refused to ascend her back. And all that time, even now, Anton was still a rail. He seemed hungry, and as she thought this, he bit into her neck, then her breast, and then he was inside her again, moving faster than a galloping horse across the wide open field of Magda.

Afterward, Anton spoke of the only time he had tasted angel. He had had a bad reaction. Everyone knew that albinos should not eat the meat, but he had tried it anyway, pulling a gristly piece from one of the ribs and swirling it through the juices of the carving plate. This was when he was just six or seven years old. Mr. Laconovich had killed an angel in the woods between their farms, and he shared it with Anton's and Magda's families.

"In less than a minute, my tongue began to itch, and I could feel a line of tingling traveling down my throat," he said. He explained how the welts rose up on his fingertips and lips, how his breathing became labored and his eyes swelled shut. His parents were beside themselves when they discovered him on the kitchen floor. His father scolded him through his tears as Anton's mother hugged his reddening body, trying to squeeze him back to normal size.

Eventually, when his symptoms stopped getting worse, they put him to bed and checked on him every fifteen minutes, his mother sleeping on the floor beside him. There, on the brink of his own demise, he had never felt so safe. He had merely to cry out and his mother would rise from the floor to comfort him. She would give him tea or a lozenge of maple candy, believing that his satisfaction in these small deeds was a sign he would get better.

At one point, Anton woke in the night to find his parents weeping in each other's arms, clearly distraught at how close they had come to losing their only son. Behind them in the kitchen, in the light of a kerosene lamp, Mr. Laconovich and his family continued to pick over the bones for the choicest pieces of meat before it all went bad.

Nevertheless, Anton enjoyed his delirium. It became more difficult to open his eyes, so he let the fever take him wherever it wanted. He imagined that he himself was an angel, and he soared up to God to ask him for a biscuit or a pear. Even in his dreams, his desires were small and practical. It would never occur to Anton to wish for a whole orchard of pears or a silo full of grain ready to be milled.

Later, his mother announced that Anton would not be let in the house if they ever had angel again. She would not even allow him to smell the meat cooking. It was too risky. She knew that each episode would be worse than the last, and she could not imagine her son being able to gasp any more desperately than he had during the hour of his greatest discomfort.

In the morning, his eyes were crusted shut, but the swelling of his body had gone down. He no longer wished to scratch his own bones. There were large raw patches of skin leaking pus all over him, wherever he could reach; in the confusion, it had taken some time for his father to realize he should make his son wear mittens. Eventually, they had to tie him to the bed, but even then Anton took great pleasure in rolling his wrists and ankles around in the heavy ropes. All morning, his mother came in and soaked his eyes with warm rags, trying to loosen the crust so he could open them. It took a while, and when he finally did open his eyes, his father had resumed his former sternness and his mother was composed, though it was clear she had been crying.

In the window behind her, the clouds were skidding past, bulky and white, like they were fleeing the scene of some terrible crime—or heading to see what happened.

CHAPTER 70:
A BLACK FLOWER BLOSSOMING

Isabelle was not interested in culture the way some ministry wives were. She was able to enjoy paintings and the symphony, but she didn't swoon about it, and she didn't believe the women who claimed to be so moved. For Isabelle, her seat on the museum board meant she would be present at gatherings of important people. It meant she could achieve a kind of standing separate from her husband's, though, admittedly, her standing was not sustainable without him.

Isabelle had even been to parties at which the prime minister made an appearance. The officials and their wives would be mingling and watching the hors d'oeuvres circulate the room when she would hear the whacking of a helicopter as it settled on the roof. She imagined a black flower blossoming. At such times, the waiters would place a tray on the champagne flutes they had already filled for fear that the vibrations would topple them. It was all very heady. The guests fell silent. Women smoothed their dresses out. The men brushed dandruff off their shoulders. Then, because no one wants to stay quiet at a party, people began to fidget. A stray conversation resumed. That's when the prime minister entered the room, always by means of the door that Isabelle was not watching.

The prime minister was not a young man. He was perhaps thirty-eight—practically venerable. It struck Isabelle that a man not much older than herself could rise so high in so short a time.

On the first night she saw him, she tried to seem aloof as he made his way through the crowd, shaking hands and whispering favors or threats into the ears of the men in epaulettes. When he stood before Isabelle and her husband, her husband seemed more starstruck than she had hoped, and he addressed her as Mrs. Vice Minister. The two men exchanged a few pleasantries, and then the prime minister turned to Isabelle.

"It will be interesting to see what kind of exhibitions this old museum can muster," he said. "I found them a little stale last season."

Isabelle glanced at her husband as the prime minister moved on, and her husband's face was full of dread. They both knew it might be a terrible thing for the prime minister to take an interest in someone's wife. But Isabelle gathered herself. She would see to the collection. She would make certain that their opening exhibit was sufficiently grand, though she wasn't yet sure how. She had only just joined the board, and she felt a smug satisfaction as she watched the prime minister bypass the museum director, waving to the crowd generally while staring into Isabelle's eyes. Then he and his entourage headed back to the roof.

Two minutes later, the helicopter lurched back to life, and everyone had a gulp of champagne to keep it from spilling.

That night, Isabelle thought only of the museum and how she might make it more impressive for the prime minister. She was not interested in pleasing her husband when he came to her after her bath. She felt as though the world had wobbled a bit, and she was trying to get a footing that her husband could not dislodge. He went to bed lonely, and she stayed up for hours, not moving, staring up into blackness that failed to get any deeper.

CHAPTER 71:
THE PEOPLE DON'T WANT STARS

Isabelle often toured the museum in the early morning before it opened. She preferred not to mingle with people who could simply walk in off the street. Privacy for her was always precious.

The morning after she met the prime minister, she stopped in front of *The Starry Night* and tried to imagine seeing a sky so full of glory. She herself had never seen anything like it, and she wondered how else the world was different when Vincent van Gogh was alive and painting. She read the placard that told about his self-mutilation, his hospitalization, his desperate attempt to impress a girl.

Footsteps sounded in one of the adjacent galleries. It was a woman's walk, although with the echoing in the marble rooms, Isabelle could not tell if the woman was coming closer or moving further away.

I suppose he must have been terrified to wake in the night and find a sky like that above him, she said to herself.

Although she enjoyed the painting, Isabelle could not imagine such fiery movement above her. It would lead to dreams of a destroyed world, the starlight like a flame crackling down a fuse.

Isabelle felt an itch between her shoulder blades, and she crossed the arms of her jacket to scratch it. She considered her position in the world. She was a smart woman living in the center of Moscodelphia. She was married to a vice minister, but she would never rise above the level of wife and museum board member. She would never see anything like van Gogh's stars. True, her girlhood in the suburbs had acquainted her with the idea of stars, but because she lived so close to Moscodelphia, the night sky never approached majesty; millions of windows were always blazing. And she had been to the beach, to the resort towns along the sea. The smog was rarely a problem there, but the lights of the boardwalks and attractions drowned out the night sky. There was nothing but a washed-out blackness above the towns, crossed by the occasional twinkling of a jet.

One time, though, in her youth, Isabelle visited a seaside resort with her parents. They were dining in an open-air restaurant, the water lapping against the pilings that held them up, when there was a power failure. It was not in their restaurant alone, but all up and down the coast. The restaurant was situated in the center of a concave line of beach towns, and her family was able to watch as one town after another went black until they were sitting in what might as well have been a cave. There was a commotion of gasping and dropped plates. Children began to weep. Parents scolded. Then, after a minute in the darkness, when everyone realized it was best to just stay still, Isabelle looked up and saw the summer sky. For the first time, she could see that some stars were blue while others were red. Some were blazing white. There was no moon in the sky, which intensified the effects. There was also a faint band of light above them. At first she thought it was a cloud. But when an actual cloud floated by, it was clear that the glowing band was really something else, something like many small and uncountable stars.

"What are all these lights?" she asked her parents.

"I'm not sure," said her father. "I've never seen anything like this."

"But they must be stars," said her mother. "What else could they be?"

They sat watching the display above the ocean. Sometimes there was a streak of light across the sky, and everyone made a noise. People became giddy. Others continued crying. Isabelle couldn't decide if she was frightened or elated. She leaned into her mother for warmth and solace, and her mother seemed pleased to be able to comfort her precocious child.

And then, perhaps an hour later, the power was restored all at once, up and down the full length of the coast. The stars they had been studying disappeared except for the brightest and most gaudy, but they looked dull now by comparison, easily missed. They were like pearls put back inside the oyster.

Isabelle relaxed her arms and took a step back from the painting. The woman in the adjacent gallery had either left or fallen to contemplation, and Isabelle wondered why there couldn't be an official turning out of the lights now and then. It could be part of a festival, a reason to go to the seaside, and the great benefit was that it would cost no money. It would be a turning off of the power, a looking upward in silence. She had mentioned this idea to her husband once.

"The people don't want stars," her husband said. "They want to be entertained. They want music and jugglers. That's why we built the resorts."

He said this in such a way that no further discussion of the matter would occur. Isabelle understood. She did not wish to anger him. And so when she wanted to see stars now, she came to the museum. The placard said that van Gogh was insane when he painted the picture. It said the sky was evidence of his hallucinations. The painter was a lesson in the danger of desire for that which can never be had.

CHAPTER 72:
HE HAD NO PROBLEM WITH
TASTING HIS OWN SPIT

Pasha leaned against his shovel to listen to the migrating geese pass over, barely visible but still audible because the wind was right. He thought of Magda. It was as if the geese had carried the idea of her across the stricken planet and dropped it into his field like a smoking meteorite.

It had been a long time since he had thought of his sister. It was painful. Mostly because he imagined her living a charmed life among the glassy towers of Moscodelphia—dining on exotic meats, being so well-fed she didn't have to bother with apple cores and potato peels. At such times, he saw her as happy. She smiled so much that when she grew contemplative, her face had wrinkles where the smile had been. It was difficult to turn such thoughts over in his mind, like he was trying to pull a burning log from the woodstove.

Thinking of Magda was painful for other reasons too—for reasons Pasha had a hard time articulating. He sometimes felt as if he were responsible for her leaving, or at least for her wishing to leave. Had she been more careful about being out in the open, the collectors might never have found her and she would be with him now, helping him rake the dung out of the chicken house. He regretted the lost work of course. But he also regretted her lost companionship. Now that both their parents were dead, Magda was the only person who knew him in any meaningful way. The town girls couldn't be bothered with him at his age, and the town men laughed at his clothes—made from animal skins and a patchwork of leftover rags. He knew they cheated him whenever he dealt with them, but there was no one he could appeal to. Everyone thought he was stupid.

Pasha eventually learned to make his own alcohol. He set up a still, and this was where he had a dog tied up. Other things on the farm might be stolen by passersby, but the liquor he distilled was truly valuable, and it was easier to carry a few bottles into town than to carry a bushel of corn. Pasha spit inside the bottles he intended to sell. It made him feel better about getting cheated, and when the tinkers and merchants opened the bottle and asked him to join them, as a way of ensuring he'd put nothing foul inside, he had no problem with tasting his own spit.

Still, the geese had the right idea. They were able to leave a place with grace and music, and there was always a field to rest beside. He liked how they waddled out into the center of his own irrigation pond as a protection against the wildcats and coyotes that came stalking on nightly rounds. It must be something to sit in the center of filth and know you are safe, that no one will wade in to get you—no matter how good you taste.

CHAPTER 73:
THE SOFT AND SLIPPERY CRESCENTS

Anton had thought about returning, of waiting for a time when the crop failures were well past, when it would be safe for him to travel openly through the countryside. It would be easy, for he had seen the maps. He knew that the place he came from was known as Sector 26. He was able to find the train track he had traveled on; he saw where the spoke exited the city and penetrated the countryside. He traced his finger along the track until he recognized the river he used to fish in, the bend on the outside of town, the slight and unusual compression of topographic lines that indicated the hill beside his family's farm.

Anton entertained the fantasy of returning only when he was drunk, and he was drunk whenever he couldn't meet with Magda. He had to at least see her. A glimpse of her silhouette in the windows of her home could satisfy him for a day. Other times he stood watching her smoke a cigarette on the music hall's steps. When the intermission bells rang, he saw her drop the still-burning cigarette beside one of the columns; and when everyone had gone back inside, Anton would cross the street, pick up the cigarette, and finish it. He felt close to her. He could smell the perfume from her fingers where the cigarette had rested, and this made him happy.

The train would stop at Laurelensk. This was the name of the town near his old farm, according to the maps. There was a depot there, which the collectors used when they made their stops to extract the wealth of the surrounding countryside. *This is strange,* thought Anton. No one he knew had called the town Laurelensk. As best as he could remember, there wasn't any name attached to the town. He had never even considered it a possibility. Everyone he knew called it only "the town."

Who had named it thus? And what did it mean? And why, now that he had read this name, did he think differently about the place he came from?

When he returned, he imagined that he would stride up the long dirt driveway to his farm carrying bags of delicacies from the city: shampoo, chewing gum, cans of peaches in a thick syrup. He would explain to his mother that she need not eat them right away. She could leave them on the shelf for months, years even, and they would still be fresh when she cut into the can. He would show them the can opener he had brought with him, and he would let them practice opening one of the cans. Anton would warn them about the sharpness of the removed lid, and then he would pour the peaches into a bowl for everyone to enjoy. The soft and slippery crescents would be a success. His family would eat them in one sitting, and they would take turns scooping up the syrup into a spoon and sharing it. Later, when his mother took the bowl to the sink, he would watch her run a finger around the bowl's circumference to be sure she had gotten the last of it.

Then it would be time for their questions, and Anton would answer them all—about the tallness of the buildings, the people milling about like ants, the density of the smog.

"They have different ideas in the city," he would say. "They don't believe in angels."

"Don't poke fun at us," his mother would respond. "We're not so foolish that you can get us to believe such things."

Sometimes, during this daydream, Anton would press his point, emphasizing the vast knowledge that Moscodelphians possessed, or pointing up to the sky and saying that the silvery angel was actually an airplane. In one version of the fantasy, he brought binoculars with him and taught them to look upward. Then he would show them the photographs of planes taking off and landing.

Other times, he let them believe he was kidding them. He knew it could be painful at this late stage to unlearn the way they had lived. If he left for Laurelensk tomorrow, if they were still alive, they'd be in their fifties, and who at such an advanced age would even be interested in the truth of things?

Anton would have to reckon with the possibility of Pasha. In all likelihood, he would still be plowing the ground up in the next farm over. Anton would bear his old neighbor no malice at this late date. He would open the locket and offer him a nail. There would be no accusations and no apologies. Pasha would accept the gift while plotting the taking of another finger, which Anton would need to be clever about. He could not hold someone accountable for having a natural impulse.

But when Anton gave the subject serious thought, he was sure his parents were dead. It had been too long. He had moved far away to save himself while his parents sank deeper into the poverty of their farm. He was a bad son.

CHAPTER 74:
A LIGHT WENT ON IN THE
FAR END OF THE HOUSE

Anton got out of his van and started walking toward the enclave of ministry homes. This was acceptable as long as it wasn't completely dark. He wanted to see Magda, if only from the street, as she passed by chance before the lighted windows of her home.

A large gray dog charged a fence and began barking at him. Other dogs answered from far away, but only half-heartedly. As the dog followed the length of its yard, banging against the fence and threatening to jump over it, Anton reached into his pocket and threw a handful of sand into the dog's barking face. He did this without looking back or to the side, just a flick of his wrist and the dog stood down, whimpering and pawing at its eyes.

He could see Magda's house up ahead. Josef's clod-like head floated in the living room window. He was staring into his terminal screen and did not look up when Magda entered the room, carrying a plate of food.

Then a light went on in the far end of the house—the bedroom, Anton assumed. He saw Magda draw the curtains, and for a moment he watched her shadow doing something near the window, making up the bed or getting changed. He couldn't tell.

At the end of the block, Anton crossed the street and circled back to make another pass at the house. He would have to get back to the van soon, as the sky was softening quickly. If he were in the country, it would be the color of certain bird eggs that were found on the forest floor after the hatching, after the mother bird had cleaned out the nest that floated unseen in the trees above. The sky was just dim enough for a star, but only if you were looking for it, only if you were in the country, surrounded by the scent of manure and rustling corn.

Josef's head was gone from the window now, and Magda's shadow could not be seen behind any of the curtains. Anton had told Magda he would be walking by, that, in fact, he had been doing so on and off for weeks. He wanted her to be watching him from one of the rooms, to give him a sign that she had seen him, that she had been waiting. But of course that would be dangerous, and he found himself wishing she would do no such thing, that she would instead go rub her husband's feet to draw off any suspicion that she was unfaithful.

The dog next door was still scratching at its eyes. There was an occasional bark in the distance, but nothing to draw anyone outside to see what might be happening. Anton saw the guardhouse up ahead—the small booth in the middle of the street that led into the ministry neighborhood. The light inside was still off, so he didn't have to worry about being stopped. He would get in the van and drive away. After all, he had done nothing wrong. No one could blame him for enjoying the twilight on such a beautiful street, and yet he had to admit that it was strange that no one who lived here was out among the flowering branches of their yards. The azaleas were covered in pink and white despite the gray rain that fell on them. Anton's delivery job took him to all corners of the city, and for the past week, the azaleas had been out in force wherever people could afford them. They were a dependable bush, well-suited to the meager soil of the city, which Anton suspected did not run very deep. But here, among the ministry homes, they were ignored. Even the windows were all closed, and the humming of air conditioners filled the spaces between the houses.

Just then, a woman stepped out onto her porch. She held a drink and seemed unsteady as she leaned against the banister. Anton thought she might be looking at him, so he tipped his hat in deference, but she seemed to be looking past him. He turned to see what she saw.

The house just past her gaze had a light on in every window, and in the bedroom to the left, a woman was combing her hair before a mirror. She appeared to be nude, or at least topless, and Anton wondered if he had interrupted an evening routine of brushing and watching. The woman looking in was older, past her prime, and he could imagine her remembering her own youth and how it was misspent. Youth was always misspent. There was always another girl to taste, and the reasons we did not do so were many and insincere.

"I saw what you did," she called across the street.

Anton stopped, though he couldn't be sure if he was being addressed.

"I saw what you did to that dog," she said.

Anton said she must be mistaken and set off again, trying to be conscious of his former pace, and taking care to step over a toad that had smashed into the sidewalk some days earlier.

"The police will know what do to with you," she cried.

But Anton could barely hear her. The blood was banging in his ears now, and he had turned a corner, trying to put something more substantial than ministry air between himself and this woman—and her rising voice.

His van was up ahead, waiting like a bullet in someone's ammunition drawer.

PART 5

CHAPTER 75:
A SINGLE COBALT TILE FLOATING
IN THE MORTAR OF JOSEF'S LIFE

Magda had the driver leave her at the base of the museum steps. She wanted to be by herself, and this was a place where none of her acquaintances would find her. Going to the museums was one of the pleasures of her station, and this was the kind of thing she would be giving up if she ran away with Anton. If she could tell her mother that this is how she spent her days, she would be incredulous. Her mother would have called it "high-class laziness" because she could not conceive of anything useful that came from looking at old paintings or sculptures of women who showed their bottoms.

Such thoughts made Magda wince. She had never returned to her family farm, as Raisa had. Josef had never offered to let her return, but then again, Magda had never asked. Now the point was moot. Both of her parents were surely dead. It would be extraordinary for either to live beyond fifty, and they would be fifty-five by now. She could put the question to Josef. She could formulate the plan that would send her south. But there were a thousand other places she would rather be—on the steps of a museum, in the wooded grove along the river, in the arms of Anton.

The exhibit this time was full of mosaics. They were pictures composed of little tiles called "tesserae." The tesserae didn't actually touch one another. Instead, the mortar showed between the pieces, and this was done on purpose—a deliberate technique that exposed the artifice of the picture and showed how much the viewer's mind helped assemble the pieces into something coherent. This, at least, is what the placard said at the entrance to the collection. Magda wasn't sure if she believed all that, but when she looked at a mosaic up close, she found it was meaningless. It was only when she stepped back, allowing herself some distance, that the picture became clear.

It reminded her of the graininess of newsprint photographs. She had seen them once when her father tore open a wall of their house to kill a family of raccoons. Inside the walls there were many crumpled newspapers jammed in for insulation. Magda spent hours smoothing out the pages and studying the strange headlines that were more than a century old. They talked of melting ice caps and gas warfare, and beautiful women lay about the house, wearing elaborate undergarments and disdainful expressions. Most of the print was so tiny that Magda was obliged to borrow her mother's magnifying glass. That's when she noticed how the photographs became a gibberish of little dots. They only made sense unmagnified, and they became clearer the farther back she held her face. For a while, Magda's father allowed her to keep some of the old newspapers in her room. She'd take them out and read about important men and wonder at the hairstyles of women who drove around in shiny cars. She thought it was a kind of storybook, like the Bible, which was full of things that could never happen. Unfortunately for Magda, everyone else in her family found the papers more useful as a form of kindling, and slowly, despite Magda's protests, the pile of papers in her room was turned into kitchen smoke. She missed the papers so much that she considered breaking through the plaster in her room to pull out more of the insulation. But she knew that her father would never stand for it. She still thought back now and again to those first pages she had carefully uncrumpled, trying to keep the paper from becoming flakes, the flakes from becoming dust.

Magda wished she could step far enough back from her own life to achieve the same effect. She would like to know how killing her father's prize turtle and dining on angel thigh and running off with Anton had anything in common beyond their own randomness. If she could just see her life and all its mistakes and all its glories from the right distance, it would gather a sense of purpose and coherence. She was sure of it.

But at other times, Magda was less certain of whether she wanted this all-focusing perspective. Figuring things out had rarely given her much solace. For instance, she could now see that the farm her parents lived on all their lives had slowly killed them. The endless cycles of drought and storm and weevil infestation eventually forced them to succumb. It was not possible for Magda to see how that pathological effort to survive, for which she had never properly thanked them, had given meaning to their lives.

If Magda's life was a mosaic, what was the mortar that both fragmented it and held it all together? And if she could figure that out, how would that be of comfort? The old Greek mosaics had almost all been destroyed. People valued the colored tiles too highly and pried them out. Some mosaics had been discovered as a mortar sheet of mostly pockmarks where the tesserae had been. In some cases, it was still possible to get the general idea of such a mosaic across, but she had to stand further back, and even then, she could never be sure without the tiles. The portraits could just as easily be of saints or heretics. At a certain point, Magda stopped caring which.

Leaving the museum that afternoon, Magda thought of herself as a single cobalt tile floating in the mortar of Josef's life. The home he had provided prevented her from touching any other tiles. She felt as though she had been pressed into the gray mortar, and the mortar had forced her into one unendurable position. Now, Anton had popped her out of the cement and would whisk her into the mountains and beyond if she let him, and she would end up in a place she could never have anticipated. She wondered if there would be toads that sang in the springtime. She wondered if the bushes would surprise her with new kinds of flowers. Most of all, she wondered about the silvery stars that had been absent from the sky she stood beneath. Would she remember them? Would they form the same pictures? Or might they have rearranged themselves after all her years in Moscodelphia?

CHAPTER 76:
EVEN THE RIVERS TERMINATED ABRUPTLY

Magda looked at the map Anton had spread like a tablecloth too small to cover the desk. It spanned hundreds of miles, and it was the kind of map you could get in trouble for having. Moscodelphia was a tiny gray stain at the center of it, the size of a fingernail. Anton pointed to the southernmost reaches of the map.

"That's where we lived," he said. "Somewhere in this patch of green, near this bend in the river."

Magda was not good with maps. She would have to trust him. Trying to read a map was like trying to draw a picture with her left hand. She always had trouble envisioning herself anywhere but where she was.

"Show me again where we will go," she said.

Anton pointed to the top of the map, where there was no detail—no roads, not even the greenness that denoted forest and farmland. These were the Outer Territories: the places beyond the direct control of the ministries. It was unclear if they were under the control of some other city undepicted or whether the landscape was wild beyond the imagination. There were rumors of large bears and musk oxen, and Anton conjectured that this is where they must live. The map became useless at the outer reaches though. Even the rivers terminated abruptly, but Anton had seen enough of the world to know a river didn't simply end. It had to find an ocean.

"That's where we have to go," he said. "If we can get to the Outer Territories, no one will try to follow us. We can start our own farm. We know how to do that."

Magda was always hopeful when he said these words. She believed they could farm whatever land was there.

"But what if there are people already there?" she asked. "What if the superstitions of the south are the same in the north?"

Anton stepped away and refilled their whiskey glasses. For all he knew, there would be people waiting for him who liked nothing more than to kill albinos. They might see him as a kind of angel.

"If we stay here," he said, "I'll have to murder Josef."

This was true and summed up why they were looking at a stolen map. Josef had become impossible. His brutality could not be endured now that she knew the gentleness of Anton still existed. But Magda could not ask Anton to murder Josef, and she herself was unable to summon the necessity. She looked up at the ceiling as if she could see through to the sky, as if the sky was not obscured by a layer of poisonous smog, as if the stars were guiding her with their cold, impersonal light. But there were no stars, and when she looked again into Anton's eyes, she saw only the fact that doing nothing was impossible.

Anton picked up the two whiskey glasses, and the map rolled back on itself, as if it had been waiting for the chance to hide the message it had now delivered. He passed Magda her glass, and they drank it down without looking at each other, letting the heat of the whiskey spread out inside them.

CHAPTER 77:
THERE WILL BE MOUNTAINS FIRST

Every moment of Magda's life had led inexorably to this one. That seemed impossible when she thought about it, yet how could it not be true? The errand to retrieve a tool had led to the kissing in the corn, which led to the amputation of Anton's finger, which led them both to Moscodelphia. Now they were planning their escape in a secret hotel room.

"There will be mountains first," Anton said. "Then we'll be free."

It was a simple and irrefutable formulation.

"From what I've heard," Anton said, returning the map to its box, "the weather is different up north. It is colder."

"Perhaps it will not have locusts," said Magda.

It was a sensible thing to say. When they had lived in the country, the locusts were never a problem in the winter months, but what if it were winter all the time in this new place? How would they grow corn and soybeans? Neither of them asked these questions out loud. They would have to make a go of it. They would take the jars of seeds that Anton had been accumulating, and they would plant them the same way they did before they came to Moscodelphia. If the ground rejected them, or if the ground was full of rocks and ice, they would make another plan.

"Did you think you'd be running away with me in our old age?" asked Magda. "Did you think when you tricked me into the corn that you'd eventually have to steal me from a Subminister of Opulence?"

Anton sat back down with her on the bed. He recognized the plea in her voice. He heard it whenever the time had come to part. It wasn't safe for them to stay in one place long.

"I did not," he said. "You gave the impression that you were much easier than all this."

She slapped his hands away and stood before him so that he could approve. It was their ritual now for him to check over her body and her dress to ensure there was no evidence of their tryst. Was everything tucked in? Was her hair in order? When she was certain that all was right with her appearance, she went back to pretending that she would stay with Josef.

Magda always left the hotel first, by way of the elevator when there was one. Anton followed ten minutes later, after straightening the room. Then he walked down the stairs, entered the bustling lobby, and pushed through the revolving door. The air of Moscodelphia was gray as usual, and the smog began at ten stories or at ninety, depending on the weather.

"It's a wonder anyone stays," he muttered. "It's a wonder it was built at all."

CHAPTER 78:
A LITTLE MORE SUGAR

Magda remembered picking blueberries in the cool shade of the pine woods, when the sun had only just risen and the berries and surrounding grasses were slick with dew. There was a plumpness to them, a tightness to the skin, and she loved that kernel of sweetness when she burst one with her tongue. That sweetness had been sucked out of the soil all around her, the same soil that animals had defecated and died upon. A blueberry bush was the closest thing to resurrection she could imagine. Of course the same thing was happening on her farm with soybeans and corn, but they were cultivated. There was something artificial about the fruit they produced. Blueberries were wild. They were doing it on their own, without plow and irrigation pipe, without a clearing away of weeds or the placement of a hive.

Magda took the blueberries and sprinkled them over Josef's cereal. They were a disappointment—partially deflated and lacking an essential glossiness. It had been a long time since she had pulled a berry off an actual bush, and she wondered if she was romanticizing this part of her history. She had done it before, and she wanted to be careful about what she felt. It was dangerous and strange to pine for the countryside. Simply being away so long had allowed her to forget that she grew up wanting to flee. She was now where she had always hoped to be. She needed to remember that.

The blueberries in Josef's cereal were shriveled, practically raisins. They were simply too delicate to make the journey from the countryside without this degradation. They reminded her of stars, of anti-stars really, the way they dotted her husband's oatmeal. It was a photographic negative of what she remembered a night sky could be.

"Your breakfast is ready," she called down the hallway.

Josef emerged with his mustache trimmed and his hair slicked back. He was creased in all the right places. Sitting down, he swung his necktie over his right shoulder and ate a spoonful of the cereal.

"A little more sugar," he said, and Magda spooned it over his bowl, being careful to hit each part of the oatmeal so that every mouthful would be sufficiently sweet.

Josef finished his breakfast and began gathering his papers and briefcase.

"I'll need you to call about these toads," he said before he left.

When Magda went to clear the morning's dishes, she found a berry at the bottom of Josef's bowl. She put it in her mouth and used her tongue to burst it behind her teeth. There was a tiny sweetness, but hardly like the sweetness she remembered.

Later, when she was done with the cleaning up, she looked at her calendar and saw that she had nothing to do. The cat wove in and out between her legs, hoping to be fed. The crows were cackling in one of the Constantinopolises' trees. The city was careening forward, and would do so regardless of what she did next. It was an odd sensation. It made her feel both completely insignificant and utterly free, and it would be a while before she realized that the two feelings always went together. Despite what she may have once wished, significance and freedom were an impossible combination for a woman in Moscodelphia.

CHAPTER 79:
OLD LADIES IN THE COUNTRYSIDE
USED TO READ TEA LEAVES

Magda often had trouble sleeping in the early-morning hours. Some days, when she was sore or sleepless, she got out of bed and sat in the living room by the picture window, tilting the blinds to let the darkness in. Then she'd step stealthily into the kitchen to make her tea. It would not be helpful to wake Josef before his time, for the effects of the night's wine would not have worn off yet.

She allowed herself a full spoonful of sugar, but she made sure to use the lemon wedge a second time before throwing it away. Josef would chastise her for such thrift, but she was never certain of their circumstances—its depth or its duration—and so she maintained the thriftiness she grew up with. She hid her miserly ways from her husband only because he would laugh at her. She sat down in her chair by the window and sniffed at her fingers, catching the full aroma of the lemon she had pinched above her cup.

At first her reflection dominated the windowpanes, her body crossed with horizontal bars as if she were sitting in a cage. But the sky began to lighten, and it was difficult to say for sure from which direction the sun was rising. At daybreak the smog was often at ground level, and it was very effective at scattering the location of the sun. It created a picturesque grayness that enveloped the entire neighborhood. She could not see her neighbors' houses; she could not see the street out front. It reminded her of fall mornings on the farm, when mists rose out of the ponds and swamps and seemed to cleanse the earth of its sorrow and filth. Certainly, when she went to use the outhouse, the grass was cold and slick and the seat was covered with a stippling of dewdrops she found refreshing.

The air outside her home in Moscodelphia was poisonous. She did not smell the sulfur in it because the air conditioner's filters had just been changed. In a few weeks they would be a deep yellow, and she would have to hold them under a rush of scalding water to remove the oily film. After that, the filters would not work as well, but they had little choice. Josef's position earned them one set of filter changes per year. They considered themselves lucky. The officials still below Josef's rank had no such filters in their homes, and Magda recognized the benefit of not having to smell the industrial seizure of the city at every hour of the day.

Magda took a deep drink of her tea. It was weak. She was using the teabag for the second time, and it was losing its force. She lifted it by a corner and shook it vigorously, but the bag gave way and the tea leaves filled her cup. She muttered to herself, getting up to grab a second cup, over which she spread a square of cheesecloth. Then she poured the tea into the new cup, catching all the detritus from the burst bag. She was about to shake the cheesecloth into the trash when she took a closer look.

Old ladies in the countryside used to read tea leaves, but Magda put no stock in the practice. The tea leaves never said anything that she herself had not already guessed. Reading the leaves, she later realized, was just a socially acceptable way to tell on your neighbor. At different times, she remembered the old women announcing things like "The leaves are saying Mr. Petrovich sleeps with a whore every fourth Saturday night," or "The leaves are saying Katrina Gorky spends too much time alone in the barn." If anyone objected, the old women just blamed it on the leaves.

When Magda leaned in to examine the mess, she found a horsefly and a piece of red plastic among the leaves. This was fairly common judging from the other tea bags she had seen break open. It's why she preferred the tea where she grew up. In the country, she used a perforated metal spoon with two sides that clapped together. The tea was better back then. She could pick from the fallow field exactly the things she wanted her tea to taste like.

The mesh of the bags hides what's really there, Magda thought, and she spit a fleck of some unidentified leaf into the sink. Just then she heard Josef stirring, and she reached for the egg that would quiet him.

CHAPTER 80:
ROAST CHICKEN AND PRAWNS
AND FRESHLY SHUCKED RAW CORN

Magda went to the window and scanned the street. Anton was taking a great risk by walking past her house to glimpse her lighted curtains. He was taking an even greater risk by running away with her. Even if Josef were inclined to let her go, he would have to make a show of finding them. It would be expected.

She looked over at the Ministry of Opulence, which rose many stories into the clouds. Josef's office was high above her. If he looked out the window, he would see only a blanket of smog and poison, and perhaps he would wonder how the toads were generated from this foul quilt atop the city where he lived and thrived.

Magda had been up there once, at a party for the officials. There was a long table filled with roast chicken and prawns and freshly shucked raw corn. She recognized the lavish bounty, and she was proud of her husband's station. She saw that life with Josef would be a life of prosperity. She need only smile as he rose through the ministry ranks.

That night, after the party, Josef had made love to her, and he was gentle. It reminded her of the times when they were first married. It was like the courting she had read about in her romance stories. He was solicitous. He was careful to kiss every inch of her body before entering her, and he did not choke her or slap at her bottom. It was like the way things were now between herself and Anton. She felt like a present being opened with care.

Magda ran over the many ways that Anton's plan might go awry. The van could break down before they got out of the city. Mrs. Constantinopolis could denounce her after she saw her get into the van. There could be on her person or in her effects some as-yet-undiscovered tracking device that would lead the soldiers and helicopters to their place of refuge. And finally, Anton himself could turn into a lie. All men, she knew, were kind in the beginning, but the years together can make them bored, and bored men have few options. Perhaps she would be abandoned at that time. Perhaps he would try to rekindle his interest by brutalizing her in perverse and original ways.

Magda pulled the curtain back into place and began straightening the room. She did not believe Anton would turn into such a man. She remembered kissing him in the cornfield, and spending many hours with him in the loft above his workbench, and walking through the pine woods around their farms—and how he never coerced her further than she wished to go. This despite the fact he could have done so. He was stronger than she was. He could catch her if she ran. And she saw now, with the wisdom of her years, that he had done the right thing by abandoning her to the farm. Moscodelphia was a bewilderment. Had she arrived back then, alone, at the age of sixteen, she would likely have been installed in some brothel. Her youth would make her prized, which in turn would make her doomed. She had seen these girls sitting in their lighted windows as the drunken men hooted and caroused and openly discussed what they would do to each of them before paying their admission and stepping inside. What else could Magda have done? She would have had to eat, and Anton would have been powerless before the will of the city.

But instead she had had the great luck of being caught out in the open on her own farm by the collectors, enabling her to arrive in the city when she was seventeen. Magda had been very pretty back then. She had never had a case of the pox, and so was able to marry a man of high station. She had become plump—the unmistakable sign of her class—and she had the luxury of being able to smile without bitterness. In fact, Josef had made sure to get her teeth fixed after they were married. They were straight enough, but there were several bad cavities that had lingered for years, and her enamel had lost some of the brightness that was so prized by city-dwelling officials. No matter. Josef had paid for a whitening, which she agreed was an improvement, but which made her teeth hurt for days afterward—if she smiled into the wind, if she took a sip of Chardonnay and swirled it around her mouth to capture its woody chill.

Now Magda was thirty-three—the age of Jesus in his final hours, as the old saying went. No one much remembered Jesus at this point. Certainly, they did not talk about him openly. He was an emblem of treason and despair. The older generation was always saying that he encouraged welfare and charity, which of course were among the worst sins a city dweller could commit. Power and selfishness were the new virtues, and as long as you were in the class of ministers and officials, it seemed a well-wrought world.

Magda felt she had already lived two lifetimes, and how much time could she have left anyway? To live past fifty would be highly unusual. It would be impractical to hope for more, and although she would like to have a child, she had been unable to carry one to term. Every month she felt her ovaries spit out a single egg, and the blood still came with the same regularity she had known since she was fourteen. It was time to run off, to find a new life on the other side of the mountain range that Anton talked about as if it were Eden. It was a place where the trains did not reach. It was a place that, because of the prevailing winds, never saw the sulfurous smog of the city in which they lived.

Anton liked to tell her that the stars at night would be like the stars of their youth. Magda was ashamed to confess that she had not paid more attention to the night sky when she was younger. Yes, the stars were present and beautiful, but she often ignored them at the end of the day because sleep was the best way to ward off hunger. She could not clearly remember any of the pictures the stars formed in the sky. It was something you forgot after a dozen years—like the taste of fresh cream. Perhaps, if she went out to use the outhouse in the middle of the night, she would marvel at the blobs of winter light like glowing grains of salt. But more likely, she would use the chamber pot her father had bought her as a present. Every girl had wanted one back then. It was the custom—a way of acknowledging that the bleeding would start soon, that she was becoming a woman, that she would need to keep clean.

When Magda received her chamber pot, her mother told her that in the city they had toilets that flushed away the water and waste, that it was very ladylike to wake in the night and use the toilet and then go back to your room without any stink or mess. She referred to it as "civilization," the apex of human striving and culture. Magda thought wistfully of this city where people ate cows and used toilets and went up something called "elevators," which took them to the tops of buildings made of brick, where they could see the world stretch out before them like a smoking heap of plenty.

Magda returned to the window and peeked out again between the blinds. She would have to be patient. A dinner must be cooked before it can be eaten.

CHAPTER 81:
SO MANY UNDILUTED STARS

Isabelle continued to see Magda in the most cultured parts of the city—smoking on the symphony steps, strolling through a sculpture garden, even staring into the mosaics at her own museum.

How ironic that this country girl and I walk in the same circles, she thought. When she was feeling cruel and powerful, Isabelle saw Magda as an interloper, someone who was pretending to belong in her station. At other times she stared at Magda with envy. Magda was not tied to her husband the way Isabelle was. True, she was foolish enough to risk losing everything by conducting this affair. But Isabelle could also see how it was brave, how Magda was willing to pursue the thing she wanted despite the risk of beatings and even execution.

There were times when Isabelle considered paying a visit to Josef to tell him how his wife had made him a laughingstock, consorting with a ghostly man who looked like he might evaporate if the clouds ever left the sky above Moscodelphia. Why shouldn't she? It seemed unnatural not to destroy someone when they had left themselves open to the possibility, when they had been careless enough to be found out. That was the galling part for Isabelle—that Magda had not been more careful. It was as if she were counting on the goodwill of strangers to ignore her treason.

But other times, say, when she was preparing some meat to her husband's liking, she felt a grudging admiration for Magda. She had seen real stars out in the countryside, and she had seen them nightly. They were common enough that Magda's memory of them was unremarkable. That's what Josef had told Isabelle about his wife's time in the country. Isabelle, on the other hand, clung to the memory of a single night as she waited for her shrimp scampi to arrive. Could her charmed life really have been that impoverished? Can she have been so misguided that she worked her entire life to end up in a city where almost no one had ever seen a star, not even the pale impersonations of stars she saw from her suburban bedroom as she imagined forcing some boy to do things simply because he was disinclined.

One night, weeks after she and Josef had had their luncheon, Isabelle showed up at the symphony for the annual performance of *The Rite of Spring*. It marked the arrival of the season in Moscodelphia more reliably than the weather, which was always subdued, and Isabelle looked forward to its insinuations and discord. On the steps leading up to the music hall, she saw Magda and the ivory man sharing a cigarette. There was less discretion between them than usual, and Isabelle decided it was time to be bold.

"May I borrow your matches?" Isabelle asked Anton.

Instead of handing them to her, Anton produced a flame and cupped it before her face. Isabelle leaned in.

"A perfect gentleman," she said, smiling. She looked over at Magda as if to acknowledge that she knew they were together and to make it clear that she approved of this man despite the oddness of his appearance.

"I've seen you here before," she said to the air between Anton and Magda. "I wonder what it's like to know that your life could end at any moment."

It sounded more like a threat than she intended, but that was only because she did not want them to hear the envy in her voice.

Anton took half a step to block Isabelle's view of Magda. "There is no reason to ask that of me when you yourself must know the answer," he said. "We are all about to attend a symphony, and the world out here could burn to the ground as we sit inside, distracted by the strings, the breathless pining of the flutes."

The pinkness of his eyes were disconcerting to Isabelle. But it was a good answer, despite its poeticisms, and Isabelle looked past Anton so that she could see Magda's face more clearly. She seemed girlish despite her years, and her eyes shone with a mixture of fear and joy that Isabelle had never felt. She thought that she herself might look that way if she had been lucky enough to have seen so many undiluted stars before this moment.

It was a treasure that Isabelle had no way of stealing.

CHAPTER 82:
LIKE A BRIGHT PLANET THAT BLINKED

Josef's earliest memory was of the silvery planes that flew above his suburb. He watched as they climbed high above the trees in his yard and then began banking to the left and away from where he stood. As a boy, Josef believed that the planes were watching him, that had he not noticed them, they would have continued toward his house and not veered away. It didn't occur to Josef that the pattern he saw in the sky was the result of his home being thirty miles to the west of a busy airport, that what he was seeing was a never-ending line of departures headed for someplace else.

Sometimes, he would be outside playing with a ball or destroying some city of the ants, and he would look up late and see a plane that had not banked to the left. Such moments confirmed his sense of destiny, of secret kingship. Important people were watching him because he himself was important. He reasoned he must be the son of a far-away monarch, that he was sent to live in the suburbs with this strange family because it would be safer for him. There was wind of a coup, perhaps of all-out revolution. If he stayed with his true parents, he would be killed and the line of succession would end. They had sent him away because they loved him.

This fantasy never fully evaporated from the pan of Josef's brain. He looked at all planes, helicopters, satellites, strangers, and tinted windows as if they had a direct bearing on his life and future trajectory. Even as a grown man, part of him would not be surprised if he was whisked into some room and told he was now the leader of everything, that everyone sitting before him awaited the orders hiding in his throat like gold coins he might regurgitate into their palms—now that the truth was out, now that the gears of the world had settled into their proper grooves.

"Have you noticed that helicopter?" asked Magda.

Josef got up from his puzzle and came to the window where Magda was drying a dish. He could hear its far-off whacking at the air.

"Where is it?" he asked.

"Above that tree," she said, pointing.

It was just visible to Josef—like a bright planet that blinked.

"It has been floating there, for thirty minutes at least." She handed the dried dish to Josef so that he could place it on the highest shelf. "They must be looking for someone."

Josef brought his empty hand back to Magda, and she put another dish in it. "If it has been there that long," he said, "they have already found what they wanted."

Magda understood. Many times she had watched the helicopters in search of a traitor on the run, the smoggy air making it appear as though the helicopters were held aloft by a cone of hardened light. They would float over the city, seemingly at random, until they found the one they were searching for. Then they stopped and floated in place until soldiers on the ground could make their way to the spot. At such times, dozens of sirens seemed to be converging on a single alley or a single backyard. Sometimes additional helicopters floated nearby and made their beams converge. It reminded Magda of what Pasha used to do to earthworms with his magnifying glass. She imagined that anyone caught in that tightening circle of light must think the world beyond it had disappeared.

Magda wondered if this is what it would be like with her when she left Josef. Would he send out helicopters to find her? Would she come to be pinned by a searchlight's beam? Would gunshots ring out briefly, as they were right now, giving the pilots permission to disperse from where they hung like spiders, to return to their families and cooling dinners?

Josef's thoughts led down a different path. If he ever found himself inside such a beam, he would wait patiently for the men to arrive and anoint him.

It didn't occur to him that they might take advantage of his stillness, firing a single bullet into his heart, which was the usual method of dispatching someone on the run, someone who was an enemy of the state. But Josef was no enemy. He had risen to the subminister level. His grooming for the coronation he suspected was coming was all but complete. He wondered if he would shout or whisper his first orders.

He decided it should be a whisper. He would make them lean in close to hear the names of the men they must now destroy.

CHAPTER 83:
HE BEGAN TO TASTE ANTON IN HIS MOUTH

Pasha felt a great congestion in his chest and sat back in the baking heat of the upper loft. He had spent all morning stacking bales, which he was winching up by hand from the wagon below. His skin was crawling with sweat and dust and particles of rat dung. Now, suddenly, his arms were powerless and his vision contracted so that it looked like he was near the exit of a tunnel, walking backward into the darkness. He tried to get up, but the weight of a giant thumb pushed him back.

He heard the ox moving in the stall below him. He heard the clucking of the hens patrolling their yard. The crows, of course, continued their maniacal calling across the fields.

Pasha took the dried finger of the albino and pressed it to his lips. It had been a long time since there was any luck in it. It felt like stone. After a minute, he was able to lift the chain over his head using only his right hand. He removed the finger and placed it in his mouth. There was no taste except for his own accumulated grime, and he wedged it between his cheek and gums as if it were a wad of tobacco. The barn flies kept leaping from the bales to his arms, from the winch to his face. He didn't have the strength to brush them away.

As the finger softened, he began to taste Anton in his mouth. He thought of the albino working in the fields, how everything had seemed easy for him. He remembered snipping the finger from his hand and how that had made Magda hate him.

"How could you do this to him?" she had demanded. "How could you do this to me?" Pasha had worried that his sister would try to kill him. She had thrown a coffee mug at him, and it ricocheted painfully off his shoulder. They were in the kitchen, and Magda made a move to find a knife in one of the drawers.

Pasha could have fled. He could have left the room and let her come to terms with what he had done. After all, Magda was young and foolish, and Anton was only an albino. She didn't understand the world. He could have just given her some time. Instead, he walked over to where she was rummaging through the drawer, and, as her fingers found the knife, Pasha punched her in the side of the head with all his might. She fell to the floor, stunned but still conscious. When it was clear her anger had not dissipated, he kicked her in the stomach, which took the wind out of her. This made even her weeping stop. She had no air to continue her rage.

Pasha felt the last of the luck leaching out of the withered digit. He seemed to be moving toward the opening of the tunnel now. The world was widening again. The heaviness in his chest floated away like a canoe someone had forgotten to tie off on the bank of a windless lake. Whatever had happened inside of him was being repaired. He had dissolved the skin and ligament and ingested it. He made a point of gathering the saliva in his mouth, and then he swallowed one of the bones.

When he was finally able to stand, the sun was setting. From the loft door, he saw a great many people milling about the yard. They were gray and transparent, and he recognized his father and mother in the small crowd. They would not answer when he called, and they seemed not to care at all when he stumbled into the dusk among them. They were his dead ancestors, roving over the land they used to work.

It was the magic of Anton's finger that allowed them to be seen. That's what he told the people in town the next day when he tried to sell the remaining finger bone, which he had scrubbed and polished and displayed inside his mother's old ring box. No one believed him of course. He was a crazy old man. A thirty-five-year-old farmer dressed in animal skins was not someone to be believed. He was someone to be turned away because he didn't have the sense to bathe. He was someone for whom no credit would be extended.

Pasha could see that the people of the town did not require magic as they went about their day. It was an odd and difficult truth. He dropped the ring box on the street outside the tinker's shop and put the bone inside his pocket. Then he walked back down the long ribbon of dirt, returning to his farm.

CHAPTER 84:
THEN SHE TOOK OUT A BEIGE SCARF

Magda took down a box from the bedroom closet. It had a wig inside. Josef had bought it for her years ago when he wanted her hair to be red one night. It was real hair. Magda didn't ask where it had come from, but probably someone poor had sold it to the wigmaker. She would have been young, likely just a girl. Even an official's wife could not have hair this rich and touchable. Magda took the wig out of the box and put it on. She tucked her own hair up under the faux scalp and attached it with little pins. After looking at herself in the bedroom mirror from every angle, she shook her head and swung her body as if she were dancing. She wanted to be certain the wig would not fall off.

Then Magda rummaged around in her dresser and took out a beige scarf. She wrapped it around her head. A woman could not walk about outside the home with hair this radiant. Many would notice, and someone would follow. She mustn't look like an official's wife, for such women would be stopped, detained, asked for papers. It was a matter of security. Anyone who was with her might be in danger.

Sometimes Josef would still tell her to put on the wig. She liked it when he did this, for it became easier to imagine that it was not she pinned beneath the body of her sweating husband. It was some other woman who had to endure his choking and his rebukes. It was some other woman who had to please him.

Magda wondered if Anton would like her to wear such a wig, and whether she might act differently before him. She thought of the old days when Josef would fit a collar around her neck and tell her to crawl around on her hands and knees, naked, and how she had liked it. Would it disappoint her to learn that Anton harbored the same dark impulses as the man she was plotting to leave?

Magda went to the window to see what the trees were doing. She put her finger into the blinds and spread them apart. Just then, a toad smacked onto her front porch. Its belly was split, and it made a single dazed hop into the garden where it would die. Magda unpinned the wig and returned it to its box.

What she really needed were clothes from the country. Her wardrobe would betray her station regardless of how she hid her hair or masked her eyes behind large sunglasses. The sunglasses, in fact, would probably draw more attention to her than not. Nobody wore them anymore, because the smog above Moscodelphia was reliably thick most days of the year. On the rare occasions when a storm blew in and cleared the air for a few hours, most people were content to squint into the brilliant sky between the buildings. It seemed sinful not to.

Magda decided that she would give Anton money to buy her clothes, but if Josef found them in the house, he would question her. He might even make her wear them as she pleased him, and this was something she needed to avoid. Her new wardrobe would be her disguise, the mask she was preparing for the next life, and she did not want Josef to sully it.

Yes, she would give Anton the money, and he would buy the clothes, holding them for her until the moment they fled. She would put on the new clothes as Anton drove out of the city, and she would sit beside him like the stranger she wanted to be.

It was exciting—the possibility of suddenly starting another life. She used to think such thoughts as she lay hidden beneath the floorboards of the barn, listening to the collectors inventory the poverty of her family, trying to decide how much they could take without starving the lot of them. She remembered wondering once whether the man she was forced to marry would be handsome as well as brutal, or whether he would be ugly and brutal. Those were the only options she could imagine back then. Now, a third option was rising in her consciousness like an unexpected moon. It was like the brightening she had witnessed in the forest beside her farm once. The crickets had long since shut off, and Magda was up in her bedroom staring out her window. She saw a light building low in the trees, making her think a city was turning all of its lights on, one by one, or perhaps that an enormous fire of white flames was slowly advancing toward her. She went downstairs and stepped into the dewy grass beside the outhouse. That's when she realized it was only the moon, blazing in the trees, illuminating all that was hoping to make it through the night without being eaten or found.

CHAPTER 85:
THE LIGHT THE ANGEL GAVE OFF
BEFORE IT STRUCK

In his youth, Anton had seen the same jets as Josef, but he thought they were angels. In many ways, Anton's conclusion made more sense. He had actually seen angels, and when he was tiny and his family was starving, he had tasted one despite his father's warnings. Anton should not have been left alone with the shreds of meat still sticking to the ribs. He raked his fingernails up and down the bone until he had a mouthful of the oily meat.

Anton's parents were sitting on the couch in the next room, listening to their stomachs gurgle and churn the angel meat into that night's dreams. When Anton fell over, they rushed to the kitchen and understood at once what had happened. He already had a fever, and the welts rising up all over his skin made him look like a pink leopard. He was lucky it was only a mouthful, and when he was better in a couple of days, his mother slipped him an extra pear, an extra ladle of soup whenever her husband wasn't looking.

Later, when he was older, Anton had even seen the angel hurtling through the sky before it banged through the roof of the Puzanovs' barn. He remembered pointing to show his grandfather and how pleased he was to see the silvery smoke streaking across the sky. This was the light the angel gave off before it struck, and it was not unlike the flashing of the planes high above their farms. In those days, no one in the country had ever seen a plane up close. They wouldn't have believed it if they were told, and it was common to think they were angels flying across the heavens, deciding which part of the world they would menace on behalf of God.

"Do you remember what it was like?" asked Magda. "When you realized that the angels were planes? That the world was something you couldn't have guessed?"

For Anton, it had happened when he first arrived in the city and saw the airport from the train, the big planes moving like chess pieces across the tarmac. And then, as his train was still jogging toward the railyard, a plane roared and lifted off the earth and into the air, hauling its silvery skin higher than Anton thought anything earthly could go.

"I worried they would burn themselves on the sun," he laughed. "It seemed safer to fly at night."

Magda confessed to thinking the same thing. It was odd how wise she now seemed. And yet for all her new knowledge, Josef would not allow her to state her views. He would never listen, for instance, to a story about dining on angel meat and how their tongues were black, and how angels were murderous if they found you alone while they still lived. To the citizens of Moscodelphia, the idea of angels was worse than superstition. It was stupidity. If she brought it up with Josef, he grew stern.

"This is how you repay me?" he would ask, incredulous. "You wish to make a mockery of me by showing my colleagues that my wife is backward?"

Josef always went further than he had to. A simple request would be enough, but Josef lived in fear that the tiny world he had created would come flying apart as it spun in the cold blackness of space, which Magda still did not believe in. The Earth was plainly flat to her, and the Sun turned round the Earth. Naturally, she would not say anything about this in front of the people Josef worked with, but she would not disbelieve her own eyes, either.

Now toads were falling from the sky. To Magda, they were a message. To Josef, they were a problem for the Ministry of Sanitation.

Some days, Magda would step out onto the front porch and, from the safety of the eaves, would scan the sky of the city, the coasts of billowing smog that traveled just over the trees. She would try to guess where the next toad would emerge. Always, it came straight down, and always it seemed to be traveling faster than if it had merely fallen. The toads seemed flung, with anguish and purpose. As she stood sipping at her morning tea, ready to give up on the game, thinking that perhaps today was the day the toads would stop falling from the sky, one would appear in the periphery of her vision. Many times, she would be unable to say for certain that it was a toad. Perhaps it was a trick of her eyes, or a small bird that had died midflight. But sometimes there was indisputable confirmation: the thudding of the toad against a car roof, a fluttering of leaves as it passed through the branches of the tree in front of her porch.

And what was the message? And was it the same for everyone? Or was it only for Magda? Some days, Magda felt like she knew the answers to all these questions. Other days, she stepped back inside the house and cleaned out the cat box.

CHAPTER 86:
NO ONE BEGRUDGED HER THE EGG

More and more, Magda enjoyed remembering the boredom of the farm. At the time, it seemed tedious—to be asked, for instance, to slice and bury a hundred chunks of potato so that they would spread and become harvestable. She would dig the holes for them in the mornings, before the sun made it over the trees. It was cooler that way, and her trowel often sliced an earthworm in half. Many times she had seen the front half hurrying into its tunnel, while the back half wriggled in the dirt, waiting for someone to smash it.

She used to dread this chore because it hurt her knees. Now, as she considered the boredom of her life with Josef, she felt that the old loneliness she experienced on the farm was actually luxuriant. She would give many things if she were able to take a spade to black soil again. Here, she was forced to wipe down the same counters a dozen times a day, and when she went to buy the groceries, there was a depressing sameness to them. The eggs, when they were available, tasted old. More likely, one found powdered eggs and had to mix them with water from the tap, giving them a metallic taste, as if you had just lost a tooth. On the farm, the eggs were oblong and multicolored, and if perchance she found one with a crack in it beneath a hen, that was her lucky day; it meant she could eat it right away for her breakfast. No one begrudged her the egg.

These days, Magda spent her time polishing utensils she never used. There was always the threat of a large party, of having to entertain important people from the ministry who would, in part, judge Josef's chances for advancement on the dinner his wife presented. She did not understand why their utensils were made of silver. They tarnished easily and became undesirable even when they were never used. On the farm, she thought, the spoons stayed reliably gray, but here in the city, because no one wanted to put a black spoon in his mouth, she sat at the kitchen table and set about polishing the utensils, the gravy bowl, the soup ladle. She rubbed the old rag into the metal until her face appeared inside the spoon, upside down and small enough to make invisible whatever feeling she wanted to hide.

In all those years, there was only one time when Josef brought his colleagues home for dinner. Their wives came too of course, and there was just enough room for the six of them around the dining room table Josef had selected at the start of their life together. Magda had to find the leaf up in the crawl space, wrapped in an old blanket since the day they had purchased it. When she inserted the leaf, she saw that it was still pristine, whereas the table that surrounded it was full of little nicks and dents from where a plate had been dropped or a bottle had been slammed down. It was a blond wood, which they could not finish because the varnish factory had burned to the ground, and the red wine stains and coffee rings reminded her of the tracks of competing animals. They had never bothered to get it finished after the new plant came online because they'd already begun living with the table. And if they were to varnish it, they would have to have it sanded. And if they did that, they would have to take it to someone's shop, they would have to rent a van. It all became more trouble than either of them could bear, and thus, by staring at the table with the leaf inserted, Magda could tell exactly how much she herself must have changed since coming to live with Josef.

Magda was shrewd. She covered the whole thing with a large tablecloth she had been saving for the occasion. Regardless, the dinner party was not a success. Josef drank too much, and the wives of his colleagues were both city-born. They had made this fact known to Magda with a dozen small gestures and smiles, a dozen words for which they could have found others. When they finally left, Josef threw a wine bottle at Magda. It ricocheted off the table and went through the window.

But Magda did not think of her own safety. She thought only of the leaf, how now it too was damaged, how it seemed like part of a table the two of them had earned.

CHAPTER 87:
ITS HIGH, UNIGNORABLE NOTE

It had been raining toads for weeks. Magda swept them off the porch and tested the air with her tongue. It tasted of flies, as it had the day before, when she pushed the night's bounty of exploded amphibians into the calendulas. The downpour was not biblical, a sudden torrent that covered the streets and jammed the rain gutters. Rather, it was an occasional thud on the roof, all night long, without pattern or predictability—as if someone had hidden many malfunctioning clocks, and the minutes ticked off at random.

Or perhaps it was biblical. Who was Magda to say that what rained down on Egypt wasn't the same as what rained down right now on Moscodelphia? The plague of a weak God. A God too busy to follow through.

Magda made a conscious effort to cut off the argument she was having with herself. It had been years since she had read about Moses in the illegal Bible her parents kept hidden in the flue of the fireplace—the one in her brother's bedroom that never got used because the mortar was beginning to fail. She recalled the leathery blackness of its cover, the golden edges of the pages, the heft of it that insisted it be read with two hands or a tabletop. She used to read it as a little girl, and she wondered if it was still there in the flue. Her parents were likely dead by now. If her brother had sold the farm, the new owners would find it when they tried to start a fire and drive out the cold. Would they see it as a gift or as a sign of treason?

Magda surveyed the lawn. It would have to be raked. Her neighbors had done so yesterday and their yards still looked good, but now the streets were lined with low mounds of decomposing toads, waiting for the city to clear them away. The crows glutted themselves, strutting the pavement before her house as if they were on a buffet line. The sky was gray, and there wasn't any breeze. Magda heard a toad slipping through the leaves of her neighbor's sugar maple.

"Magda, I need my tea," called Josef. He stood in the hall mirror, tightening the tie around his neck. "I'll be late."

Magda went to the kitchen, where she could tell the kettle was just about to whistle its high, unignorable note. She poured the water into Josef's thermos, at the bottom of which were three teabags and two spoonfuls of raw sugar. She twisted the top, shook it, and took it to her husband.

There were days when Magda wondered what her life would be like if she had never been taken from the farm, if she had never been bid on by Josef. She thought about this after enduring another night of his wine-stunned weight on top of her. Would she simply have been rewashing a different set of dishes for the last sixteen years? Or would she feel like the piano music tripping out of the parlor window at the Constantinopolis house—something to quicken the air and the people it surrounded?

"Your lunch is in your briefcase," she said as Josef was pulling on his jacket. He nodded into the mirror and went to the door, taking an umbrella from the coat stand. He left without kissing her, and Magda watched as he expanded a black tulip above his head and took off at a brisk pace toward the Ministry of Opulence. It was a large gray building where he had a desk and a title, a secretary who did what she was told.

Magda stayed at the door until Josef disappeared around the corner. Part of her hoped she might see a falling toad spatter on the sidewalk in front of him, ruining the leg of his trousers, which Josef had insisted she iron a second time because the crease was not precise. Josef registered his dissatisfaction with Magda's work almost every day, and afterward there was nothing for Magda to do but climb beside him inside the covers of the bed she had made that morning.

CHAPTER 88:
THE COLOR OF MEN AND LIONS

In bed beside Josef's snoring, Magda sometimes thought back to the mosaics she had seen at the museum. It was odd, she thought, that the ministries would provide the city with such a distraction. It seemed strange to build a beautiful building that housed only enigmas. They seemed to have no purpose, and yet she was drawn to them. It was among her favorite things to do—to walk through the museum unimpeded, browsing the mosaics.

She thought, *If I were to pry out one of the red tiles and replace it with one of the blue tiles, no one would be the wiser.* This bothered her. A thing that could be admired should not also be mutable. This was the theory, anyway, she was turning over in her mind. *How many tiles would I have to swap out before someone recognized the change? Who is to say the tiles haven't already been swapped out?*

The older mosaics seemed deliberate. They were symmetrical and realistic. There were men and lions in profile, and they were the color of men and lions. But later mosaics were less so. There might be a man, but his body was blue, or he floated over a lake while dangling below a giant dandelion. "Surreal" was the word on the placard for that one. It was an art that mixed reality and dream, but without fully mixing them together—like the vinegar and oil in her cruet of salad dressing, which, no matter how hard she shook it, would revert to their separate layers before the meal had ended, sometimes even before she had finished pouring.

Often, Magda felt Josef's hand reach over and begin groping her through the sheets. He was still in a state of semi-sleep, and she had learned that he'd slip back into a deeper unconsciousness if she simply played dead as her mother had long ago advised. This happened almost every night, and as long as she resisted the urge to roll away from him or tighten the sheets around herself, she knew that Josef's hand would be confused and forget it was in pursuit.

The last mosaics in the exhibit were the most troubling of all. These were said to be "abstract," and the tiles sometimes formed a geometric design, devoid of people, devoid of trees. These made Magda think of empty buildings. It is what she imagined the museum would feel like if she fainted in the ladies' room and everyone went home before she revived. She would wander the hallways, lit only by security lights, searching for a door. Other mosaics had no discernible pattern, and these disturbed her even more. She wondered if, perhaps, the mosaic was originally a man's portrait that had been dropped by the men in charge of moving the exhibit. She imagined the tiles dashed over the museum floor. The men knew they would be beaten, or worse, so they glued the tiles back together at random. When they found an ear or a nostril more or less intact, they broke it into its component pieces and reassembled them elsewhere. Perhaps it was one of these men who wrote the description of the "abstract mosaic"—as a kind of joke, as a way of laughing at the ministerial class for all its airs and foolishness.

Magda could not believe that. She would not. The abstract mosaics, despite their seeming randomness, their unwillingness to be explicated, were the most powerful pieces in the exhibit. And while it was true that she could imagine prying out a red tile and replacing it with a blue one, she believed it would somehow ruin the picture, or at least change its effect, for reasons she could not articulate. She felt this strongly—in the marrow of her ribs. This sense of confused beauty was among her most treasured feelings. She could count on one hand the times she had felt something similar: when she first saw the bronze eye of a toad at close range, when she felt Anton removing her clothing in the pitch dark of the barn, when the whip-poor-wills started up beneath the stars on the night of her first bleeding. What brought all these things together and made her think of mosaics? She couldn't say, and she was glad of it.

Later in the night, she would hear Josef's snoring get terribly loud and then cut off, as if a switch had been flicked inside his lungs. In such moments she heard the distant traffic of the highways, or perhaps the sound of a night bird that had somehow found itself inside the city limits. This was her chance to drift off, before the snoring began again.

And so she thought of Anton's ivory skin coming toward her through the corn.

CHAPTER 89:
THE FEW MUST BE SACRIFICED
FOR THE WELFARE OF THE MANY

Enemies of the state were taken to the tops of the tallest buildings and thrown out a window. It was a matter of needless frugality, of not wasting bullets. In Moscodelphia, bullets and terror were never in short supply. The garb of the prisoners was pure white, as a sign of their surrender, and the presence of white-clad bodies crumpled on the sidewalk encouraged the superstitious to think of them as wingless angels. This effect was heightened by the fact that prisoners always wore gowns. It was a matter of efficiency: Stitching a gown was simple, one size always fit all.

The falling convict hurtled toward the layer of smog, which might start at the fortieth floor and end at the tenth. The moment he emerged from the cloud was the moment he could see his fate racing up toward him. The brain had barely the time to process the disaster. And then it was over. Not even pain really. Just a sudden jolt that the brain interpreted as every cell of the body slamming into something simultaneously, and then a winking out. Unintentionally, it was more humane than most methods of execution the state had employed—beheadings and burnings; firing squads with the prisoner bleeding and tied to a post, waiting for the soldiers to reload because too many shots had missed.

There were some in the ministries who began to take advantage. They heard what people whispered, so they arranged to have the prisoners fall into the courtyards at the busiest times, a way to maximize the publicity. The subministers didn't care if the convict struck someone as he walked dully toward his lunch. It was fate. Or there was something amiss in the struck person, some reason for correction. They even went so far as to hack large wounds into the prisoners' shoulder blades—to make it seem like their wings had been shorn off, like God had torn them away and this was the reason they fell to earth. Sometimes, they even dumped out a bucket of swan feathers after forcing the prisoner over the ledge.

It became Josef's job to push the prisoners out the window. It was upsetting and dangerous. The prisoners would resist of course, and they would cling to furniture and legs, anything to keep themselves from getting near the window. Once, by accident, a ministry worker had gone out the window with the convict. He had been grabbed at the last moment, and it could easily have been Josef if he was on duty that day.

After that, the people involved in the executions began drugging the convicts, or forcing them to drink a liter of vodka with their last meal. It was a way to ensure compliance, and it was much simpler than threatening their families or getting their daughter in front of them and telling the man that if he resisted the daughter would be thrown over as well. Sometimes they threw the child out anyway. Orphans were a tax on the state. The few must be sacrificed for the welfare of the many. In fact, that was the motto of the Ministry of Opulence. It was carved into the cornerstone. It was embossed on the letterhead.

Naturally, Josef had suggested binding the hands of the prisoners, but this was forbidden by his superiors. They did not explain the reason for the prohibition, but the reason was clear anyway. The difficulty of pushing men out the window, men who could resist, ensured that the subministers remained loyal, dedicated to the task of keeping in power the men who sat along the back wall watching.

When Josef came home after a day of throwing men out the window, he was in a black mood. The crimes for which they had been convicted were ambiguous at best: plotting to undermine the unity of citizens, extravagance in the face of shirked duties, possession of books, inability to conduct one's life for the good of the state. Josef pined for the embodiment of unadulterated evil as he took possession of the prisoner—a murderer, a thief. But these were not the crimes the state was interested in suppressing. And so, Josef would throw a begging man out the window, often as he began urinating all over himself. And then Josef would go home and Magda would ask him how his day had been, and he would grow angry because he did not wish to relive such a day. He made her bring him wine. He told her how the meal she served could be improved.

The higher that Josef rose through the ranks of the ministry, the more monstrous his own actions appeared to him. He worried he had become the type of man that children fear. He would be thinking this as he struck his wife or forced himself upon her. All of this would happen as the cat stood watching from the corner, its tail switching back and forth. Later, as Magda applied ice to the bruise upon her jaw, the cat came over and rubbed itself through her legs.

The cat liked Magda for her long nails, and it wanted to be scratched.

CHAPTER 90:
SHE COULD NOT DISCOUNT
THE FACT OF ANGELS

Now when Magda walked over the small woods that ran through the city park like a coffee stain and found a toad staring up at her from the leaves like a lump of living dirt, she had to wonder whether this was a toad that had always lived there or a toad that had fallen from the sky and was merely dazed, collecting itself, adjusting to the strangeness of the earth.

One day she spotted a toad in the leafy world beside the path. It seemed unlikely to have fallen. Magda looked up. Here and there, she saw a toad skewered on a branch or found one splattered against a wide rock. Would it be possible to survive the landing if it occurred in a deep enough pile of dead leaves and loam? Magda couldn't say for sure. Once she had seen a toad slam into the flagstones of her porch, and it had lived long enough to hop its way to the garden, leaking urine and blood as it went. It surely died a short time later, but she could not rule out the possibility that a toad could survive its arrival under the right circumstances.

Magda considered that there were even stories of people surviving after a great fall. Shortly after she came to the city, she had heard the legend of the woman who fell out of a plane, who survived by somehow steering herself into the silvery light of a lake in Josef's childhood suburb. And of course, Magda could not discount the fact of angels who, though they were flung downward by the powerful hand of God, still survived long enough to murder their discoverers—or nurse themselves back to health in some-body's barn, feeding on the blood of goats, the lickings of the trough.

Magda bent down to examine the toad, and it did not hop away. She admired the copper foil of its eyes, bulging out and perfectly clean as it blinked and breathed, slowly expanding its body like something in the dirt was trying to get out—a mole or some other creature digging its way to the surface. The serenity of the toad was remarkable. It made Magda think it had a message for her, that it was an emissary from some other world.

Magda got down on her hands and knees, and still the toad did not move. Perhaps its instinct was to rely on camouflage for as long as possible. She reached out and let her hand linger just above its nose. There was still no movement save for the steady breathing, the unhurried blinking, but only with one eye at a time, as if the toad wanted to keep Magda within its gaze, as if the toad wanted to see coming whatever mayhem Magda might be planning.

When Magda finally grabbed at the toad, it still didn't try to get away, although it immediately began peeing all over her hands. This was a good sign, one she remembered from her girlhood when she used to gather them up in buckets to see how many she could find. She thought it must surely be a normal toad, a toad that had lived in this park, not one that had arrived as a bit of strange language from the sky.

She was staring into the coppery ball bearing of its eye when the toad opened its mouth and a black beetle came crawling out of it, preening the toad's saliva from the long whiplike antennae probing at the air. She lay the toad back down in the leaves, watching as one beetle after another emerged from its mouth. Each of them rested for a moment on the edge of the toad's jaw, then opened the black shells of its wing casings and took flight into the trees on some mysterious mission. When she examined the toad again, it had completely deflated, and the light had left its pretty eyes. She had never seen anything like this, and she wiped her hands through the dirt to clean them.

Before she went home, she kicked leaves over the dead toad. She searched the air above her and walked home, mulling over this message and why it was meant for her. The beetles' wings had made a faint whirring as they took off and rose into the trees, and now she felt she could hear that same sound everywhere she went—if only she stopped and gave her full attention to the air that surrounded her. Even if she was at home and far away from where a beetle might be, she could hear it in the background, like the workings of a boiler in a cold house or the sound of wind moving across an acre of ruined soybeans.

Magda wondered how she had not noticed it before.

CHAPTER 91: HIS LAST EVENING ON EARTH

Magda was a sly thief. Every night, she took a penny or a nickel from Josef's change purse. She checked his pockets before she did the laundry. She had a pebble at the ready if they happened to be walking by the river and Josef told her to make a wish, pressing a coin inside her palm. It was always warm, and when in winter she slipped the coin into her own pocket, it felt invisible, like she had inserted a disk of warm air. Magda saved these coins, and she skimmed the money he gave her for the week's groceries. There was always something held back.

It was a heavy plan, and she realized she could never travel with so large a cache. It would make her slow and conspicuous. So each week, as she ran her errands, she converted her little coins to larger coins, converted her larger coins to paper bills. The paper money was sewn into her coat, her favorite hat, the padding inside her brassiere.

Magda wanted to be ready to run when the opportunity arose. Perhaps Josef would have to travel on ministry business. Perhaps he would ask her to take care of his parents if one of them cracked a hip. It would all depend. If she could not get at least a twelve-hour head start, the entire plan seemed ill-advised. If she ran, and he caught her, he would probably kill her. That's what would be expected, and of course, Magda was getting old. Her body was less powerful. If her life came down to a foot race, death would surely catch her.

Magda had seen it happen. When her childhood friend Raisa Vyachev ran away from Bartov, a man high up in the Ministry of Freshness, he tracked her down the same day and had her flogged in front of the cameras the police held up from many angles. It all played out live on television, as did many pursuits of traitors and disobedient wives. When Raisa was thoroughly defeated and contrite, Bartov himself came into the frame and put a bullet in her mouth.

Raisa had been close to Magda, which was unusual. She was two stations higher than Magda because her husband was two stations higher than Josef. But Raisa had come from the countryside, like Magda, and she had a way of carrying herself in public that let Magda know she could be trusted in a way that other women could not.

When Magda thought things out, she could see how Raisa had brought it all down upon herself. She had not even gotten out of the city when the search began, and she was discovered at the apartment of the man she was hoping to run away with: Sascha Karlov. He had been delayed at work and could not leave his post for fear of drawing suspicion. For this, he got to see his mistress murdered on live television. Suddenly he saw his address on the screen. He heard his name.

There was little Sascha could do. He picked a knife up out of the break room sink and hurried out the back door of his offices. But already the sirens were converging, and he heard the deep whacking of the helicopter blades coming toward his quadrant. He ran up the alley and peeked out into the street to see what was happening. Everywhere, he could see his face on the monitors and electronic billboards. They were offering a reward—a frozen turkey—and that's when he knew this was his last evening on Earth.

With some manhunts, the rewards started out low and unimpressive—dinner at a restaurant, a liter of vodka, and so forth. But turkey was among the greatest delicacies there were. Everyone liked to eat something with wings. Sascha thought of his neighbor imagining the golden skin as he smoothed the butter into it. He imagined the triumph of the family who found him and turned him in, and as he was thinking this, a window was thrown open and someone shouted that they had found the man on the billboards. Ordinary citizens began running toward him. He took out the knife and stood ready to slash at his attackers, but he was struck in the back of the head by what turned out to be a brick. Then the largest of the men began fighting over who would get the reward as Sascha's eggshell head kept trying to recohere. By the time the police showed up, he was unconscious.

Later, Raisa's husband arrived and put a bullet in Sascha's mouth as well. There was little effect, other than to make an even larger mess of the alley between the two buildings, the roofs of which were covered in pigeons that erupted at the shot and began circling the gray world beneath them that only became grayer in the fading light of April.

CHAPTER 92:
IT WOULD NOT TAKE THEM LONG
TO CLEAN THE ENTIRE YARD

Magda heard a toad hit the roof, and she thought of Anton's hands all over her—the foolishness of resisting, the foolishness of proceeding. Soon enough, he would knock at the door as if he were making a delivery, and she would ask him to bring the package inside. Then she would take the suitcases from their hiding place in the guest bedroom; she would give the cat a final scratch behind the ears.

Magda began straightening up. She did not wish to leave Josef with a dirty house. She had changed the sheets on their bed and scoured the toilet and put all the cups still warm from the dishwasher back upon their shelves. She could not decide where she should leave her note, the one that would explain the inexplicable: that she had fallen in love, that she was leaving him. Anton did not want her to leave the note.

"But he will think I am dead," she had said.

"It would be better if he did," Anton replied.

But Magda believed that she owed Josef this courtesy. After all, it was she who was running off to live in the countryside, in the wild poverty she had always wished to escape.

And then Magda became fearful. Josef had provided well for her. They had lived many years in this enclave of brick houses. Magda and Josef had meat twice a week, and they could buy as much rice and coffee and sugar as they wanted. It was a life of luxury.

The men who tended her yard were often skeletal. Magda would find them eating out of her trash cans. She did not have the heart to stifle them, though she could have. Being the wife of an official brought with it many powers. If she chose to call the police, they would come to her house quickly. They would do as she bid them. It could even happen without words if that is what she wished. The police would arrive, and she would watch them from the curtains as they collected the men, one by one, and beat them like monkeys.

But then she thought of Josef coming home that evening. He would drop his briefcase on the floor as if he'd been carrying bricks. He would walk past the mirror without looking into it. He would walk past Magda and proceed to the jug of wine, filling the largest mug in the cabinet.

There was a knock at the door, but it was early. Anton would not come early. His plan had been precise. He would arrive with a package, and then she would stand on the porch and demand that he take her to the boutiques to go shopping. Her driver, she would explain to anyone who asked, was not available. Then he would take the suitcases, which had been placed inside delivery boxes, and carry them to his truck. This was the only way. It would be impossible to leave at night when Josef was there. Besides, the checkpoints were more numerous and diligent once darkness had taken over the streets.

Magda peeked through the curtain. It was Mrs. Constantinopolis. Magda grabbed a towel and wrapped it around her head as if she had stepped from the shower. She opened the door.

"Hello, Mrs. Constantinopolis. What can I do for you?" Magda positioned herself in the half-opened door to block the woman's entry, but she came in anyway.

"I'm just drying my hair," Magda said. "What is it you need?"

"My husband and I are having guests tomorrow night," she said. As she surveyed the living room, the cat fled down the hall. "We'd like you and Josef to stop by as well. Mical has been promoted to a vice minister's position. We are going to celebrate."

"It is good for you both," said Magda. "Of course we will be there." Magda's hands floated up to her towel and cinched it more tightly into place.

"I wonder if you have any olives I can borrow?" she said, scanning the living room as if it were an extension of her own. As Magda went to look, a van pulled up to the street in front of her house, and two senile old men began cleaning up the toads. The taller of the two held a bag open as the other man speared the toads with a long metal rod and wiped them into the waiting bag with his gloved hand. It would not take them long to clean the entire yard.

Magda produced a can of green olives. The label was gone, but someone had written "green olives" in black marker on top of it. Mrs. Constantinopolis shook the can next to her ear and felt the olives jiggling inside. She wanted to be sure it wasn't soup or dog food or mashed potatoes. One never knew for sure with cans like this, but she seemed pleased.

"Come by around seven," she said. "Wear your red tunic."

CHAPTER 93:
LIKE THE BREAKING OF A FLU

In their youth, Isabelle had left Josef for practical reasons: He was not as powerful as his name had promised; she was attracted to a ruthlessness that Josef could not sustain. When Josef found himself alone after graduating from the academy, he wallowed for a week. He cried so hard that spots appeared before his eyes—faint gray blurs that raced around in front of him as he stared at an undecorated wall or a blank computer screen. After a couple of days, he stopped taking notice of the spots and accepted that they would accompany him as a manifestation of his weakness. Josef did not try to win Isabelle back. She had already moved away, engaged to be married to a man whose station was slightly higher than Josef's.

Now Magda had left Josef in the same manner—secretly, with a head start, in a direction he could not guess. When he had found the note, he was too sleepy with wine to read it. He felt the crisp paper beneath his pillow, and the old dread spread over him. When he finally read it the following morning, he realized that she must already have gotten to wherever she hoped to be.

"She has gone to visit her people in the country," he said when Mical Constantinopolis inquired about his wife at the party.

"You must be happy for your freedom," Mical joked. "Perhaps we will patronize the brothels together before she returns?"

The lie was pleasing to Josef. He decided he would keep up the charade for a couple weeks and then announce her death on the family farm. He need only decide the method of her demise, and in a way he realized that this was his only revenge. She could die by infection or by bandits or in the spinning gears of farm machinery. He enjoyed playing the various scenarios out in his mind. He wanted her to suffer, and he kept coming back to amoebic dysentery. He would tell people she expired in a puddle of her own unstoppable defecation. It seemed fitting for someone who would betray him like this.

Still, Josef was grateful she had left the cat, which grew more affectionate now that Magda was gone—the cat could see it would not be fed except by Josef. She wove in and out of his drunken legs. She curled into his lap to steal his warmth.

And then one day, more than a week after Magda had left, Josef heard from Mical Constantinopolis that the toads had stopped falling. Because the toads were often left to rot in the public squares and residential lawns, and because they fell infrequently and without pattern, it took a while for the stoppage to be noticed and confirmed. It was like the breaking of a flu. One coughed for the last time, and then, hours later, one realized the coughing had stopped. The sanitation department scooped up the last of the toads piled in low fly-filled mounds along the streets, and suddenly there was nothing waiting for them the following week.

"You will have to change the stories again," said Mical gravely. "We can no longer say the toads were a blessing."

Josef understood. He would revise again a small bit of history in a book that nobody read, and he would do so without realizing that his wife, apparently, had played a part in its unfolding. He did not know the moment of her first infidelity, and so he saw no correlation with her departure. If he had known, he would have to acknowledge that he had lived as a cuckold beneath his own roof while his adulterous wife continued to eat his food and spend his generous allowance. It was a possibility too humiliating to contemplate, so he didn't.

The smog remained above Moscodelphia, of course. There was nothing to be done about that.

CHAPTER 94:
THE SCENT OF PINE TREES FILLED THE VAN

There was still plenty of daylight left in the sky, and this made Magda anxious. She peered into her sideview mirror at the city receding behind them.

"It's almost gone," she said, and Anton glanced over at his own mirror.

Moscodelphia was turning into a smoky stain on the horizon, though there were faint twinklings of light coming out of it as the circling jets pointed briefly in their direction. The last time she had seen it like this was when she had traveled from the south, by train, after being captured by the collectors.

"By this time tomorrow, we won't be able to see it at all," Anton said.

This was both a comfort and a worry to Magda. Obviously, if they could not see the city, the city could not see them. It meant the chances of Josef finding them, or even pursuing them, were greatly reduced. But it also meant they must keep to their new and difficult path. Magda tucked her chin into the fabric of her gray dress. It was part of the costume she would wear in her new life and which Anton had gotten for her. It was a little big, and she inhaled the scent of the last woman who must have worn it, trying, like a dog, to learn what she was like.

"It's funny that we're running away to start a farm," she said. She looked over at Anton as he drove. It had been more than an hour since they had seen a car. "My youth was spent dreaming of Moscodelphia. Now I am fleeing it."

Anton understood. Part of him felt like he was about to pick up a snake that might still be alive. He was always suspicious of things that looked like rock, like death. He preferred to let someone else give it a try.

"We'll find out what kind of choice we've made soon enough," he said. Then he reminded her that once they were over the mountains, they probably wouldn't have enough fuel to return, even if they wanted.

"Then it's settled," she said. "I won't bring it up again."

Magda began to wonder about Pasha. It had been a long time since she had done so, and it was odd to think that he was in large part responsible for where she had come to be. Had he not stolen Anton's finger, he might not have fled to Moscodelphia. Certainly, she would have taken more care when the collectors made their rounds.

Magda tried to push these thoughts aside. It was something like affection that filled her as she thought of Pasha, and she did not wish to honor him that way. She imagined him having to bury their mother and father, having to whip and butcher the animals without any help, having to chide himself for using too many shotgun shells. With no one there to beat Pasha, she felt confident the farm would have fallen into disrepair, that her cruel brother would rule over both a wilder and diminishing patch of land.

And then she thought of Benjamin deep in the ground where Pasha still walked. Benjamin had been a sweet boy while he lasted, and she couldn't think of a worse brother for him to have. And yet, if anyone was tending the grave after all these years, it would have been Pasha. If Pasha were still alive, he'd make sure the marker stone stayed straight after the frost heaves of winter. He'd make sure the goats weren't allowed to rove over the cemetery to eat the flowering weed heads and soil the bed of their brother's last sleeping. There were so many uncertainties in the world, but Magda knew that she'd never see Pasha again. Moscodelphia was the last link between them, and now the chain was broken. She felt both guilty and relieved.

The van lurched across a patch of crumbling road, jostling Magda out of her reverie. She looked again into her sideview mirror. The sky was beginning to purple, and Moscodelphia seemed slightly lower behind them because they were starting up the long sloping plateau that led to the mountains. They passed another burned-out car rusting into the sand by the side of the road. Then they entered a towering forest that blotted out most of the light and had to slow down. The road inside the forest was not maintained. Large chunks of asphalt were missing or had crumbled. The scent of pine trees filled the van.

"The map gave no indication the road might disappear," said Anton.

CHAPTER 95:
THE CRICKETS CROWDING
THE FIELD AROUND THEM

For a long time, the occasional toad still fell from the sky. They littered the paved highway and later, but less frequently, the dirt roads. Once, when a toad hit the windshield, Anton flicked on the wiper, and the toad's exploded belly smeared across the glass before the wind took it tumbling. They just kept driving, headed deeper and deeper into the poverty Anton had promised her: a farm with real animals, manure to be raked, the electricity unpredictable. They did not stop to eat. Magda broke bread apart for both of them, and she had a wheel of sheep's cheese that she fed to Anton in little pinches. It was a luxury. Either the wheel was very old or someone had maintained a secret flock somewhere in the country. Or perhaps it was made of dog's milk. It was only the label and the strangeness of the taste that made Magda believe it might have come from sheep.

"How will we know when we are there?" asked Magda.

"We have to drive over the mountains first."

Mountains. Another thing Magda had never known, though she had seen pictures of them. "It's a shame we'll be crossing them at night," she said.

"You'll know you're in the mountains when your ears begin to pop," he said, thinking of the times he'd taken an elevator almost to the top of the ministry buildings—how his ears had hurt until suddenly they didn't, and how that was a small pleasure of his job delivering packages all over the city.

Magda could not tell if he was teasing her, but she was too tired to wonder for very long. She curled into herself and fell asleep as the belts and gears of the van continued their relentless humming. She dreamed of the black beetles crawling out of the toad she had found in the park, how they floated up into the highest branches of the trees and disappeared. Had they stopped there or simply continued rising—above the buildings, above the clouds—until they had merged with the pure blackness that existed only in a starless patch of country sky?

Magda woke with a strange crackling in her ears, as if she were under-water, and felt a need to relieve herself.

"I have to go. Can't we pull over now?" she asked.

The van that Anton had taken was old. He had chosen it because it wouldn't be missed right away, but he worried it might not start again if he ever took out the key. Besides, someone might think they had broken down and then recognize them when they pulled up to help. But these were crazy thoughts. If they could be caught here, more than three hundred miles from Magda's home at two in the morning, they would never be safe.

Anton turned off the engine and cut the headlights. Together they listened to the night sounds before he let her get out of the van—the ticking of the motor, the crickets crowding the fields around them, the wind moving through branches. Magda remembered this music arising from the darkness, but she was afraid to acknowledge it. They opened their respective doors, and the cabin light ruined whatever night vision they had developed. Anton began emptying cans of gasoline into the tank, while Magda relieved herself on the other side of the van, holding the fender in one hand and her bunched-up dress in the other. They were in the mountains now, but not above tree line. Magda could tell that the road kept going up.

She made her way to Anton through the blackness, one hand feeling the air in front of her and the other tapping along the outside of the van.

Anton pulled her to him. She could smell the sweat and the weariness in his clothes, but his embrace was warm. She felt she could fall asleep standing there while the breezes drifted over them in the moonless air.

"You won't leave me the way I've left Josef?"

Anton adjusted his arms so that he could lock his hands at the small of her back.

"Please don't," she said.

Magda closed her eyes and listened to the wind moving through the trees. She heard it start from far off, slowly make its way across the mountain, and then move on to who knows where. But before it disappeared completely, another breeze had begun making its way toward them, canceling the sound of the old one. It seemed like a great and personal sibilance—something intended only for the two of them. They stood there on the side of the road for a while, each of them trying to hear two breezes at once. Finally, when a breeze arrived overhead, Magda opened her eyes so that she might see the branches bending. She let out a little gasp.

"You can see them now," said Anton.

Magda's eyes had adjusted. High above them, over the entire sky, the stars had come out. She thought they looked like a city floating there between the branches, ready to tumble down on top of them. She thought they looked like the skyline of Moscodelphia that she and Josef once enjoyed as they walked beside the river, throwing pennies in for wishes. The sky was beautiful, just as Anton reminded her it would be. They could hear whip-poor-wills calling back and forth in the valley, and the night was full of honeysuckle that seemed to rise up from below.

That's when they saw a bright streak cross the sky and thud into the mountain ahead of them. The smoke trail was silvery, unmistakable. Magda remembered back to the first full belly of her life, and Anton remembered the welts rising up on his lips, the tingle on his tongue, going deeper.

They would need to be ready. They got back inside the van and continued north.

ACKNOWLEDGMENTS

Sections of this novel were published as stories in *The Southern Review,* *Ghost Parachute, Isthmus, Connotations Press,* and *Brilliant Flash Fiction.* In addition, I would like to thank Jessica McEntee for her close reading and excellent notes on an early draft of the book.